H. G. Wells

THE INVISIBLE MAN
A Grotesque Romance*

Edited by
MACDONALD DALY
University of Nottingham

'Being but dark earth
though made diaphanall'*

EVERYMAN
J. M. DENT · LONDON
CHARLES E. TUTTLE
VERMONT

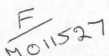

Introduction and other critical apparatus
© Macdonald Daly 1995

This edition first published in 1995

Reprinted 1999

Text copyright by the Literary Executors
of the Estate of H. G. Wells

Chronology compiled by
John Lawton

J. M. Dent
Orion Publishing Group
Orion House, 5 Upper St Martin's Lane,
London WC2H 9EA
and
Charles E. Tuttle Co., Inc.
28 South Main Street,
Rutland, Vermont 05701, USA

Typeset in sabon by CentraCet Ltd, Cambridge
Printed in Great Britain by
The Guernsey Press Co. Ltd, Guernsey, C.I.

British Library Cataloguing-in-Publication Data
is available upon request

ISBN 0 460 87628 7

CONTENTS

NOTE ON THE AUTHOR AND EDITOR

H. G. WELLS was born in Bromley, Kent in 1866. After working as a draper's apprentice and pupil-teacher, he won a scholarship to the Normal School of Science, South Kensington, in 1884, studying under T. H. Huxley. He was awarded a first-class honours degree in biology and resumed teaching, but had to retire after a kick from an ill-natured pupil, at football, afflicted his kidneys. He worked in poverty in London as a crammer while experimenting in journalism and stories, and published textbooks on biology and physiography (1893), but it was *The Time Machine* (1895) that launched his literary career. Many scientific romances and short stories began to be paralleled with sociological and political books and tracts, notably *Anticipations* (1901), *Mankind in the Making* (1903), and *A Modern Utopia* (1905). His full-length, largely autobiographical novels began with *Love and Mr Lewisham* (1900), *Kipps* (1905), *Tono-Bungay* and *Ann Veronica* (1909), the last promoting the outspoken, socially and sexually liberated 'New Woman'. He married his cousin Isabel in 1891, but later eloped with, and subsequently married, Catherine Robbins, 'Jane'. A constant philanderer, he invited scandal by including his lightly concealed private affairs in *Ann Veronica* and *The New Machiavelli* (1911). Shaw and the Webbs had invited him into the Fabian Society and soon regretted it. Wells increasingly used fiction as a platform for the ideas and visions of a world-state which preoccupied him, but he foresaw that the Novel itself would decline to be replaced by candid autobiography. After about 1920, critical attention was turning towards his natural successor Aldous Huxley and the 'pure', non-journalistic novels of Joyce and Virginia Woolf. His mass public dwindled, though it welcomed *The Outline of History*, of that year, and long continued to do so. The Second World War and the cataclysm of Hiroshima confirmed the pessimism which had throughout accompanied his exuberant hopes and visions. His last book was titled, with some personal significance, *Mind at the End of its Tether* (1945), but his vigour continued almost to his death in 1946. In his last two decades he had produced some forty books.

MACDONALD DALY was born in Glasgow in 1963, and is Lecturer in Modern Literature at the University of Nottingham. He has edited the Everyman edition of D. H. Lawrence's *Sons and Lovers*, and the Penguin edition of Elizabeth Gaskell's *Mary Barton*. He has published a large number of academic articles and, with Ellis Sharp, a book of short stories, *Engels on Video* (Zoilus Press, 1995). He is currently writing another book of stories, a volume of essays, and a monograph on D. H. Lawrence's early writings.

NOTE ON THE TEXT

The Invisible Man was serialised in the June and July 1897 numbers of *Pearson's Weekly* before its appearance in book form the following September (London: C. Arthur Pearson, 1897). The Epilogue did not appear in either the serial or the English first edition, but was added to the American first edition (New York: Edward Arnold, 1897), in which there was also a large number of smaller changes. This Everyman edition reprints the American text, with the exception of obvious errors, some of which are mentioned in the Notes, and its adherence to Everyman house style.

CHRONOLOGY OF WELLS'S LIFE

Year   *Age* *Life*

1866   Born 21 September, Bromley, Kent, to a working-class
                family: father a gardener, shopkeeper and cricketer; mother
                a maid and housekeeper

1873   7   Entered Thomas Morley's Bromley Academy

CHRONOLOGY OF HIS TIMES

Year	Arts & Science	History & Politics
1865	Mendel's *Law of Heredity*	End of American Civil War; Lincoln assassinated
1866	Dostoevsky's *Crime and Punishment*	Russia defeated Austria at Sadowa
1867	Ibsen's *Peer Gynt*; Lister experiments with sterile surgery	Dominion of Canada founded
1868	Browning's *The Ring and the Book*; typewriter first patented	Gladstone Prime Minister
1869	Juies Verne's *Twenty Thousand Leagues Under the Sea*; Flaubert's *L'Education Sentimentale*; John Stuart Mill's *On the Subjection of Women*	Suez Canal opened
1870	Charles Dickens dies; T. H. Huxley's *Theory of Biogenesis*	Franco-Prussian War; Prussia defeats France at Sedan; fall of Napoleon III; Education Act, introducing elementary education for 5–13-year olds
1871	Lewis Carroll's *Through the Looking Glass*; George Eliot's *Middlemarch*; Charles Darwin's *The Descent of Man*	Paris Commune suppressed; the Chicago Fire; unification of Germany
1872	Edison's duplex telegraph	The Secret Ballot Act
1873	Tolstoy's *Anna Karenina*; James Clarke Maxwell's *Electricity and Magnetism*	Napoleon III dies in exile in Kent; David Livingstone dies in what is now Zambia
1874	Thomas Hardy's *Far from the Madding Crowd*; first Impressionist exhibition in Paris	Disraeli Prime Minister; Factory Act introduces fifty-six-and-a-half-hour week
1875	Bizet's *Carmen*	London Medical School for Women founded
1876	Alexander Graham Bell's telephone; Twain's *Tom Sawyer*	Battle of Little Bighorn; death of General Custer; Queen Victoria becomes Empress of India

Year   *Age Life*

1880   14   Apprenticed to Rodgers and Denyer, Drapers, at Windsor

1881   15   Pupil-teacher at Alfred William's school at Wookey,
                 Somerset; pupil at Midhurst Grammar School; apprenticed
                 to Southsea Drapery Emporium

1883–4   Under-master at Midhurst Grammar School; wins
                 scholarship and bursary at the Normal School of Science,
                 South Kensington

1884–7   Studies under T. H. Huxley at the Normal School of
                 Science; begins to write; first published work appears in
                 May 1887 in the *Science Schools Journal* – 'A Tale of the
                 Twentieth Century'

1887   21   Teacher at Holt Academy, Wrexham

1888   22   Returns to London after illness, working as a teacher; 'The
                 Chronic Argonauts' published in *Science Schools Journal*

1890   24   B.Sci degree

1891   25   Tutor for University Correspondence College; marries his
                 cousin, Isabel Wells; 'The Rediscovery of the Unique'
                 published in the *Fortnightly Review*

Year	Arts & Science	History & Politics
1877	Thomas Edison's phonograph	Britain annexes the Transvaal
1879	Dostoevsky's *The Brothers Karamazov*	Zulu Wars, South Africa
1880	Electric light devised by T. A. Edison (USA) and by J. W. Swan (Scotland)	Boer uprising in the Transvaal
1881	Henry James's *Portrait of a Lady*	President Garfield murdered, USA
1882	R. L. Stevenson's *Treasure Island*	Married Woman's Property Act
1883	Death of Karl Marx; William Thomson (later, Lord Kelvin) publishes *On the Size of Atoms*; first skyscraper in Chicago	Fabian Society founded
1884	Twain's *Huckleberry Finn*; invention of Maxim machine gun	Berlin Conference on division of Africa; Gladstone's Reform Act extends vote to country householders
1885	Zola's *Germinal*; Pasteur's vaccine to cure hydrophobia; Karl Benz's automobile	Battle of Khartoum; death of General Gordon
1886	R. L. Stevenson's *Dr Jekyll and Mr Hyde*; Rimbaud's *Les Illuminations*	Lord Salisbury Prime Minister
1887	H. W. Goodwin's celluloid film invented; speed of light measured	Queen Victoria's Golden Jubilee
1888	Kipling's *Plain Tales from the Hills*; Eastman's box camera; Dunlop's pneumatic tyre; Hertz discovers electromagnetic waves	Kaiser Frederick III dies after only three months as Emperor of Germany; accession of Wilhelm II
1889	Death of Robert Browning; T. H. Huxley's *Agnosticism*; Eiffel Tower built	Archduke Rudolf, heir to the Emperor, commits suicide at Mayerling, Austria
1890	Emily Dickinson's *Poems*; discovery of tetanus and diptheria viruses	Bismarck dismissed by the Kaiser; the 'O'Shea' scandal; Charles Parnell resigns as leader of Irish party
1891	Wilde's *The Picture of Dorian Gray*; Hardy's *Tess of the D'Urbervilles*	

Year		Life
1892	26	Meets Amy Catherine Robbins – 'Jane'
1893	27	Elopes with Jane; in poor health; first published book, *A Text Book of Biology*; lives by writing for the rest of his life
1895	29	Marries Jane; they settle in Woking; meets George Bernard Shaw; *The Time Machine*; *Select Conversations with an Uncle*; *The Wonderful Visit*; *The Stolen Bacillus*
1896	30	*The Island of Doctor Moreau*; *The Wheels of Chance*; meets George Gissing
1897	31	*The Invisible Man*; *The Plattner Story and Others*; *Thirty Strange Stories*; *The Star*
1898	32	In poor health again; travels to Italy; meets Edmund Gosse, Henry James, Joseph Conrad, J. M. Barrie; *The War of the Worlds*
1899	33	*When the Sleeper Wakes*; *Tales of Space and Time*
1900	34	Now rich enough to have house built at Sandgate, Kent; *Love and Mr Lewisham*
1901	35	*Anticipations*; *The First Men in the Moon*; birth of first son 'Gip', G. P. Wells

Year	Arts & Science	History & Politics
1892	Kipling's *Barrack Room Ballads*; Diesel's internal combustion engine	Keir Hardie wins first seat in Parliament for Labour (ILP)
1893	Henry Ford's first automobile	Gladstone's Irish Home Rule Bill defeated
1894	Shaw's *Arms and the Man*; Edison's Kinetoscope Parlour, New York; Émile Berliner's gramophone disc	Death of Alexander III, Tsar of Russia; accession of Nicholas II
1895	Conrad's *Almayer's Folly*; Freud's *Studies in Hysteria*; Wilhelm Röntgen introduces X-rays; Gillette's safety razor.	Hispano-Cuban war; London School of Economics founded; Jameson Raid, South Africa
1896	Chekhov's *The Seagull*; Nobel Prizes instituted; William Ramsay discovers helium. Rutherford publishes researches into magnetic detection of electrical waves; Becquerel determines radioactivity of uranium	Cecil Rhodes resigns as PM of Cape Colony
1897	Shaw's *Candida*; The Webbs's *Industrial Democracy*; Havelock Ellis's *Studies in the Psychology of Sex*; Robert Ross discovers the cause of malaria; Marconi's first radio transmission	Queen Victoria's Diamond Jubilee; Indian revolt on North-West Frontier
1898	Zola's *J'Accuse*; Wilde's *The Ballad of Reading Gaol*; Henry James's *The Turn of the Screw*; the Curies discover radium	Cuban-American War; death of Bismarck; Battle of Omdurman, Sudan; General Kitchener retakes Khartoum
1899	Wilde's *The Importance of Being Earnest*	Dreyfus pardoned; Boer War begins
1900	Conrad's *Lord Jim*; Chekhov's *Uncle Vanya*; Freud's *The Interpretation of Dreams*; Planck's Quantum Theory; deaths of Ruskin and Wilde	Boxer Rebellion in China
1901	Kipling's *Kim*; Thomas Mann's *Buddenbrooks*; Marconi transmits radio communication across the Atlantic	Assassination of President McKinley, USA; Theodore Roosevelt succeeds; Queen Victoria dies; accession of Edward VII

Year	Age	Life
1902	36	*The Sea Lady*; *The Discovery of the Future*
1903	37	Joins Fabian Society, the Coefficients, and the Reform Club; birth of second son, Frank; *Twelve Stories and a Dream*; *Mankind in the Making*
1904	38	*The Food of the Gods*
1905	39	*Kipps*; *A Modern Utopia*
1906	40	Affairs with Amber Reeves and Rosamund Bland; meets Gorky in New York; *In the Days of the Comet*; *Socialism and the Family*; *The Future in America*; *This Misery of Boots*; *The So-called Science of Sociology*
1908	42	Resigns from the Fabians; *First and Last Things*; *The War in the Air*; *New Worlds for Old*
1909	43	Birth of Wells's daughter, Anna, to Amber Reeves; Wells and Jane move to Hampstead; *Tono-Bungay*; *Ann Veronica*
1910	44	*The History of Mr Polly*

Year	Arts & Science	History & Politics
1902	Conrad's *Heart of Darkness*; Bennett's *Anna of the Five Towns*; William James's *The Varieties of Religious Experience*; Caruso's first record	End of the Boer War
1903	The Wright Brothers succeed in powered flight; Henry Ford starts Ford Motors; Samuel Butler's *The Way of All Flesh*; Shaw's *Man and Superman*	Bolshevik-Menshevik split in Russian socialists; Lenin becomes Bolshevik leader
1904	Picasso's *The Two Sisters*; Freud's *The Psychopathology of Everyday Life*; Chekhov's *The Cherry Orchard*	Russo-Japanese War begins; Theodore Roosevelt re-elected
1905	Einstein's Special Theory of Relativity; Debussy's *La Mer*; Cézanne's *Les Grandes Baigneuses*; Edith Wharton's *The House of Mirth*; Shaw's *Major Barbara* forbidden by New York police	Russia defeated by Japan; riots in St Petersburg, 'the Potemkin' mutinies
1906	J. J. Thompson wins Nobel Prize for Physics	American occupation of Cuba; Liberal victory in General Election – maj. 218; Labour win 54 seats
1907	First Cubist exhibition in Paris; Kipling wins Nobel Prize for Literature; Conrad's *The Secret Agent*	Defeat of Labour bill to give votes to women; arrest of fifty-seven suffragettes in London
1908	Arnold Bennett's *The Old Wives' Tale*; E. M. Forster's *A Room with a View*; Rutherford wins Nobel Prize for Physics; Wright Brothers tour Europe	Asquith Prime Minister; Mrs Pankhurst imprisoned
1909	Diaghilev's Russian Ballet in Paris; Peary Expedition at North Pole; Blériot flies the Channel	Murderer Dr Crippen arrested
1910	Marie Curie's *Treatise on Radiography*; Stravinsky's *Firebird*; Roger Fry's Post-Impressionist Exhibition in London; E. M. Forster's *Howards End*; Tolstoy dies	Death of Edward VII; accession of George V

Year	Age	Life
1911	45	*The New Machiavelli*; *The Country of the Blind and Other Stories*; *Floor Games* (for children); moves to Easton Glebe, Essex
1912	46	Meets Rebecca West; *Marriage*
1913	47	*The Passionate Friends*; *Little Wars*
1914	48	Birth of Wells's son, Anthony, to Rebecca West; visits Russia with Maurice Baring; *The Wife of Sir Isaac Harman*; *The World Set Free*; *An Englishman Looks at the World*; *The War That Will End War*
1915	49	*Boon* (originally published under the pseudonym Reginald Bliss); break with Henry James; *The Research Magnificent*; *Bealby*
1916	50	Visits Western Front in France and Italy; *Mr Britling Sees it Through*; *The Elements of Reconstruction*; *What is Coming?*
1917	51	*The Soul of a Bishop*; *War and the Future*; *God, the Invisible King*
1918	52	*Joan and Peter*; joins Ministry of Information under Lord Northcliffe
1919	53	*The Undying Fire*; *History is One*; contributor to *The Idea of a League of Nations*

Year	Arts & Science	History & Politics
1911	Amundsen at South Pole; Rutherford's *Theory of Atomic Structure*; D. H. Lawrence's *The White Peacock*; Ezra Pound's *Cantos*; Rupert Brooke's *Poems*	Lords Reform Bill passed in Lords after intervention of the King; Liberals announce first measures for National Insurance
1912	Schoenberg's *Pierrot Lunaire*; Jung's *The Theory of Psychoanalysis*	The *Titanic* disaster; Woodrow Wilson elected US President
1913	Vitamin A isolated at Yale, by Elmer McCollum; Lawrence's *Sons and Lovers*	Panama Canal opened; hunger strikes by suffragettes in prison
1914	J. H. Jean's *Radiation and the Quantum Theory*; James Joyce's *Dubliners*	Assassination of Archduke Franz Ferdinand of Austria in Sarajevo; the Great War starts
1915	D. W. Griffith's film *Birth of a Nation*; Somerset Maugham's *Of Human Bondage*; Lawrence's *The Rainbow* banned; Joseph Conrad's *Victory*	The Allied failure at Gallipoli; Zeppelins attack London; the *Lusitania* sinking; Coalition Government formed in Britain
1916	Death of Henry James; James Joyce's *Portrait of the Artist as a Young Man*; Dadaism in Zurich	The battle of Verdun; the Easter Rising, Dublin; Battle of Jutland; President Wilson's plea for peace; Lloyd George Prime Minister
1917	Freud's *Introduction to Psychoanalysis*; T. S. Eliot's *Prufrock*	America enters the war; Russian Revolution; Lenin in power; Woodrow Wilson re-elected
1918	Matisse's *Odalisques*; Joyce's *Ulysses*	Collapse of the Central Powers ends the Great War; Versailles Peace Conference; vote given to women over thirty and men over twenty-one; first woman elected to Parliament – Countess Markiewicz (Sinn Fein)
1919	Thomas H. Morgan's *The Physical Basis of Heredity*; Thomas Hardy's *Collected Poems*; Maugham's *The Moon and Sixpence*; J. M. Keynes's *The Economic Consequences of the Peace*; Bauhaus founded; Alcock and Brown fly the Atlantic	Herbert Hoover takes control of European Relief; Prohibition in America; Versailles Treaty signed; President Wilson awarded Nobel Peace Prize; socialist uprising in Berlin crushed by troops; murder of Rosa Luxemburg

Year	Age	Life
1920	54	Visits Russia; meets Lenin and Moura Budberg; *The Outline of History*; *Russia in the Shadows*
1921	55	Vsits USA; *The Salvaging of Civilization*
1922	56	*A Short History of the World*; *The Secret Places of the Heart*; unsuccessful as a Labour Parliamentary candidate for London University
1923	57	*Men Like Gods*; *The Story of a Great Schoolmaster*; *The Dream*; stands for Parliament again but defeated
1924	58	Begins affair with Odette Keun
1925	59	*Christina Alberta's Father*
1926	60	*The World of William Clissold*
1927	61	Death of Jane Wells; *Meanwhile*; *Collected Short Stories*; *Democracy Under Revision*; collected *H. G. Wells* (Atlantic edition)
1928	62	*The Open Conspiracy: Blue Prints for a World Revolution*; *Mr Blettsworthy on Rampole Island*; introduction to *The Book of Catherine Wells*

Year	Arts & Science	History & Politics
1920	Eddington's *Space, Time and Gravitation*; F. Scott Fitzgerald's *This Side of Paradise*; Sinclair Lewis's *Main Street*; Edith Wharton's *The Age of Innocence*	America rejects the League of Nations; National Socialist Workers' Party (NAZI) publishes manifesto, Germany
1921	Einstein wins Nobel Prize for Physics	Victory of Red Army in Russian Civil War
1922	T. S. Eliot's *The Waste Land*; first transmissions by BBC	Mussolini establishes dictatorship in Italy; Irish Free State established
1923	Gershwin's *Rhapsody in Blue*; E. N. da C. Andrade's *The Structure of the Atom*; Freud's *The Ego and the Id*; W. B. Yeats awarded Nobel Prize for Literature	Hitler's Nazi coup fails in Munich; Stanley Baldwin Prime Minister; Matrimonial Bill passed, allowing wives to divorce husbands; British Mandate in Palestine
1924	E. M. Forster's *A Passage to India*; Thomas Mann's *Magic Mountain*	Lenin dies; Minority Labour government; Ramsay MacDonald Prime Minister
1925	John Logie Baird's successful television experiments; Eisenstein's film *Battleship Potemkin*; Chaplin's *The Gold Rush*; Fitzgerald's *The Great Gatsby*	Hitler publishes *Mein Kampf*
1926	Fritz Lang's film *Metropolis*; William Faulkner's *Soldier's Pay*; Kafka's *The Castle*; Hemingway's *The Sun also Rises*; R. H. Tawney's *Religion and the Rise of Capitalism*	British troops withdraw from the Rhineland; British Commonwealth instituted; General Strike
1927	Lindbergh's flight from New York to Paris; Abel Gance's film *Napoleon*; Virginia Woolf's *The Lighthouse*; *The Jazz Singer* (first talkie); completion of Proust's *A la Recherche du Temps Perdu*	Trotsky expelled from Russian Communist Party
1928	J. L. Baird demonstrates colour TV; Eisenstein's film *October*	Vote given to women over twenty-one – equal rights; Chiang Kai-shek President of China

Year	Arts & Science	History & Politics
1929	Robert Graves's *Goodbye to All That*; Hemingway's *A Farewell to Arms*; Thomas Mann wins Nobel Prize for Literature	Crash of New York Stock Exchange, Wall Street; second minority Labour Government; thirteen women elected to Parliament; Nazi victory in Bavarian elections
1930	Freud's *Civilization and its Discontents*; W. H. Auden's *Poems*; Robert Frost's *Collected Poems*; Sinclair Lewis wins Nobel Prize for Literature; Amy Johnson's flight from London to Australia; death of D. H. Lawrence	Haile Selassie (Ras Tafari) becomes Emperor of Ethiopia; Gandhi's Salt March, India; Nazi party becomes second largest in Germany
1931	Death of Edison; Empire State Building completed; Chaplin's *City Lights*; Schweitzer's *My Life and Thoughts*; Faulkner's *Sanctuary*	World slump begins with the collapse of the Credit Anstalt bank, Vienna; first woman elected to the American Senate; National Government, Britain
1932	James Chadwick discovers the neutron; Fritz Lang's film of Huxley's *Brave New World*; Galsworthy's Nobel Prize for Literature	Franklin D. Roosevelt wins US Presidential election; New Deal initiated; Stalin purges begin, Russia
1933	A. N. Whitehead's *Adventures of Ideas*; Jung's *Psychology and Religion*; Orwell's *Down and Out in Paris and London*	Hitler becomes Chancellor; start of anti-Jewish measures in Germany; first concentration camps; Germany leaves League of Nations
1934	Gershwin's *Porgy and Bess*; Graves's *I, Claudius*	'Night of the Long Knives' massacre in Germany; Hitler assumes title of 'Führer', after plebiscite
1935	The Curies awarded Nobel Prize for Chemistry, having synthesized radioactive elements; The Webbs's *Soviet Communism; A New Civilization*; Graham Greene's *England Made Me*; T. S. Eliot's *Murder in the Cathedral*	Hitler denounces Versailles Treaty, forms Air Force and imposes conscription; Russian show trials; Italy invades Abyssinia

Year	Age	Life
1936	70	Awarded Hon. D. Litt by London University; *The Anatomy of Frustration*; *The Croquet Player*; *The Man Who Could Work Miracles*; *The Idea of a World Encyclopaedia*
1937	71	*Brynhild*; *Star Begotten*; *The Camford Visitation*
1938	72	*Apropos of Dolores*; *World Brain*; *The Brothers*
1939	73	Visits Sweden; *The Fate Of Homo Sapiens*; *Travels of a Republican Radical In Search of Hot Water*; *The Holy Terror*
1940	74	In London during Blitz; speaking tour of USA; *The Commonsense of War and Peace*; *Babes in the Darkling Wood*; *All Aboard for Ararat*
1941	75	*Guide to the New World*; *You Can't be Too Careful*
1942	76	*Phoenix*; *Science and the World Mind*; *The Conquest of Time* (final revision of *First and Last Things*)
1943	77	*Crux Ansata*

Year	Arts & Science	History & Politics
1936	Chaplin's *Modern Times*; Alexander Korda's film *Things to Come*; Dylan Thomas's *Twenty-Five Poems*; Kipling, Houseman and Chesterton die; A. J. Ayer's *Language, Truth and Logic*	Hitler reoccupies the Rhineland; Spanish Civil War begins; Rome-Berlin Axis announced; death of George V; Edward VIII accedes in January, abdicates in December; 'Battle of Cable St' in London's East End
1937	Picasso's *Guernica*; Steinbeck's *Of Mice and Men*; Orwell's *The Road to Wigan Pier*; Sartre's *La Nausée*; Wallace Carothers invents nylon	Stalin purges high Party and military officials; Japanese Imperialism in China, Peking and Shanghai captured
1938	Orson Welles's radio feature of H. G. Wells's *The War of the Worlds* terrifies America	Austria falls to Hitler; Munich Conference over Czecho-slovakia; Appeasement policy confirmed; Franco's victories in Spain; Roosevelt appeals to the dictators for peace
1939	Death of Freud; Joliot-Curie shows the potential of nuclear fission; Henry Moore's *Reclining Figure*; Joyce's *Finnegans Wake*; Steinbeck's *The Grapes of Wrath*; death of Yeats, and of Ford Madox Ford	Germany invades Poland; Second World War begins; Hitler-Stalin Pact; Russia invades Finland and Poland; fall of Madrid to Franco
1940	Koestler's *Darkness at Noon*	Churchill Prime Minister; Dunkirk and collapse of France; Battle of Britain; start of Blitz on London; murder of Trotsky
1941	Welles's *Citizen Kane*; Carol Reed's film *Kipps*	Hitler invades Russia; Japan bombs Pearl Harbor; America enters the war
1942	Evelyn Waugh's *Put Out More Flags*	Japan invades Burma, Malaya, Dutch East Indies; Singapore surrenders; Americans bomb Tokyo; Stalingrad siege begins; Montgomery wins El Alamein; start of Hitler's 'Final Solution'
1943	Henry Moore's sculpture *Madonna and Child*	Russian victory at Stalingrad; Warsaw Ghetto killings; Allies finally conquer North Africa; fall of Mussolini, Italy surrenders

Year   *Age* *Life*

1944   78 *'42 to '44: A Contemporary Memoir*; thesis for Doctorate
                of Science (*On the Quality of Illusion in Continuity of the
                Individual Life in the Higher Metazoa with Particular
                Reference to the Species Homo Sapiens*); in London during
                rocket attacks

1945   79 *Mind at the End of Its Tether*; *The Happy Turning*

1946   Dies in London, 13 August

Year	Arts & Science	History & Politics
1944	T. S. Eliot's *Four Quartets*	Leningrad relieved; Allies capture Rome and land in Normandy; de Gaulle enters Paris; V1 and V2 rocket raids on London
1945	Orwell's *Animal Farm*; Nobel Prize for Medicine to Alexander Fleming, E. B. Chain and Howard Florey, for discovery of penicillin	Yalta Conference; Russians capture Warsaw and Berlin; Mussolini executed, Hitler's suicide; United Nations Charter; end of the Second World War in Europe; death of President Roosevelt; atomic bombs dropped on Hiroshima and Nagasaki; Japan surrenders; Labour win General Election; Attlee Prime Minister
1946	Electronic Brain constructed at Pennsylvania University; Cocteau's film *La Belle et La Bête*; Eugene O'Neill's *The Iceman Cometh*	First General Assembly of the United Nations; nationalization of Civil Aviation, coal and the Bank of England; Churchill's 'Iron Curtain' speech
1947	Transistor invented	GATT established
1948	Norman Mailer's *The Naked and the Dead*	National Health Service; Israel founded; East German blockade of Berlin; Allied airlift into Berlin
1949	Orwell's *1984*	West Germany established, confirming division of Europe
1950	Death of Orwell	Start of Korean War

INTRODUCTION

He has come, the being who was an object of fear to primitive races, whom anxious priests tried to exorcize, whom sorcerers called up at midnight without ever yet seeing him in visible form, to whom the temporary lords of creation attributed in imagination the shape, monstrous or attractive, of gnomes, spirits, fairies or goblins. After the vulgar ideas inspired by prehistoric fears, scientific research has clarified the outlines of man's presentiment. Mesmer guessed it and in the last ten years doctors have discovered the exact nature of this being's power before its manifestation. They have experimented with this weapon of the new lord of the world, the imposition of a dominant will on the human soul, which thus becomes its slave. To this power they have given the name of magnetism, hypnotism, suggestion, and what not. I have seen them playing with it like silly children playing with fire. Woe to us! Woe to mankind. He has come . . . [1]

In a certain respect, there is nothing very odd, novel, or absurd about an invisible man – that is, in the house of fiction. All fictional characters are, strictly, invisible. If, from the flow of words that makes up a narrative, there emerges a figure, human features, a face, its presence can be explained only as the product of a reader's imagination, actively at work, 'translating' the body of textual signs into this mental-visual form. Maupassant's narrator surmises (when he is not convinced that it has the objective reality he claims for it in the passage quoted above) that the invisible being haunting him is the hallucinatory effect of 'a deep fissure in my mind and in the logical processes of my thought. Phenomena of this kind occur in dreams, in which we are not surprised at the most wildly fantastic happenings, because our critical faculty and power of objective examination are dormant, while the imaginative mechanism is awake and active.'[2] What is true of dreams is true of fiction. Readers, like dreamers, do not require an elaborate mechanical or techno-

logical edifice to buttress fantasy. Fantasy is precisely that which
floats free of such 'real' determination.

Or is it? Even to claim that *The Invisible Man* is a 'fantasy' –
and the term is routinely applied to Wells's scientific romances
– is in the first place to risk dropping into a paradoxical abyss.
The term itself, etymologically, denotes 'a making visible'
(*OED*). Wells must have smiled when Joseph Conrad wrote to
him, placing the book in the category of 'the Fantastic'. The
story, after all, enacts 'a making *in*visible' of its protagonist,
Griffin, in which respect it could only be termed an anti-fantasy.
But Conrad's remark was not without an inbuilt paradox of its
own: 'Impressed is *the* word, O Realist of the Fantastic! whether
you like it or not,' was his declared response to *The Invisible
Man*. 'And if you want to know what impresses me it is to see
how you contrive to give over humanity into the clutches of the
Impossible and yet manage to keep it down (or up) to its
humanity, to its flesh, blood, sorrow, folly. *That* is the achieve-
ment! In this little book you do it with an appalling complete-
ness.'[3] Conrad's praise is drawn forth not simply by the
'fantastic' elements of the text, but by the 'realist' grounding
they are given. He is presumably lauding Wells's strenuous
efforts to render his unlikely tale 'plausible', both by locating its
action in an 'ordinary' social and geographical setting, and by
offering an apparently rational, 'scientific' explanation for Griffin's discovery of invisibility. The point implicit in Conrad's
response, I think, is that the yoking of the 'fantastic' to the
'realistic' produces a narrative dynamism between two modes of
representation which is, by definition, absent in unbridled
fantasy. In other words, the fantastic is heightened, its qualities
more keenly evidenced, by its sharp juxtaposition with the
realistic. This is what Wells, at any rate, was to claim for his
scientific romances almost four decades later.[4]

Whether or not this proposal is valid can only be confirmed
by individual readings of *The Invisible Man*. Radical fantasists
and super-realists might argue that the co-presence of realism
and fantasy within the boundaries of a single text leads to a
mutual neutralisation, rather than intensification, of each. Both
are also likely to be perplexed as to why a novel, whose verbal
form determines that the invisibility of characters is pre-given,
should expend so much effort attempting to convince readers
that invisibility is technically possible. There can be no doubt,

however, that it was a prime intention of Wells to effect such readerly conviction. Indeed, in retrospect, he thought he might have failed to do so, as he told Arnold Bennett in the month after the book first appeared:

> There is another difficulty . . . which really makes the whole story impossible. I believe it to be insurmountable. Any alteration in the refractive index of the eye lens would make vision impossible. Without such alteration the eyes would be visible as glassy globules. And for vision it is also necessary that there should be visual purple behind the retina and an opaque cornea and iris. On these lines you would get a very effective short story but nothing more.[5]

But the letter also indicates that Wells was prepared to sacrifice the demands of technical 'plausibility' when they fundamentally impeded his yarn-spinning impulses. Only *Griffin*'s 'story', the narrative Griffin tells Kemp, can be 'impossible' for the reasons offered. *Wells*'s story none the less manages to get written by recourse to the time-honoured device of simply omitting to mention these difficulties.

Where Wells differs from the out-and-out fantasist is in refusing the obvious fall-back position of simple reliance on the reader's suspension of disbelief. Instead, he throws up a haze of technological and pseudo-scientific detail, replete with jargon and up-to-the minute buzz words, conveniently attenuating his technical descriptions when they come close to what would be an embarrassing complexity. Here, for instance, is a typical Griffin speech, delivered mid-way through the expositional discourse which is at the heart of the book:

> 'I will tell you, Kemp, sooner or later, all the complicated processes. We need not go into that now. For the most part, saving certain gaps I chose to remember, they are written in cypher in those books that tramp has hidden. We must hunt him down. We must get those books again. But the essential phase was to place the transparent object whose refractive index was to be lowered between two radiating centres of a sort of ethereal vibration, of which I will tell you more fully later. No, not these Röntgen vibrations – I don't know that these others of mine have been described. Yet they are obvious enough. I needed two little dynamos, and these I worked with a cheap gas engine. My first

experiment was with a bit of white wool fabric. It was the
strangest thing in the world to see it in the flicker of the flashes
soft and white, and then to watch it fade like a wreath of smoke
and vanish.' (p. 86)

This speech is only apparently expository. Its rhetorical strat-
egies all point to the actual ineffability of what Wells purports
to describe. Thus Griffin is made to delay ('I will tell you, Kemp,
sooner or later, all the complicated processes. We need not go
into that now ... I will tell you more fully later'), to claim
forgetfulness ('for the most part, saving certain gaps I chose to
remember, they are written in cypher in those books'), to retreat
into imprecise generalities ('two radiating centres of a sort of
ethereal vibration'), to decline the opportunity to furnish particulars ('they are obvious enough'), and to indulge in casual
name-dropping which only serves to distract from the paucity
of information he has vouchsafed ('these Röntgen vibrations').[6]
Naturally, these informational deficiencies are not restored later
in the novel. The postponed explanation never happens, the
books are not recovered, and so on. Rather, the narrative
proceeds swiftly *as if* a sufficient theoretical exposition of
invisibility has been given here. By the end of the paragraph,
indeed, Griffin has breezily moved the discussion on to practi-
calities. The exposition that has been staged is a mere simula-
crum. It represents a genuine theory only as much as Griffin's
pantomime mask represents a real face.

Wells thus creates a twofold problem for himself. Firstly, a
theory of invisibility is not required to validate Griffin's 'auth-
enticity'. For the reader, and for Kemp, he is already invisible
beyond doubt. From this point of view the exposition of the
theory is a potentially prolix excrescence or indulgence. This
'fantasist' objection might seem to be answered by the 'realist'
counter-argument that what Griffin's invisibility generates is not
doubt but *mystery*, and that what is desired is not evidence to
prove that Griffin is genuinely invisible (the reader and Kemp
both know that he is) but disclosure of the 'plausible' methods
whereby he has achieved this state: '"But how was it all done?"
said Kemp, "and how did you get like this?"' (p. 74); '"Before
we can do anything else," said Kemp, "I must understand a little
more about this invisibility of yours"' (p. 80). This is where
Wells meets his second difficulty, for Griffin's account does not,

in fact, reveal his secrets, or does so in such an obscure and partial manner that the enigma is only redoubled thereby. In short, Wells's 'realist fantasy' runs the risk of falling foul of both fantasist and realist readers alike.

What might be the benefits of taking such chances? We can examine this dilemma in the light of a comparison with a narrative which was, without doubt, a major source of inspiration for *The Invisible Man*. This is the tale of Gyges the Lydian, as told by Socrates in Book II of Plato's *The Republic*:

They relate that he was a shepherd in the service of the ruler at that time of Lydia, and that after a great deluge of rain and an earthquake the ground opened and a chasm appeared in the place where he was pasturing; and they say that he saw and wondered and went down into the chasm; and the story goes that he beheld other marvels there and a hollow bronze horse with little doors, and that he peeped in and saw a corpse within, as it seemed, of more than mortal stature, and that there was nothing else but a gold ring on its hand, which he took off and went forth. And when the shepherds held their customary assembly to make their monthly report to the king about the flocks, he also attended wearing the ring. So as he sat there it chanced that he turned the collet of the ring towards himself, towards the inner part of his hand, and when this took place they say that he became invisible to those who sat by him and they spoke of him as absent; and that he was amazed, and again fumbling with the ring turned the collet outwards and so became visible. On noting this he experimented with the ring to see if it possessed this virtue, and he found the result to be that when he turned the collet inwards he became invisible, and when outwards visible; and becoming aware of this, he immediately managed things so that he became one of the messengers who went up to the king, and on coming there he seduced the king's wife and with her aid set upon the king and slew him and possessed his kingdom. If now there should be two such rings, and the just man should put on one and the unjust the other, no one could be found, it would seem, of such adamantine temper as to persevere in justice and endure to refrain his hands from the possessions of others and not touch them, though he might with impunity take what he wished even from the market-place, and enter into houses and lie with whom he pleased, and slay and loose bonds from whomsoever he would, and in all other things conduct himself among mankind as the equal of a god.[7]

Socrates recounts the Gyges story as an example of anti-social licence and its ethical consequences. Plainly parabolic, the narrative properly ignores the mechanism of the invisibility-inducing ring. It is only interested in this supernatural marvel insofar as it disrupts the moral order of the everyday world. As such, the tale is one of absolute corruption caused by the possession and exercise of power. The thesis is not countenanced that Gyges must already have been morally corrupt to so use the power he accidentally acquired. The most just of men, Socrates claims, would do exactly the same.

The Invisible Man is obviously related to the Gyges tale, but in complex ways. It too is a parable of moral decadence, but where does Griffin's corruption begin? He tells Kemp that, once the technical possibility of personal invisibility dawned on him, '"I beheld, unclouded by doubt, a magnificent vision of all that invisibility might mean to a man – the mystery, the power, the freedom. Drawbacks I saw none"' (p. 84). Was the failure to see 'drawbacks' here the first seed of moral decomposition, or a sign that it was already established? Once he has *made* himself invisible, to be sure, Griffin's sense of egoistic potency is enormously magnified: 'I was invisible, and I was only just beginning to realise the extraordinary advantage my invisibility gave me. My head was already teeming with plans of all the wild and wonderful things I had now impunity to do' (p. 93). Between these two points he not only confesses to a number of outrageous crimes, but demonstrates a marked nihilism in accounting for them: he robs his father of money belonging to someone else, and his father commits suicide ('"I did not feel a bit sorry for my father. He seemed to me to be the victim of his own foolish sentimentality"' (p. 85)); he tortures a cat, and then lies to its owner, his neighbour ('"a drink-sodden old creature with only a white cat to care for in all the world . . . She had to be satisfied at last and went away again"' (p. 87)); and deliberately sets fire to a lodging house full of people ('"no doubt it was insured"' (p. 93)). This moral degeneration is, like the chemical process which effects invisibility, gradual and cumulative. Griffin's becoming invisible is a literal textual event, but it is also a metaphor for the complete withdrawal from social life which his moral bankruptcy signifies. The narrative then prompts twin questions, one on the literal, one on the metaphorical plane: (a) is invisibility reversible?; and (b) is there a degree of moral corruption beyond which an individual is no longer redeemable?

Like the Gyges tale, then, *The Invisible Man* sets out to ignite an ethical debate around the concentration of great power in individual hands. But we are perhaps now in a position to appreciate one of the narrative functions of Wells's decision to do what Socrates does not – that is, to construct a technical edifice around a fantastic notion. For one thing, Griffin's methodical pursuit of the goal of invisibility serves to establish that his turpitude is not the result of mental derangement. Indeed, his intellectual grasp of the technical issues and his relaxation of principles increase in direct proportion to each other. Eventually, mere expediency becomes his only behavioural touchstone. The following is his attempt to justify to Kemp the treatment he has meted out to one of his unfortunate victims, the costumier whom he knocks unconscious and ties up in a sheet. Kemp invokes '"common conventions of humanity"' to judge this act. But those, Griffin retorts, '"are all very well for common people"':

'My dear Kemp, it's no good your sitting and glaring as though I was a murderer. It had to be done. He had his revolver. If once he saw me he would be able to describe me —'

'But still,' said Kemp, 'in England – today. And the man was in his own house, and you were – well, robbing.'

'Robbing! Confound it! You'll call me a thief next! Surely, Kemp, you're not fool enough to dance on the old strings. Can't you see my position?'

'And his too,' said Kemp.

The Invisible Man stood up sharply. 'What do you mean to say?'

Kemp's face grew a trifle hard. He was about to speak and checked himself. 'I suppose, after all,' he said with a sudden change of manner, 'the thing had to be done. You were in a fix. But still —'

'Of course I was in a fix – an infernal fix. And he made me wild too – hunting me about the house, fooling about with his revolver, locking and unlocking doors. He was simply exasperating. You don't blame me, do you? You don't blame me?'

'I never blame anyone,' said Kemp. 'It's quite out of fashion.' (p. 109)

Kemp *does*, of course, blame him. His seeming dismissal of moral concerns is merely a subterfuge to maintain Griffin in dialogue until his would-be captors (whom Kemp has already summoned) arrive. What is intriguing about the passage is Griffin's reaction. He is clearly still shaken by the possibility that ethical judgments ('the old strings') might ensnare him. It is not so much that he displays a residual moral sense, but rather that he seems to perceive the potential *power* of moral evaluation – its power, that is, to mobilise society to resistance against him. It is not a lingering conscience which disturbs Griffin here, but the prospect of collective co-operation overwhelming his own individual might. It is as logical as it is reprehensible that he should proceed to propose a 'Reign of Terror' which will 'terrify and dominate' the community (p. 115). The 'scientific' elements of the tale help to establish that Griffin may be vicious, but that he is not mad.

None the less, Wells could clearly have staged this kind of moral debate, as Plato does, without recourse to a spurious scientific explanation of invisibility: one of the funniest moments in the history of literary criticism, after all, is Mario Praz's complaint about Mary Shelley's failure to specify how Frankenstein enlivened dead tissue to make his monster.[8] Undoubtedly the technological dimension is there partly to forestall accusations of unoriginality. Wells was hardly the first to make a fiction out of bodily invisibility, but to present it as scientifically explicable was entirely new. Maupassant's story leaves the existential status of 'Le Horla' in suspension: it might easily be read as the delusion of a demented narrator. In Fitzjames O'Brien's 'What Was It?', on the other hand, the invisible being is a decidedly objective fact and, moreover, the story contains the following speculative conversation between the narrator, Harry, and his friend, Dr Hammond:

'Let us reason a little, Harry. Here is a solid body which we touch, but which we cannot see. The fact is so unusual that it strikes us with terror. Is there no parallel, though, for such a phenomenon? Take a piece of pure glass. It is tangible and transparent. A certain chemical coarseness is all that prevents its being so entirely transparent as to be totally invisible. It is not *theoretically impossible*, mind you, to make a glass which shall not reflect a single ray of light, – a glass so pure and homogeneous in its atoms that the rays from the sun will pass through it as they do through the air, refracted but not reflected. We do not see the air, and yet we feel it.'

'That's all very well, Hammond, but these are inanimate substances. Glass does not breathe, air does not breathe. *This* thing has a heart that palpitates, – a will that moves it, – lungs that play, and inspire and respire."⁹

But the pair get no further than this: as the title of the story suggests, the physical reality of the invisible being remains a matter of note and query rather than explanation. Wells clearly identified the need to put more scientific flesh on these unseen bones.

Yet there is more to *The Invisible Man*'s contrived scientificity than a wish on Wells's part to differentiate his story from those who had earlier dealt with the theme. Without it, the novel would not be the comic satire that it is. For, just as Griffin's intellectual advances are made at the price of moral regression, so his lust for power, evidenced as much by his desire to transform himself as to assume control over others, is inflated by comparison with the little that his invisibility does, pathetically, achieve for him. Essentially, *The Invisible Man* is an inversion of the tale of Gyges. Griffin does not obtain real power. He is lucky enough even to receive attention:

'The more I thought it over, Kemp, the more I realised what a helpless absurdity an Invisible Man was – in a cold and dirty climate and a crowded civilised city. Before I made this mad experiment I had dreamt of a thousand advantages. That after-noon it seemed all disappointment. I went over the heads of the things a man reckons desirable. No doubt invisibility made it possible to get them, but it made it impossible to enjoy them when they were got. Ambition – what is the good of pride of place when you cannot appear there? What is the good of the love of woman when her name must needs be Delilah? I have no taste for politics, for the blackguardisms of fame, for philanthropy, for sport. What was I to do? And for this I had become a wrapped-up mystery, a swathed and bandaged caricature of a man!' (pp. 111–12)

It is in passages like these that *The Invisible Man* reads like a 'realist' critique of 'fantasy', the very genre in which Wells is, putatively, working. Griffin's failure to consider the English weather and urban crowding is a trope for his active renunciation of the material basis of all collective life. His ambition is to break free of what are undoubtedly material causes of his social isolation, particularly albinism and poverty. But he has not the foresight to perceive that the visual effacement of his body will not be a solution to either. Instead of being recognised as 'other' because of his skin's lack of pigmentation, his invisibility simply leads to his not being recognised at all. Money, moreover, has no value other than in exchange; but to exchange with others one must be capable of being acknowledged by them. In the first instance, Griffin is thus forced to *dissemble* a visual presence, in a stunning reversal of the tale of the emperor's new clothes, by becoming a man of garments. Next, he hatches a plan, 'A way of getting back! Of restoring what I have done' (p. 112). He is learning, but learning too late, that one's social identity is fundamentally rooted in the material of the body. To forget that is to live, so to speak, in a fantasy: it is this 'realist' lesson which Wells's tale, paradoxically, 'makes visible'.

The fact that *The Invisible Man* is in part a fictional critique of the Nietzschean 'will to power' is yet another sign of Wells's extraordinary topicality. Patrick Bridgwater has pointed out that in the month the novel began to be serialised (June 1897) Thomas Common defended Nietzsche against Wells's 'accusation of "blackguardism", a charge which Wells made in *Natural Science* (April 1897): "The tendency of a belief in natural selection as the main factor of human progress, is, in the moral field, towards the glorification of a sort of rampant egotism – of blackguardism in fact, – as the New Gospel. You get that in the Gospel of Nietzsche."'[10] Bridgwater agrees that Wells's reading of Nietzsche was sorely misguided. But misunderstanding of the German philosopher's work was the norm rather than the exception in this period, and need not detain us. The more important fact is that Wells, according to Bridgwater, was the first English artist to pay serious attention to Nietzsche (who was not to die until 1900).

What Wells achieves in the character of Griffin, whose name itself indicates a unity of different species,[11] – is an assimilation of the Nietzschean 'beyond-man' (the word with which Tille clumsily translated the German *Übermensch*) to the Marlovian overreacher. Griffin, a 'singular person', falls 'out of infinity into Iping' (p. 13), just as Nietzsche's prophet Zarathustra descends from the mountains to preach his parody of the New Testament and the coming of the superman. But Griffin is at once a more minatory and more absurd figure than Zarathustra. He believes himself to be the superman as well as the prophet of his arrival. His growing megalomania culminates in the proclamation of a new dynasty, with himself as emperor: 'Port Burdock is no longer under the Queen, tell your Colonel of Police, and the rest of them; it is under me – the Terror! This is day one of year one of the new epoch – the Epoch of the Invisible Man. I am Invisible Man the First.' Typically, however, this edict arrives at Kemp's house in 'a strange missive, written in pencil on a greasy sheet of paper ... on the addressed side of it the postmark Hinton-dean, and the prosaic detail "2d. to pay"' (p. 123) – hardly an auspicious style in which to issue such an historic declaration. The episode is representative: Wells's satirical subversion of his superman is consistently a matter of juxtaposing Griffin's de-socialised ambitions and bombastic rhetoric with the 'prosaic detail' of English provincial society and the necessities of material life. Like Marlowe's Doctor Faustus,[12] Griffin, in the event, barters his life and happiness for a career of farcical ignominy and a final, tragic solitude.

The Invisible Man is undoubtedly the least 'romantic' of Wells's scientific romances. Like every romance, it is centrally concerned with a character whose story is decidedly 'out of the ordinary'. But it throws into crisis this hero's experience, and the genre of romance itself, by engineering a collision between the anticipatedly 'fantastic' and the recognisably 'realistic'. Wells had done this before in *The Wonderful Visit* (1895), but his more typical devices were the creation of an alternative world or radical alteration of that which was familiar. Thus the protagonists of *The Time Machine* (1895) and *The Island of Doctor Moreau* (1896) were both deliberately displaced from late Victorian England (the first temporally, the other geographically), and in *The War of the Worlds* (1898) and *In the Days of the Comet* (1906) England itself would be drastically transformed. *The Invisible Man* eschews these possibilities, however, and is therefore 'a grotesque romance' in a number of senses. Firstly, it is a romance whose hero is a grotesque: one member of the novel's panoply of opinionated rustics, Silas Durgan, indeed proposes the only career for Griffin that the denizens of Iping would be likely to sponsor: '"if he choses to show enself at fairs he'd make his fortune in no time"' (p. 20). Secondly, *The Invisible Man* grotesquely distorts the romance genre by cross-fertilising it with its antithesis: Griffin falls out of the infinity of romance into the incongruously particular realism of a West Sussex village in 1896.[13] Bruce Beiderwell has, thirdly, related Wells's novel to the specific conception of the grotesque found in John Ruskin's *The Stones of Venice* (1851-3):

> He notes that the grotesque is composed of two complementary elements, 'one ludicrous, the other fearful.' The difficulty in distinguishing between these two elements, Ruskin maintains, arises from the fact that 'the mind, under certain phases of excitement, *plays* with *terror*, and summons images which, if it were in another temper, would be awful, but of which, either in weariness or in irony, it refrains for a time to acknowledge the true terribleness.' A tension between play and terror (along with a resistance to the full recognition of terror) functions as the central technique in *The Invisible Man*.'[14]

This 'attempted combination, as it were, of Thurber and Kafka'[15] makes the reading of Wells's novel a curiously contradictory and indecisive experience. In it, we witness the boundaries between certain seemingly fixed and opposed categories – romance and realism, exuberance and fear, sensationalism and seriousness, and (Wells's major preoccupations) science and art – begin to corrode and dissolve, and the possibilities of new and better syntheses emerge. In a very proper sense of the epithet, *The Invisible Man* was an experimental fiction.

MACDONALD DALY

References

1. Guy de Maupassant, 'Le Horla' (1887), trans. H. N. P. Sloman, *The Mountain Inn and Other Stories* (Harmondsworth: Penguin, 1955), pp. 49–50.
2. *ibid.*, p. 45.
3. Quoted in Patrick Parrinder (ed.), *H. G. Wells: The Critical Heritage* (London: Routledge and Kegan Paul), p. 60.

4. See Wells's preface to *The Scientific Romances of H. G. Wells* (London: Gollancz, 1933), pp. vii–x (reprinted in the Appendix).

5. Harris Wilson (ed.), *Arnold Bennett and H. G. Wells* (London: Hart-Davis, 1960), pp. 34–5.

6. On Röntgen, see the note to p. 86.

7. Plato, *The Republic*, trans. Paul Shorey (London: Heinemann, 1937), pp. 117, 119. Wells read *The Republic* as a youth and records, in *Experiment in Autobiography* (London: Gollancz and the Cresset Press, 1934), p. 177, 'its immense significance' for him. See also Philip Holt, 'H. G. Wells and the Ring of Gyges', *Science-Fiction Studies* 19 (July 1992), pp. 236–47.

8. Mario Praz, 'Introductory Essay', *Three Gothic Novels* (Harmondsworth: Penguin, 1968), pp. 25–7. To be fair to Praz, his distinction is between pseudo-scientific novelists who 'try to lift the veil, be it only for a moment' and those who make no attempt whatsoever to explain scientific processes. He mentions Wells to include him in the former category.

9. Fitzjames O'Brien, 'What Was It?', *The Diamond Lens and Other Stories* (London: Ward and Downey, 1887), p. 261.

10. Patrick Bridgwater, *Nietzsche in Anglosaxony* (Leicester: Leicester University Press, 1972), p. 56. Bridgwater argues that specific Nietzschean influence is observable in Wells's *The Island of Doctor Moreau* (1896) and *When the Sleeper Wakes* (1899), and concludes that Wells read Alexander Tille's edition of *The Collected Works of Friedrich Nietzsche*, the first two volumes of which had been published the previous year: vol. VII, *Thus Spake Zarathustra: A Book for All and None* (trans. Alexander Tille), and vol. XI, *The Case of Wagner: Nietzsche* Contra *Wagner; The Twilight of the Idols; The Antichrist* (trans. Thomas Common) (2 vols., London: H. Henry, 1896).

11. On the name, see the first note to p. 72.

12. 'Sweet Mephistophilis, so charm me here,/That I may walk invisible to all,/And do whate'er I please unseen of any' – *Doctor Faustus*, III.iii.11–14.

13. On the date of the events of the novel, see the first note to p. 13.

14. Bruce Beiderwell, 'The Grotesque in Wells's *The Invisible Man*', *Extrapolation* 24, 4 (1983), p. 302.

15. Bernard Bergonzi, *The Early H. G. Wells: A Study of the Scientific Romances* (Manchester: Manchester University Press, 1961), pp. 118–19.

THE INVISIBLE MAN

CHAPTER I

The Strange Man's Arrival

The stranger came early in February,* one wintry day, through a biting wind and a driving snow, the last snowfall of the year, over the down,* walking as it seemed from Bramblehurst* railway station, and carrying a little black portmanteau in his thickly gloved hand. He was wrapped up from head to foot, and the brim of his soft felt hat hid every inch of his face but the shiny tip of his nose; the snow had piled itself against his shoulders and chest, and added a white crest to the burden he carried. He staggered into the Coach and Horses,* more dead than alive as it seemed, and flung his portmanteau down. 'A fire,' he cried, 'in the name of human charity! A room and a fire!' He stamped and shook the snow from off himself in the bar, and followed Mrs Hall into her guest parlour to strike his bargain. And with that much introduction, that and a ready acquiescence to terms and a couple of sovereigns* flung upon the table, he took up his quarters in the inn.

Mrs Hall lit the fire and left him there while she went to prepare him a meal with her own hands. A guest to stop at Iping* in the winter-time was an unheard-of piece of luck, let alone a guest who was no 'haggler', and she was resolved to show herself worthy of her good fortune. As soon as the bacon was well under way, and Millie, her lymphatic* aid, had been brisked up a bit by a few deftly chosen expressions of contempt, she carried the cloth, plates, and glasses into the parlour and began to lay them with the utmost éclat.* Although the fire was burning up briskly, she was surprised to see that her visitor still wore his hat and coat, standing with his back to her and staring out of the window at the falling snow in the yard. His gloved hands were clasped behind him, and he seemed to be lost in thought. She noticed that the melted snow that still sprinkled his shoulders dropped upon her carpet. 'Can I take your hat and coat, sir,' she said, 'and give them a good dry in the kitchen?'

'No,' he said without turning.

She was not sure she had heard him, and was about to repeat her question.

He turned his head and looked at her over his shoulder. 'I prefer to keep them on,' he said with emphasis, and she noticed that he wore big blue spectacles with side-lights,* and had a bushy side-whisker* over his coat-collar that completely hid his cheeks and face.

'Very well, sir,' she said. '*As* you like. In a bit the room will be warmer.'

He made no answer, and had turned his face away from her again, and Mrs Hall, feeling that her conversational advances were ill-timed, laid the rest of the table things in a quick staccato and whisked out of the room. When she returned he was still standing there, like a man of stone, his back hunched, his collar turned up, his dripping hat-brim turned down, hiding his face and ears completely. She put down the eggs and bacon with considerable emphasis, and called rather than said to him, 'Your lunch is served, sir.'

'Thank you,' he said at the same time, and did not stir until she was closing the door. Then he swung round and approached the table with a certain eager quickness.

As she went behind the bar to the kitchen she heard a sound repeated at regular intervals. Chirk, chirk, chirk, it went, the sound of a spoon being rapidly whisked round a basin. 'That girl!' she said. 'There! I clean forgot it. It's her being so long!' And while she herself finished mixing the mustard, she gave Millie a few verbal stabs for her excessive slowness. She had cooked the ham and eggs, laid the table, and done everything, while Millie (help indeed!) had only succeeded in delaying the mustard. And him a new guest and wanting to stay! Then she filled the mustard pot, and putting it with a certain stateliness upon a gold and black tea-tray, carried it into the parlour.

She rapped and entered promptly. As she did so her visitor moved quickly, so that she got but a glimpse of a white object disappearing behind the table. It would seem he was picking something from the floor. She rapped down the mustard pot on the table, and then she noticed the overcoat and hat had been taken off and put over a chair in front of the fire, and a pair of wet boots threatened rust to her steel fender. She went to these things resolutely. 'I suppose I may have them to dry now,' she said in a voice that brooked no denial.

'Leave the hat,' said her visitor, in a muffled voice, and turning she saw he had raised his head and was sitting and looking at her.

For a moment she stood gaping at him, too surprised to speak.

He held a white cloth – it was a *serviette* he had brought with him – over the lower part of his face, so that his mouth and jaws were completely hidden, and that was the reason of his muffled voice. But it was not that which startled Mrs Hall. It was the fact that all his forehead above his blue glasses was covered by a white bandage, and that another covered his ears, leaving not a scrap of his face exposed excepting only his pink, peaked nose. It was bright, pink, and shiny just as it had been at first. He wore a dark-brown velvet jacket with a high, black, linen-lined collar turned up about his neck. The thick black hair, escaping as it could below and between the cross bandages, projected in curious tails and horns, giving him the strangest appearance conceivable. This muffled and bandaged head was so unlike what she had anticipated, that for a moment she was rigid.

He did not remove the *serviette*, but remained holding it, as she saw now, with a brown gloved hand, and regarding her with his inscrutable blue glasses. 'Leave the hat,' he said, speaking very distinctly through the white cloth.

Her nerves began to recover from the shock they had received. She placed the hat on the chair again by the fire. 'I didn't know, sir,' she began, 'that—' and she stopped embarrassed.

'Thank you,' he said drily, glancing from her to the door and then at her again.

'I'll have them nicely dried, sir, at once,' she said, and carried his clothes out of the room. She glanced at his white-swathed head and blue goggles again as she was going out of the door; but his napkin was still in front of his face. She shivered a little as she closed the door behind her, and her face was eloquent of her surprise and perplexity. 'I *never*,' she whispered. 'There!' She went quite softly to the kitchen, and was too preoccupied to ask Millie what she was messing about with *now*, when she got there.

The visitor sat and listened to her retreating feet. He glanced inquiringly at the window before he removed his *serviette*, and resumed his meal. He took a mouthful, glanced suspiciously at the window, took another mouthful, then rose and, taking the *serviette* in his hand, walked across the room and pulled the blind down to the top of the white muslin that obscured the lower panes. This left the room in a twilight. This done, he returned with an easier air to the table and his meal.

'The poor soul's had an accident or an opration or something,' said Mrs Hall. 'What a turn them bandages did give me, to be sure!'

She put on some more coal, unfolded the clothes-horse,* and extended the traveller's coat upon this. 'And they goggles! Why, he looked more like a divin' helmet than a human man!' She hung his muffler on a corner of the horse. 'And holding that handkercher over his mouth all the time. Talkin' through it! . . . Perhaps his mouth was hurt too – maybe.'

She turned round, as one who suddenly remembers. 'Bless my soul alive!' she said, going off at a tangent; 'ain't you done them taters* yet, Millie?'

When Mrs Hall went to clear away the stranger's lunch, her idea that his mouth must also have been cut or disfigured in the accident she supposed him to have suffered, was confirmed, for he was smoking a pipe, and all the time that she was in the room he never loosened the silk muffler he had wrapped round the lower part of his face to put the mouth piece to his lips. Yet it was not forgetfulness, for she saw he glanced at it as it smouldered out. He sat in the corner with his back to the window-blind and spoke now, having eaten and drunk and being comfortably warmed through, with less aggressive brevity than before. The reflection of the fire lent a kind of red animation to his big spectacles they had lacked hitherto.

'I have some luggage,' he said, 'at Bramblehurst station,' and he asked her how he could have it sent. He bowed his bandaged head quite politely in acknowledgment of her explanation. 'Tomorrow!' he said. 'There is no speedier delivery?' and seemed quite disappointed when she answered, 'No.' Was she quite sure? No man with a trap who would go over?

Mrs Hall, nothing loath, answered his questions and developed a conversation. 'It's a steep road by the down, sir,' she said in answer to the question about a trap; and then, snatching at an opening, said, 'It was there a carriage was upsettled,* a year ago and more. A gentleman killed, besides his coachman. Accidents, sir, happen in a moment, don't they?'

But the visitor was not to be drawn so easily. 'They do,' he said through his muffler, eyeing her quietly through his impenetrable glasses.

'But they take long enough to get well, sir, don't they? . . . There was my sister's son, Tom, jest* cut his arm with a scythe, tumbled on it in the 'ayfield, and, bless me! he was three months tied up, sir. You'd hardly believe it. It's regular* given me a dread of a scythe, sir.'

'I can quite understand that,' said the visitor.

'He was afraid, one time, that he'd have to have an opration – he was that bad, sir.'

The visitor laughed abruptly, a bark of a laugh that he seemed to bite and kill in his mouth. '*Was* he?' he said.

'He was, sir. And no laughing matter to them as had the doing for him,* as I had – my sister being took up with her little ones so much. There was bandages to do, sir, and bandages to undo. So that if I may make so bold as to say it, sir—'

'Will you get me some matches?' said the visitor, quite abruptly. 'My pipe is out.'

Mrs Hall was pulled up suddenly. It was certainly rude of him, after telling him all she had done. She gasped at him for a moment, and remembered the two sovereigns. She went for the matches.

'Thanks,' he said concisely, as she put them down, and turned his shoulder upon her and stared out of the window again. It was altogether too discouraging. Evidently he was sensitive on the top of operations and bandages. She did not 'make so bold as to say,' however, after all. But his snubbing way had irritated her, and Millie had a hot time of it that afternoon.

The visitor remained in the parlour until four o'clock, without giving the ghost of an excuse for an intrusion. For the most part he was quite still during that time; it would seem he sat in the growing darkness smoking in the firelight, perhaps dozing.

Once or twice a curious listener might have heard him at the coals, and for the space of five minutes he was audible pacing the room. He seemed to be talking to himself. Then the armchair creaked as he sat down again.

CHAPTER 2

Mr Teddy Henfrey's First Impressions

At four o'clock, when it was fairly dark and Mrs Hall was screwing up her courage to go in and ask her visitor if he would take some tea, Teddy Henfrey, the clock-jobber,* came into the bar. 'My sakes!* Mrs Hall,' said he, 'but this is terrible weather for thin boots!' The snow outside was falling faster.

Mrs Hall agreed with him, and then noticed he had his bag, and hit upon a brilliant idea. 'Now you're here, Mr Teddy,' said she, 'I'd be glad if you'd give th' old clock in the parlour a bit of a look. 'T is going, and it strikes well and hearty; but the hour-hand won't do nuthin' but point at six.'

And leading the way, she went across to the parlour door and rapped and entered.

Her visitor, she saw as she opened the door, was seated in the armchair before the fire, dozing it would seem, with his bandaged head drooping on one side. The only light in the room was the red glow from the fire – which lit his eyes like adverse railway signals,* but left his downcast face in darkness – and the scanty vestiges of the day that came in through the open door. Everything was ruddy, shadowy, and indistinct to her, the more so since she had just been lighting the bar lamp, and her eyes were dazzled. But for a second it seemed to her that the man she looked at had an enormous mouth wide open, a vast and incredible mouth that swallowed the whole of the lower portion of his face. It was the sensation of a moment: the white-bound head, the monstrous goggle eyes, and this huge yawn below it. Then he stirred, started up in his chair, put up his hand. She opened the door wide, so that the room was lighter, and she saw him more clearly, with the muffler held to his face just as she had seen him hold the *serviette* before. The shadows, she fancied, had tricked her.

'Would you mind, sir, this man a-coming to look at the clock, sir?' she said, recovering from her momentary shock.

'Look at the clock?' he said, staring round in a drowsy

manner, and speaking over his hand, and then, getting more fully awake, 'certainly.'

Mrs Hall went away to get a lamp, and he rose and stretched himself. Then came the light, and Mr Teddy Henfrey, entering, was confronted by this bandaged person. He was, he says,* 'taken aback'.

'Good-afternoon,' said the stranger, regarding him, as Mr Henfrey says, with a vivid sense of the dark spectacles, 'like a lobster'.

'I hope,' said Mr Henfrey, 'that it's no intrusion.'

'None whatever,' said the stranger. 'Though, I understand,' he said, turning to Mrs Hall, 'that this room is really to be mine for my own private use.'

'I thought, sir,' said Mrs Hall, 'you'd prefer the clock—' She was going to say 'mended'.

'Certainly,' said the stranger, 'certainly – but, as a rule, I like to be alone and undisturbed.'

'But I'm really glad to have the clock seen to,' he said, seeing a certain hesitation in Mr Henfrey's manner. 'Very glad.' Mr Henfrey had intended to apologise and withdraw, but this anticipation reassured him. The stranger stood round with his back to the fireplace and put his hands behind his back. 'And presently,' he said, 'when the clock-mending is over, I think I should like to have some tea. But not till the clock-mending is over.'

Mrs Hall was about to leave the room – she made no conversational advances this time, because she did not want to be snubbed in front of Mr Henfrey – when her visitor asked her if she had made any arrangements about his boxes at Bramble-hurst. She told him she had mentioned the matter to the postman, and that the carrier could bring them over on the morrow. 'You are certain that is the earliest?' he said.

She was certain, with a marked coldness.

'I should explain,' he added, 'what I was really too cold and fatigued to do before, that I am an experimental investigator.'

'Indeed, sir,' said Mrs Hall, much impressed.

'And my baggage contains apparatus and appliances.'

'Very useful things, indeed, they are, sir,' said Mrs Hall.

'And I'm naturally anxious to get on with my inquiries.'

'Of course, sir.'

'My reason for coming to Iping,' he proceeded, with a certain deliberation of manner, 'was – a desire for solitude. I do not wish to be disturbed in my work. In addition to my work, an accident—'

'I thought as much,' said Mrs Hall to herself.

'—necessitates a certain retirement. My eyes – are sometimes so weak and painful that I have to shut myself up in the dark for hours together. Lock myself up. Sometimes – now and then. Not at present, certainly. At such times the slightest disturbance, the entry of a stranger into the room, is a source of excruciating annoyance to me – it is well these things should be understood.'

'Certainly, sir,' said Mrs Hall. 'And if I might make so bold as to ask—'

'That, I think, is all,' said the stranger, with that quietly irresistible air of finality he could assume at will. Mrs Hall reserved her question and sympathy for a better occasion.

After Mrs Hall had left the room, he remained standing in front of the fire, glaring, so Mr Henfrey puts it, at the clock-mending. Mr Henfrey not only took off the hands of the clock, and the face, but extracted the works; and he tried to work in as slow and quiet and unassuming a manner as possible. He worked with the lamp close to him, and the green shade threw a brilliant light upon his hands, and upon the frame and wheels, and left the rest of the room shadowy. When he looked up, coloured patches swam in his eyes. Being constitutionally of a curious nature, he had removed the works – a quite unnecessary proceeding – with the idea of delaying his departure and perhaps falling into conversation with the stranger. But the stranger stood there, perfectly silent and still. So still, it got on Henfrey's nerves. He felt alone in the room and looked up, and there, grey and dim, were the bandaged head and huge blue lenses staring fixedly, with a mist of green spots drifting in front of them. It was so uncanny-looking to Henfrey that for a minute they remained staring blankly at one another. Then Henfrey looked down again. Very uncomfortable position! One would like to say something. Should he remark that the weather was very cold for the time of year?

He looked up as if to take aim with that introductory shot. 'The weather' – he began.

'Why don't you finish and go?' said the rigid figure, evidently in a state of painfully suppressed rage. 'All you've got to do is to fix the hour-hand on its axle. You're simply humbugging—'*

'Certainly, sir – one minute more, sir. I overlooked—' And Mr Henfrey finished and went.

But he went off feeling excessively annoyed. 'Damn it!' said Mr Henfrey to himself, trudging down the village through the thawing snow; 'a man must do a clock at times, sure lie.'*

And again: 'Can't a man look at you? – Ugly!'

And yet again: 'Seemingly not. If the police was wanting you you couldn't be more wropped* and bandaged.'

At Gleeson's corner he saw Hall, who had recently married the stranger's hostess at the Coach and Horses, and who now drove the Iping conveyance, when occasional people required it, to Sidderbridge Junction, coming towards him on his return from that place. Hall had evidently been 'stopping a bit'* at Sidderbridge, to judge by his driving. ''Ow do,* Teddy?' he said, passing.

'You got a rum un* up home!' said Teddy.

Hall very sociably pulled up. 'What's that?' he asked.

'Rum-looking customer stopping at the Coach and Horses,' said Teddy. 'My sakes!'

And he proceeded to give Hall a vivid description of his grotesque guest. 'Looks a bit like a disguise, don't it? I'd like to see a man's face if I had him stopping in *my* place,' said Henfrey. 'But women are that trustful, where strangers are concerned. He's took your rooms and he ain't even given a name, Hall.'

'You don't say so!' said Hall, who was a man of sluggish apprehension.

'Yes,' said Teddy. 'By the week. Whatever he is, you can't get rid of him under the week. And he's got a lot of luggage coming tomorrow, so he says. Let's hope it won't be stones in boxes,* Hall.'

He told Hall how his aunt at Hastings* had been swindled by a stranger with empty portmanteaux. Altogether he left Hall vaguely suspicious. 'Get up, old girl,'* said Hall. 'I s'pose I must see 'bout this.'

Teddy trudged on his way with his mind considerably relieved.

Instead of 'seeing 'bout it,' however, Hall on his return was severely rated* by his wife on the length of time he had spent in Sidderbridge, and his mild inquiries were answered snappishly and in a manner not to the point. But the seed of suspicion Teddy had sown germinated in the mind of Mr Hall in spite of these discouragements. 'You wim' don't know everything,' said Mr Hall, resolved to ascertain more about the personality of his guest at the earliest possible opportunity. And after the stranger had gone to bed, which he did about half-past nine, Mr Hall went very aggressively into the parlour and looked very hard at his wife's furniture, just to show that the stranger wasn't master there,* and scrutinised closely and a little contemptuously a sheet of mathematical computation the stranger had left. When retiring for the night he instructed Mrs Hall to look very closely at the stranger's luggage when it came next day.

'You mind your own business, Hall,' said Mrs Hall, 'and I'll mind mine.'

She was all the more inclined to snap at Hall because the stranger was undoubtedly an unusually strange sort of stranger, and she was by no means assured about him in her own mind. In the middle of the night she woke up dreaming of huge white heads like turnips, that came trailing after her at the end of interminable necks, and with vast black eyes. But being a sensible woman, she subdued her terrors and turned over and went to sleep again.

CHAPTER 3

The Thousand and One Bottles

So it was that on the twenty-ninth* day of February, at the beginning of the thaw, this singular person fell out of infinity into Iping Village. Next day his luggage arrived through the slush. And very remarkable luggage it was. There were a couple of trunks indeed, such as a rational man might need, but in addition there were a box of books – big, fat books, of which some were just in an incomprehensible handwriting – and a dozen or more crates, boxes, and cases, containing objects packed in straw, as it seemed to Hall, tugging with a casual curiosity at the straw – glass bottles. The stranger, muffled in hat, coat, gloves, and wrapper, came out impatiently to meet Fearenside's cart, while Hall was having a word or so of gossip preparatory to helping bring them in. Out he came, not noticing Fearenside's dog, who was sniffing in a *dilettante** spirit at Hall's legs. 'Come along with those boxes,' he said. 'I've been waiting long enough.'

And he came down the steps towards the tail of the cart as if to lay hands on the smaller crate.

No sooner had Fearenside's dog caught sight of him, however, than it began to bristle and growl savagely, and when he rushed down the steps it gave an undecided hop, and then sprang straight at his hand. 'Whup!' cried Hall, jumping back, for he was no hero with dogs, and Fearenside howled, 'Lie down!' and snatched his whip.

They saw the dog's teeth had slipped the hand, heard a kick, saw the dog execute a flanking jump and get home on the stranger's leg, and heard the rip of his trousering. Then the finer end of Fearenside's whip reached his property, and the dog, yelping with dismay, retreated under the wheels of the waggon. It was all the business of a swift half-minute. No one spoke, every one shouted. The stranger glanced swiftly at his torn glove and at his leg, made as if he would stoop to the latter, then turned and rushed swiftly up the steps into the inn. They heard him go headlong across the passage and up the uncarpeted stairs to his bedroom.

'You brute, you!' said Fearenside, climbing off the waggon with his whip in his hand, while the dog watched him through the wheel. 'Come here!' said Fearenside – 'You'd better.'

Hall had stood gaping. 'He wuz bit,' said Hall. 'I'd better go and see to en,'* and he trotted after the stranger. He met Mrs Hall in the passage. 'Carrier's darg,' he said, 'bit en.'

He went straight upstairs, and the stranger's door being ajar, he pushed it open and was entering without any ceremony, being of a naturally sympathetic turn of mind.

The blind was down and the room dim. He caught a glimpse of a most singular thing, what seemed a handless arm waving towards him, and a face of three huge indeterminate spots on white, very like the face of a pale pansy. Then he was struck violently in the chest, hurled back, and the door slammed in his face and locked. It was so rapid that it gave him no time to observe. A waving of indecipherable shapes, a blow, and a concussion. There he stood on the dark little landing, wondering what it might be that he had seen.

A couple of minutes after, he rejoined the little group that had formed outside the Coach and Horses. There was Fearenside telling about it all over again for the second time; there was Mrs Hall saying his dog didn't have no business to bite her guests; there was Huxter, the general dealer from over the road, interrogative; and Sandy Wadgers from the forge, judicial; besides women and children, all of them saying fatuities: 'Wouldn't let en bite *me*, I knows;' ''Tasn't right *have* such dargs;' 'Whad '*e* bite'n for then?' and so forth.

Mr Hall, staring at them from the steps and listening, found it incredible that he had seen anything so very remarkable happen upstairs. Besides, his vocabulary was altogether too limited to express his impressions.

'He don't want no help, he says,' he said in answer to his wife's inquiry. 'We'd better be a-takin' of his luggage in.'

'He ought to have it cauterised at once,' said Mr Huxter, 'especially if it's at all inflamed.'

'I'd shoot en, that's what I'd do,' said a lady in the group.

Suddenly the dog began growling again.

'Come along,' cried an angry voice in the doorway, and there stood the muffled stranger with his collar turned up, and his hat-brim bent down. 'The sooner you get those things in the better I'll be pleased.' It is stated by an anonymous bystander that his trousers and gloves had been changed.

'Was you hurt, sir?' said Fearenside. 'I'm rare sorry the darg—'

'Not a bit,' said the stranger. 'Never broke the skin. Hurry up with those things.'

He then swore to himself, so Mr Hall asserts.

Directly the first crate was, in accordance with his directions, carried into the parlour, the stranger flung himself upon it with extraordinary eagerness, and began to unpack it, scattering the straw with an utter disregard of Mrs Hall's carpet. And from it he began to produce bottles – little fat bottles containing powders, small and slender bottles containing coloured and white fluids, fluted blue bottles labelled *Poison*, bottles with round bodies and slender necks, large green-glass bottles, large white-glass bottles, bottles with glass stoppers and frosted labels, bottles with fine corks, bottles with bungs, bottles with wooden caps, wine bottles, salad-oil bottles – putting them in rows on the chiffonnier,* on the mantel, on the table under the window, round the floor, on the bookshelf – everywhere. The chemist's shop in Bramblehurst could not boast half so many. Quite a sight it was. Crate after crate yielded bottles, until all six were empty and the table high with straw; the only things that came out of these crates besides the bottles were a number of test-tubes and a carefully packed balance.

And directly the crates were unpacked, the stranger went to the window and set to work, not troubling in the least about the litter of straw, the fire which had gone out, the box of books outside, nor for the trunks and other luggage that had gone upstairs.

When Mrs Hall took his dinner in to him, he was already so absorbed in his work, pouring little drops out of the bottles into test-tubes, that he did not hear her until she had swept away the bulk of the straw and put the tray on the table, with some little emphasis perhaps, seeing the state that the floor was in. Then he half turned his head and immediately turned it away again. But she saw he had removed his glasses; they were beside him on the table, and it seemed to her that his eye sockets were extraordinary hollow. He put on his spectacles again, and then turned and faced her. She was about to complain of the straw on the floor when he anticipated her.

'I wish you wouldn't come in without knocking,' he said in the tone of abnormal exasperation that seemed so characteristic of him.

'I knocked, but seemingly—'

'Perhaps you did. But in my investigations – my really very urgent and necessary investigations – the slightest disturbance, the jar of a door – I must ask you—'

'Certainly, sir. You can turn the lock if you're like that, you know – any time.'

'A very good idea,' said the stranger.

'This stror, sir, if I might make so bold as to remark—'

'Don't. If the straw makes trouble put it down in the bill.' And he mumbled at her – words suspiciously like curses.

He was so odd, standing there, so aggressive and explosive, bottle in one hand and test-tube in the other, that Mrs Hall was quite alarmed. But she was a resolute woman. 'In which case, I should like to know, sir, what you consider—'

'A shilling. Put down a shilling. Surely a shilling's enough?'

'So be it,' said Mrs Hall, taking up the table-cloth and beginning to spread it over the table. 'If you're satisfied, of course—'

He turned and sat down, with his coat-collar towards her.

All the afternoon he worked with the door locked and, as Mrs Hall testifies, for the most part in silence. But once there was a concussion and a sound of bottles ringing together as though the table had been hit, and the smash of a bottle flung violently down, and then a rapid pacing athwart the room. Fearing 'something was the matter,' she went to the door and listened, not caring to knock.

'I can't go on,' he was raving. 'I *can't* go on. Three hundred thousand, four hundred thousand! The huge multitude! Cheated! All my life it may take me! Patience! Patience indeed! Fool and liar!'

There was a noise of hobnails* on the bricks in the bar, and Mrs Hall had very reluctantly to leave the rest of his soliloquy. When she returned the room was silent again, save for the faint crepitation* of his chair and the occasional clink of a bottle. It was all over. The stranger had resumed work.

When she took in his tea she saw broken glass in the corner

of the room under the concave mirror, and a golden stain that had been carelessly wiped. She called attention to it.

'Put it down in the bill,' snapped her visitor. 'For God's sake don't worry me. If there's damage done, put it down in the bill;' and he went on ticking a list in the exercise book before him.

'I'll tell you something,' said Fearenside, mysteriously. It was late in the afternoon, and they were in the little beer-shop of Iping Hanger.*

'Well?' said Teddy Henfrey.

'This chap you're speaking of, what my dog bit. Well – he's black. Leastways, his legs are. I seed through the tear of his trousers and the tear of his glove. You'd have expected a sort of pinky to show, wouldn't you? Well – there wasn't none. Just blackness. I tell you, he's as black as my hat.'

'My sakes!' said Henfrey. 'It's a rummy case altogether. Why, his nose is as pink as paint!'

'That's true,' said Fearenside. 'I knows that. And I tell ee what I'm thinking. That marn's a piebald, Teddy. Black here and white there – in patches. And he's ashamed of it. He's a kind of half-breed, and the colour's come off patchy instead of mixing. I've heard of such things before. And it's the common way with horses, as any one can see.'

CHAPTER 4

Mr Cuss Interviews the Stranger

I have told the circumstances of the stranger's arrival in Iping with a certain fullness of detail, in order that the curious impression he created may be understood by the reader. But excepting two odd incidents, the circumstances of his stay until the extraordinary day of the Club Festival may be passed over very cursorily. There were a number of skirmishes with Mrs Hall on matters of domestic discipline, but in every case until late in April, when the first signs of penury began, he over-rode her by the easy expedient of an extra payment. Hall did not like him, and whenever he dared he talked of the advisability of getting rid of him; but he showed his dislike chiefly by concealing it ostentatiously, and avoiding his visitor as much as possible. 'Wait till the summer,' said Mrs Hall, sagely, 'when the artisks are beginning to come. Then we'll see. He may be a bit over-bearing, but bills settled punctual is bills settled punctual, whatever you like to say.'

The stranger did not go to church, and indeed made no difference between Sunday and the irreligious days, even in costume. He worked, as Mrs Hall thought, very fitfully. Some days he would come down early and be continuously busy. On others he would rise late, pace his room, fretting audibly for hours together, smoke, sleep in the armchair by the fire. Communication with the world beyond the village he had none. His temper continued very uncertain; for the most part his manner was that of a man suffering under almost unendurable provocation, and once or twice things were snapped, torn, crushed, or broken in spasmodic gusts of violence. He seemed under a chronic irritation of the greatest intensity. His habit of talking to himself in a low voice grew steadily upon him, but though Mrs Hall listened conscientiously she could make neither head nor tail of what she heard.

He rarely went abroad by daylight, but at twilight he would go out muffled up invisibly, whether the weather were cold or not, and he chose the loneliest paths and those most over-shadowed by trees and banks. His goggling spectacles and ghastly bandaged face under the penthouse of his hat came with a disagreeable suddenness out of the darkness upon one or two home-going labourers, and Teddy Henfrey, tumbling out of the Scarlet Coat* one night, at half-past nine, was scared shamefully by the stranger's skull-like head (he was walking hat in hand) lit by the sudden light of the opened inn door. Such children as saw him at nightfall dreamt of bogies,* and it seemed doubtful whether he disliked boys more than they disliked him, or the reverse, but there was certainly a vivid dislike enough on either side.

It was inevitable that a person of so remarkable an appearance and bearing should form a frequent topic in such a village as Iping. Opinion was greatly divided about his occupation. Mrs Hall was sensitive on the point. When questioned, she explained very carefully that he was an 'experimental investigator', going gingerly over the syllables as one who dreads pitfalls. When asked what an experimental investigator was, she would say with a touch of superiority that most educated people knew such things as that, and would thus explain that he 'discovered things'. Her visitor had had an accident, she said, which temporarily discoloured his face and hands, and being of a sensitive disposition, he was averse to any public notice of the fact.

Out of her hearing there was a view largely entertained that he was a criminal trying to escape from justice by wrapping himself up so as to conceal himself altogether from the eye of the police. This idea sprang from the brain of Mr Teddy Henfrey. No crime of any magnitude dating from the middle or end of February was known to have occurred. Elaborated in the imagination of Mr Gould, the probationary assistant in the National School,* this theory took the form that the stranger was an Anarchist* in disguise, preparing explosives, and he resolved to undertake such detective operations as his time permitted. These consisted for the most part in looking very hard at the stranger whenever they met, or in asking people who had never seen the stranger, leading questions about him. But he detected nothing.

Another school of opinion followed Mr Fearenside, and either accepted the piebald view or some modicication of it; as, for instance, Silas Durgan, who was heard to assert that 'if he choses to show enself at fairs he'd make his fortune in no time,' and being a bit of a theologian, compared the stranger to the man with the one talent.* Yet another view explained the entire matter by regarding the stranger as a harmless lunatic. That had the advantage of accounting for everything straight away.

Between these main groups there were waverers and compromisers. Sussex folk have few superstitions, and it was only after the events of early April that the thought of the supernatural was first whispered in the village. Even then it was only credited among the women folks.

But whatever they thought of him, people in Iping, on the whole, agreed in disliking him. His irritability, though it might have been comprehensible to an urban brain-worker, was an amazing thing to these quiet Sussex villagers. The frantic gesticulations they surprised now and then, the headlong pace after nightfall that swept him upon them round quiet corners, the inhuman bludgeoning of all the tentative advances of curiosity, the taste for twilight that led to the closing of doors, the pulling down of blinds, the extinction of candles and lamps – who could agree with such goings on? They drew aside as he passed down the village, and when he had gone by, young humourists would up with coat-collars and down with hat-brims, and go pacing nervously after him in imitation of his occult bearing. There was a song popular at that time called the 'Bogey Man'; Miss Statchell sang it at the schoolroom concert (in aid of the church lamps), and thereafter whenever one or two of the villagers were gathered together and the stranger appeared, a bar or so of this tune, more or less sharp or flat, was whistled in the midst of them. Also belated little children would call 'Bogey Man!' after him, and make off tremulously elated.

Cuss, the general practitioner, was devoured by curiosity. The bandages excited his professional interest, the report of the thousand and one bottles aroused his jealous regard. All through April and May he coveted an opportunity of talking to the stranger, and at last, towards Whitsuntide,* he could stand it no longer, but hit upon the subscription-list for a village nurse as an excuse. He was surprised to find that Mr Hall did not know his guest's name. 'He give a name,' said Mrs Hall, an assertion which was quite unfounded, 'but I didn't rightly hear it'. She thought it seemed so silly not to know the man's name.

Cuss rapped at the parlour door and entered. There was a fairly audible imprecation from within. 'Pardon my intrusion,' said Cuss, and then the door closed and cut Mrs Hall off from the rest of the conversation.

She could hear the murmur of voices for the next ten minutes, then a cry of surprise, a stirring of feet, a chair flung aside, a bark of laughter, quick steps to the door, and Cuss appeared, his face white, his eyes staring over his shoulder. He left the door open behind him, and without looking at her strode across the hall and went down the steps, and she heard his feet hurrying along the road. He carried his hat in his hand. She stood behind the door, looking at the open door of the parlour. Then she heard the stranger laughing quietly, and then his footsteps came across the room. She could not see his face where she stood. The parlour door slammed, and the place was silent again.

Cuss went straight up the village to Bunting the vicar. 'Am I mad?' Cuss began abruptly, as he entered the shabby little study. 'Do I look like an insane person?'

'What's happened?' said the vicar, putting the ammonite* on the loose sheets of his forthcoming sermon.

'That chap at the inn —'

'Well?'

'Give me something to drink,' said Cuss, and he sat down.

When his nerves had been steadied by a glass of cheap sherry, the only drink the good vicar had available, he told him of the interview he had just had. 'Went in,' he gasped, 'and began to demand a subscription for that Nurse Fund. He'd stuck his hands in his pockets as I came in, and he sat down lumpily in his chair. Sniffed. I told him I'd heard he took an interest in scientific things. He said yes. Sniffed again. Kept on sniffing all the time; evidently recently caught an infernal cold. No wonder, wrapped up like that! I developed the nurse idea, and all the while kept my eyes open. Bottles – chemicals – everywhere. Balance, test-tubes in stands, and a smell of – evening primrose. Would he subscribe? Said he'd consider it. Asked him, point-blank, was he researching. Said he was. A long research? Got quite cross. "A damnable long research," said he, blowing the cork out, so to speak. "Oh," said I. And out came the grievance. The man was just on the boil, and my question boiled him over. He had been given a prescription, most valuable prescription – what for he wouldn't say. Was it medical? "Damn you! What are you fishing after?" I apologised. Dignified sniff and cough. He resumed. He'd read it. Five ingredients. Put it down; turned his head. Draught of air from window lifted the paper. Swish, rustle. He was working in a room with an open fireplace, he said. Saw a flicker, and there was the prescription burning and lifting chimneyward. Rushed towards it just as it whisked up chimney. So! Just at that point, to illustrate his story, out came his arm.'

'Well?'

'No hand, just an empty sleeve. Lord! I thought, *that's* a deformity! Got a cork arm, I suppose, and has taken it off. Then, I thought, there's something odd in that. What the devil keeps that sleeve up and open, if there's nothing in it? There was nothing in it, I tell you. Nothing down it, right down to the joint. I could see right down it to the elbow, and there was a glimmer of light shining through a tear of the cloth. "Good God!" I said. Then he stopped. Stared at me with those black goggles of his, and then at his sleeve.'

'Well?'

'That's all. He never said a word; just glared, and put his sleeve back in his pocket quickly. "I was saying," said he, "that there was the prescription burning, wasn't I?" Interrogative cough. 'How the devil," said I, "can you move an empty sleeve like that?" "Empty sleeve?" "Yes," said I, "an empty sleeve."'

'"It's an empty sleeve, is it? You saw it was an empty sleeve?" He stood up right away. I stood up too. He came towards me in three very slow steps, and stood quite close. Sniffed venomously. I didn't flinch, though I'm hanged if that bandaged knob of his, and those blinkers, aren't enough to unnerve any one, coming quietly up to you.

'"You said it was an empty sleeve?" he said. "Certainly," I said. At staring and saying nothing a barefaced man, unspectacled, starts scratch.* Then very quietly he pulled his sleeve out of his pocket again, and raised his arm towards me as though he would show it to me again. He did it very, very slowly. I looked at it. Seemed an age. "Well?" said I, clearing my throat, "there's nothing in it." Had to say something. I was beginning to feel frightened. I could see right down it. He extended it straight towards me, slowly, slowly, just like that, until the cuff was six inches from my face. Queer thing to see an empty sleeve come at you like that! And then—'

'Well?'

'Something – exactly like a finger and thumb it felt – nipped my nose.'

Bunting began to laugh.

'There wasn't anything there!' said Cuss, his voice running up into a shriek at the 'there'. 'It's all very well for you to laugh, but I tell you I was so startled, I hit his cuff hard, and turned round, and cut out of the room – I left him—'

Cuss stopped. There was no mistaking the sincerity of his panic. He turned round in a helpless way and took a second glass of the excellent vicar's very inferior sherry. 'When I hit his cuff,' said Cuss, 'I tell you, it felt exactly like hitting an arm. And there wasn't an arm! There wasn't the ghost of an arm!'

Mr Bunting thought it over. He looked suspiciously at Cuss. 'It's a most remarkable story,' he said. He looked very wise and grave indeed. 'It's really,' said Mr Bunting with judicial emphasis, 'a most remarkable story.'

CHAPTER 5

The Burglary at the Vicarage

The facts of the burglary at the vicarage came to us chiefly through the medium of the vicar and his wife. It occurred in the small hours of Whit-Monday, the day devoted in Iping to the Club festivities. Mrs Bunting, it seems, woke up suddenly in the stillness that comes before the dawn, with the strong impression that the door of their bedroom had opened and closed. She did not arouse her husband at first, but sat up in bed listening. She then distinctly heard the pad, pad, pad of bare feet coming out of the adjoining dressing-room and walking along the passage towards the staircase. As soon as she felt assured of this, she aroused the Rev. Mr Bunting as quietly as possible. He did not strike a light, but putting on his spectacles, her dressing-gown, and his bath slippers, he went out on the landing to listen. He heard quite distinctly a fumbling going on at his study desk downstairs, and then a violent sneeze.

At that he returned to his bedroom, armed himself with the most obvious weapon, the poker, and descended the staircase as noiselessly as possible. Mrs Bunting came out on the landing.

The hour was about four, and the ultimate darkness of the night was past. There was a faint shimmer of light in the hall, but the study doorway yawned impenetrably black. Everything was still except the faint creaking of the stairs under Mr Bunting's tread, and the slight movements in the study. Then something snapped, the drawer was opened, and there was a rustle of papers. Then came an imprecation, and a match was struck and the study was flooded with yellow light. Mr Bunting was now in the hall, and through the crack of the door he could see the desk and the open drawer and a candle burning on the desk. But the robber he could not see. He stood there in the hall undecided what to do, and Mrs Bunting, her face white and intent, crept slowly downstairs after him. One thing kept up Mr Bunting's courage: the persuasion that this burglar was a resident in the village.

They heard the chink of money, and realised that the robber had found the housekeeping reserve of gold, two pounds ten in half-sovereigns altogether. At that sound Mr Bunting was nerved to abrupt action. Gripping the poker firmly, he rushed into the room, closely followed by Mrs Bunting. 'Surrender!' cried Mr Bunting, fiercely, and then stopped amazed. Apparently the room was perfectly empty.

Yet their conviction that they had, that very moment, heard somebody moving in the room had amounted to a certainty. For half a minute, perhaps, they stood gaping, then Mrs Bunting went across the room and looked behind the screen, while Mr Bunting, by a kindred impulse, peered under the desk. Then Mrs Bunting turned back the window-curtains, and Mr Bunting looked up the chimney and probed it with the poker. Then Mrs Bunting scrutinised the wastepaper basket and Mr Bunting opened the lid of the coal-scuttle.* Then they came to a stop and stood with eyes interrogating each other.

'I could have sworn—' said Mr Bunting.

'The candle!' said Mr Bunting. 'Who lit the candle?'

'The drawer!' said Mrs Bunting. 'And the money's gone!'

She went hastily to the doorway.

'Of all the extraordinary occurrences—'

There was a violent sneeze in the passage. They rushed out, and as they did so the kitchen door slammed. 'Bring the candle,' said Mr Bunting, and led the way. They both heard a sound of bolts being hastily shot back.

As he opened the kitchen door he saw through the scullery that the back door was just opening, and the faint light of early dawn displayed the dark masses of the garden beyond. He is certain that nothing went out of the door. It opened, stood open for a moment, and then closed with a slam. As it did so, the candle Mrs Bunting was carrying from the study flickered and flared. It was a minute or more before they entered the kitchen.

The place was empty. They refastened the back door, examined the kitchen, pantry, and scullery thoroughly, and at last went down into the cellar. There was not a soul to be found in the house, search as they would.

Daylight found the vicar and his wife, a quaintly costumed little couple, still marvelling about on their own ground floor by the unnecessary light of a guttering candle.

CHAPTER 6

The Furniture That Went Mad

Now it happened that in the early hours of Whit-Monday, before Millie was hunted out for the day, Mr Hall and Mrs Hall both rose and went noiselessly down into the cellar. Their business there was of a private nature, and had something to do with the specific gravity of their beer.* They had hardly entered the cellar when Mrs Hall found she had forgotten to bring down a bottle of sarsaparilla* from their joint-room. As she was the expert and principal operator in this affair, Hall very properly went upstairs for it.

On the landing he was surprised to see that the stranger's door was ajar. He went on into his own room and found the bottle as he had been directed.

But returning with the bottle, he noticed that the bolts of the front door had been shot back, that the door was in fact simply on the latch. And with a flash of inspiration he connected this with the stranger's room upstairs and the suggestions of Mr Teddy Henfrey. He distinctly remembered holding the candle while Mrs Hall shot these bolts overnight. At the sight he stopped, gaping, then with the bottle still in his hand went upstairs again. He rapped at the stranger's door. There was no answer. He rapped again; then pushed the door wide open and entered.

It was as he expected. The bed, the room also, was empty. And what was stranger, even to his heavy intelligence, on the bedroom chair and along the rail of the bed were scattered the garments, the only garments so far as he knew, and the bandages of their guest. His big slouch hat even was cocked jauntily over the bed-post.

As Hall stood there he heard his wife's voice coming out of the depth of the cellar, with that rapid telescoping of the syllables and interrogative cocking up of the final words to a high note, by which the West Sussex villager is wont to indicate a brisk impatience. 'Gearge! You gart what a wand?'

At that he turned and hurried down to her. 'Janny,' he said, over the rail of the cellar steps, "tas the truth what Henfrey sez. 'E's not in uz room, 'e ent. And the front door's unbolted.'

At first Mrs Hall did not understand, and as soon as she did she resolved to see the empty room for herself. Hall, still holding the bottle, went first. 'If 'e ent there,' he said, 'his close are. And what's 'e doin' without his close, then? 'Tas a most curious basness.'

As they came up the cellar steps, they both, it was afterwards ascertained, fancied they heard the front door open and shut, but seeing it closed and nothing there, neither said a word to the other about it at the time. Mrs Hall passed her husband in the passage and ran on first upstairs. Some one sneezed on the staircase. Hall, following six steps behind, thought that he heard her sneeze. She, going on first, was under the impression that Hall was sneezing. She flung open the door and stood regarding the room. 'Of all the curious!' she said.

She heard a sniff close behind her head as it seemed, and, turning, was surprised to see Hall a dozen feet off on the topmost stair. But in another moment he was beside her. She bent forward and put her hand on the pillow and then under the clothes.

'Cold,' she said. 'He's been up this hour or more.'

As she did so, a most extraordinary thing happened, the bed-clothes gathered themselves together, leapt up suddenly into a sort of peak, and then jumped headlong over the bottom rail. It was exactly as if a hand had clutched them in the centre and flung them aside. Immediately after, the stranger's hat hopped off the bed-post, described a whirling flight in the air through the better part of a circle, and then dashed straight at Mrs Hall's face. Then as swiftly came the sponge from the washstand; and then the chair, flinging the stranger's coat and trousers carelessly aside, and laughing drily in a voice singularly like the stranger's turned itself up with its four legs at Mrs Hall, seemed to take aim at her for a moment, and charged at her. She screamed and turned, and then the chair legs came gently but firmly against her back and impelled her and Hall out of the room. The door slammed violently and was locked. The chair and bed seemed to be executing a dance of triumph for a moment, and then abruptly everything was still.

Mrs Hall was left almost in a fainting condition in Mr Hall's arms on the landing. It was with the greatest difficulty that Mr Hall and Millie, who had been roused by her scream of alarm, succeeded in getting her downstairs, and applying the restoratives customary in these cases.

''Tas sperits,' said Mrs Hall. 'I know 'tas sperits. I've read in papers of en. Tables and chairs leaping and dancing!'

'Take a drop more, Janny,' said Hall, ''Twill steady ye.'

'Lock him out,' said Mrs Hall. 'Don't let him come in again. I half guessed – I might ha' known. With them goggling eyes and bandaged head, and never going to church of a Sunday. And all they bottles – more'n it's right for any one to have. He's put the sperits into the furniture. My good old furniture! 'Twas in that very chair my poor dear mother used to sit when I was a little girl. To think it should rise up against me now!'

'Just a drop more, Janny,' said Hall. 'Your nerves is all upset.'

They sent Millie across the street through the golden five o'clock sunshine to rouse up Mr Sandy Wadgers, the blacksmith. Mr Hall's compliments and the furniture upstairs was behaving most extraordinary. Would Mr Wadgers come round? He was a knowing man, was Mr Wadgers, and very resourceful. He took quite a grave view of the case. 'Arm darmed ef thet ent witchcraft,' was the view of Mr Sandy Wadgers. 'You want horseshoes* for such gentry as he.'

He came round greatly concerned. They wanted him to lead the way upstairs to the room, but he didn't seem to be in any hurry. He preferred to talk in the passage. Over the way Huxter's apprentice came out and began taking down the shutters of the tobacco window. He was called over to join the discussion. Mr Huxter naturally followed over in the course of a few minutes. The Anglo-Saxon genius for parliamentary government asserted itself; there was a great deal of talk and no decisive action. 'Let's have the facts first,' insisted Mr Sandy Wadgers. 'Let's be sure we'd be acting perfectly right in bustin' that there door open. A door onbust is always open to bustin', but ye can't onbust a door once you've busted en.'

And suddenly and most wonderfully the door of the room upstairs opened of its own accord, and as they looked up in amazement, they saw descending the stairs the muffled figure of the stranger staring more blackly and blankly than ever with those unreasonably large blue glass eyes of his. He came down stiffly and slowly, staring all the time; he walked across the passage staring, then stopped.

'Look there!' he said, and their eyes followed the direction of his gloved finger and saw a bottle of sarsaparilla hard by the cellar door. Then he entered the parlour, and suddenly, swiftly, viciously, slammed the door in their faces.

Not a word was spoken until the last echoes of the slam had died away. They stared at one another. 'Well, if that don't lick everything!' said Mr Wadgers, and left the alternative unsaid.

'I'd go in and ask'n 'bout it,' said Wadgers, to Mr Hall. 'I'd d'mand an explanation.'

It took some time to bring the landlady's husband up to that pitch. At last he rapped, opened the door, and got as far as, 'Excuse me—'

'Go to the devil!' said the stranger in a tremendous voice, and 'Shut the door after you.' So that brief interview terminated.

CHAPTER 7

The Unveiling of the Stranger

The stranger went into the little parlour of the Coach and Horses about half-past five in the morning, and there he remained until near midday, the blinds down, the door shut, and none, after Hall's repulse, venturing near him.

All that time he must have fasted. Thrice he rang his bell, the third time furiously and continuously, but no one answered him. 'Him and his "go to the devil" indeed!' said Mrs Hall. Presently came an imperfect rumour of the burglary at the vicarage, and two and two were put together. Hall, assisted by Wadgers, went off to find Mr Shuckleforth, the magistrate, and take his advice. No one ventured upstairs. How the stranger occupied himself is unknown. Now and then he would stride violently up and down, and twice came an outburst of curses, a tearing of paper, and a violent smashing of bottles.

The little group of scared but curious people increased. Mrs Huxter came over; some gay young fellows resplendent in black ready-made jackets and *piqué** paper ties, for it was Whit-Monday, joined the group with confused interrogations. Young Archie Harker distinguished himself by going up the yard and trying to peep under the window-blinds. He could see nothing, but gave reason for supposing that he did, and others of the Iping youth presently joined him.

It was the finest of all possible Whit-Mondays, and down the village street stood a row of nearly a dozen booths, a shooting gallery, and on the grass by the forge were three yellow and chocolate waggons and some picturesque strangers of both sexes putting up a cocoanut shy. The gentlemen wore blue jerseys, the ladies white aprons and quite fashionable hats with heavy plumes. Woodyer, of the Purple Fawn,* and Mr Jaggers, the cobbler, who also sold second-hand ordinary bicycles, were stretching a string of union-jacks and royal ensigns (which had originally celebrated the Jubilee)* across the road . . .

And inside, in the artificial darkness of the parlour, into which only one thin jet of sunlight penetrated, the stranger, hungry we must suppose, and fearful, hidden in his uncomfortable hot wrappings, pored through his dark glasses upon his paper or chinked his dirty little bottles, and occasionally swore savagely at the boys, audible if invisible, outide the windows. In the corner by the fireplace lay the fragments of half a dozen smashed bottles, and a pungent twang of chlorine tainted the air. So much we know from what was heard at the time and from what was subsequently seen in the room.

About noon he suddenly opened his parlour door and stood glaring fixedly at the three or four people in the bar. 'Mrs Hall,' he said. Somebody went sheepishly and called for Mrs Hall.

Mrs Hall appeared after an interval, a little short of breath, but all the fiercer for that. Hall was still out. She had deliberated over this scene, and she came holding a little tray with an unsettled bill upon it. 'Is it your bill you're wanting, sir?' she said.

'Why wasn't my breakfast laid? Why haven't you prepared my meals and answered my bell? Do you think I live without eating?'

'Why isn't my bill paid?' said Mrs Hall. 'That's what I want to know.'

'I told you three days ago I was awaiting a remittance—'

'I told you two days ago I wasn't going to await no remittances. You can't grumble if your breakfast waits a bit, if my bill's been waiting these five days, can you?'

The stranger swore briefly but vividly.

'Nar, nar!' from the bar.

'And I'd thank you kindly, sir, if you'd keep your swearing to yourself, sir,' said Mrs Hall.

The stranger stood looking more like an angry diving-helmet than ever. It was universally felt in the bar that Mrs Hall had the better of him. His next words showed as much.

'Look here, my good woman—' he began.

'Don't good woman *me*,' said Mrs Hall.

'I've told you my remittance hasn't come—'

'Remittance indeed!' said Mrs Hall.

'Still, I daresay in my pocket—'

'You told me two days ago that you hadn't anything but a sovereign's worth of silver upon you—'

'Well, I've found some more—'

"Ul-*lo*!' from the bar.

'I wonder where you found it?' said Mrs Hall.

That seemed to annoy the stranger very much. He stamped his foot. 'What do you mean?' he said.

'That I wonder where you found it,' said Mrs Hall. 'And before I take any bills or get any breakfasts, or do any such things whatsoever, you got to tell me one or two things I don't understand, and what nobody don't understand, and what everybody is very anxious to understand. I want know what you been doing t' my chair upstairs, and I want know how't is your room was empty, and how you got in again. Them as stops in this house comes in by the doors, that's the rule of the house, and that you *didn't* do, and what I want know is how you *did* come in. And I want know—'

Suddenly the stranger raised his gloved hands clenched, stamped his foot, and said, 'Stop!' with such extraordinary violence that he silenced her instantly.

'You don't understand,' he said, 'who I am or what I am. I'll show you. By Heaven! I'll show you.' Then he put his open palm over his face and withdrew it. The centre of his face became a black cavity. 'Here,' he said. He stepped forward and handed Mrs Hall something which she, staring at his metamorphosed face, accepted automatically. Then, when she saw what it was, she screamed loudly, dropped it, and staggered back. The nose – it was the stranger's nose! pink and shining – rolled on the floor.

Then he removed his spectacles, and every one in the bar gasped. He took off his hat, and with a violent gesture tore at his whiskers and bandages. For a moment they resisted him. A flash of horrible anticipation passed through the bar. 'Oh, my Gard!' said some one. Then off they came.

It was worse than anything. Mrs Hall, standing open-mouthed and horror-struck, shrieked at what she saw, and made for the door of the house. Every one began to move. They were prepared for scars, disfigurements, tangible horrors, but *nothing*! The bandages and false hair flew across the passage into the bar, making a hobbledehoy* jump to avoid them. Every one tumbled on every one else down the steps. For the man who stood there shouting some incoherent explanation, was a solid gesticulating figure up to the coat-collar of him, and then – nothingness, no visible thing at all!

People down the village heard shouts and shrieks, and looking up the street saw the Coach and Horses violently firing out its humanity. They saw Mrs Hall fall down and Mr Teddy Henfrey jump to avoid tumbling over her, and then they heard the frightful screams of Millie, who, emerging suddenly from the kitchen at the noise of the tumult, had come upon the headless stranger from behind. These ceased suddenly.

Forthwith every one all down the street, the sweetstuff seller, cocoanut shy proprietor and his assistant, the swing man, little boys and girls, rustic dandies, smart wenches, smocked elders and aproned gipsies, began running towards the inn, and in a miraculously short space of time a crowd of perhaps forty people, and rapidly increasing swayed and hooted and inquired and exclaimed and suggested, in front of Mrs Hall's establishment. Every one seemed eager to talk at once, and the result was babel.* A small group supported Mrs Hall, who was picked up in a state of collapse. There was a conference, and the incredible evidence of a vociferous eye-witness. 'O Bogey!' 'What's he been doin', then?' 'Ain't hurt the girl, 'as 'e?' 'Run at en with a knife, I believe.' 'No 'ed, I tell ye. I don't mean no manner of speaking, I mean *marn 'ithout a 'ed!*' 'Narnsense! 'tas some conjuring trick.' 'Fetched off 'is wrappin's, 'e did—'

In its struggles to see in through the open door, the crowd formed itself into a straggling wedge, with the more adventurous apex nearest the inn. 'He stood for a moment, I heerd the gal scream, and he turned. I saw her skirts whisk, and he went after her. Didn't take ten seconds. Back he comes with a knife in uz hand and a loaf; stood just as if he was staring. Not a moment ago. Went in that there door. I tell 'e, 'e ain't gart no 'ed 't all. You just missed en—'

There was a disturbance behind, and the speaker stopped to step aside for a little procession that was marching very resolutely towards the house, first Mr Hall, very red and determined, then Mr Bobby Jaffers, the village constable, and then the wary Mr Wadgers. They had come now armed with a warrant.

People shouted conflicting information of the recent circumstances. ''Ed or no 'ed,' said Jaffers, 'I got to 'rest en, and 'rest en I *will*.'

Mr Hall marched up the steps, marched straight to the door of the parlour and flung it open. 'Constable,' he said, 'do your duty.'

Jaffers marched in, Hall next, Wadgers last. They saw in the dim light the headless figure facing them, with a gnawed crust of bread in one gloved hand and a chunk of cheese in the other.

'That's him!' said Hall.

'What the devil's this?' came in a tone of angry expostulation from above the collar of the figure.

'You're a damned rum customer, mister,' said Mr Jaffers. 'But 'ed or no 'ed, the warrant says "body", and duty's duty—'

'Keep off!' said the figure, starting back.

Abruptly he whipped down the bread and cheese, and Mr Hall just grasped the knife on the table in time to save it. Off came the stranger's left glove and was slapped in Jaffer's face. In another moment Jaffers, cutting short some statement concerning a warrant, had gripped him by the handless wrist and caught his invisible throat. He got a sounding kick on the shin that made him shout, but he kept his grip. Hall sent the knife sliding along the table to Wadgers, who acted as goalkeeper for the offensive,* so to speak, and then stepped forward as Jaffers and the stranger swayed and staggered towards him, clutching and hitting in. A chair stood in the way, and went aside with a crash as they came down together.

'Get the feet,' said Jaffers between his teeth.

Mr Hall, endeavouring to act on instructions, received a sounding kick in the ribs that disposed of him for a moment, and Mr Wadgers, seeing the decapitated stranger had rolled over and got the upper side of Jaffers, retreated towards the door, knife in hand, and so collided with Mr Huxter and the Siddermorton carter coming to the rescue of law and order. At the same moment down came three or four bottles from the chiffonnier and shot a web of pungency into the air of the room.

'I'll surrender,' cried the stranger, though he had Jaffers down, and in another moment he stood up panting, a strange figure, headless and handless, for he had pulled off his right glove now as well as his left. 'It's no good,' he said, as if sobbing for breath.

It was the strangest thing in the world to hear that voice coming as if out of empty space, but the Sussex peasants are perhaps the most matter-of-fact people under the sun. Jaffers got up also and produced a pair of handcuffs. Then he started.

'I say!' said Jaffers, brought up short by a dim realisation of the incongruity of the whole business. 'Darm it! Can't use 'em as I can see.'

The stranger ran his arm down his waistcoat, and as if by a miracle the buttons to which his empty sleeve pointed became undone. Then he said something about his shin, and stooped down. He seemed to be fumbling with his shoes and socks.

'Why!' said Huxter, suddenly, 'that's not a man at all. It's just empty clothes. Look! You can see down his collar and the linings of his clothes. I could put my arm—'

He extended his hand; it seemed to meet something in mid-air, and he drew back with a sharp exclamation. 'I wish you'd keep your fingers out of my eye,' said the aerial voice, in a tone of savage expostulation. 'The fact is, I'm all here: head, hands, legs, and all the rest of it, but it happens I'm invisible. It's a confounded nuisance, but I am. That's no reason why I should be poked to pieces by every stupid bumpkin in Iping, is it?'

The suit of clothes, now all unbuttoned and hanging loosely upon its unseen supports, stood up, arms akimbo.

Several other of the men folks had now entered the room, so that it was closely crowded. 'Invisible, eigh?' said Huxter, ignoring the stranger's abuse. 'Who ever heard the likes of that?'

'It's strange, perhaps, but it's not a crime. Why am I assaulted by a policeman in this fashion?'

'Ah! that's a different matter,' said Jaffers. 'No doubt you are a bit difficult to see in this light, but I got a warrant and it's all correct. What I'm after ain't no invisibility, it's burglary. There's a house been broken into and money took.'

'Well?'

'And circumstances certainly point—'

'Stuff and nonsense!' said the Invisible Man.

'I hope so, sir; but I've got my instructions.'

'Well,' said the stranger, 'I'll come. I'll *come*. But no handcuffs.'

'It's the regular thing,' said Jaffers.

'No handcuffs,' stipulated the stranger.

'Pardon me,' said Jaffers.

Abruptly the figure sat down, and before any one could realise what was being done, the slippers, socks, and trousers had been kicked off under the table. Then he sprang up again and flung off his coat.

'Here, stop that,' said Jaffers, suddenly realising what was happening. He gripped the waistcoat; it struggled, and the shirt slipped out of it and left it limp and empty in his hand. 'Hold him!' said Jaffers, loudly. 'Once he gets they things off—!'

'Hold him!' cried every one, and there was a rush at the fluttering white shirt which was now all that was visible of the stranger.

The shirt-sleeve planted a shrewd blow in Hall's face that stopped his open-armed advance, and sent him backward into old Toothsome the sexton, and in another moment the garment was lifted up and became convulsed and vacantly flapping about the arms, even as a shirt that is being thrust over a man's head. Jaffers clutched at it, and only helped to pull it off; he was struck in the mouth out of the air, and incontinently drew his truncheon and smote Teddy Henfrey savagely upon the crown of his head.

'Look out!' said everybody, fencing at random and hitting at nothing. 'Hold him! Shut the door! Don't let him loose! I got something! Here he is!' A perfect babel of noises they made. Everybody, it seemed, was being hit all at once, and Sandy Wadgers, knowing as ever and his wits sharpened by a frightful blow in the nose, reopened the door and led the rout. The others, following incontinently, were jammed for a moment in the corner by the doorway. The hitting continued. Phipps, the Unitarian, had a front tooth broken, and Henfrey was injured in the cartilage of his ear. Jaffers was struck under the jaw, and, turning, caught at something that intervened between him and Huxter in the *mêlée,** and prevented their coming together. He felt a muscular chest, and in another moment the whole mass of struggling, excited men shot out into the crowded hall.

'I got him!' shouted Jaffers, choking and reeling through them all, and wrestling with purple face and swelling veins against his unseen enemy.

Men staggered right and left as the extraordinary conflict swayed swiftly towards the house door, and went spinning down the half-dozen steps of the inn. Jaffers cried in a strangled voice, holding tight, nevertheless, and making play with his knee, spun round, and fell heavily undermost with his head on the gravel. Only then did his fingers relax.

There were excited cries of 'Hold him!' 'Invisible!' and so forth, and a young fellow, a stranger in the place whose name did not come to light, rushed in at once, caught something, missed his hold, and fell over the constable's prostrate body.

Half-way across the road a woman screamed as something pushed by her; a dog, kicked apparently, yelped and ran howling into Huxter's yard, and with that the transit of the Invisible Man was accomplished. For a space people stood amazed and gesticulating, and then came Panic, and scattered them abroad through the village as a gust scatters dead leaves. *

But Jaffers lay quite still, face upward and knees bent.

CHAPTER 8

In Transit

The eighth chapter is exceedingly brief, and relates that Gibbins, the amateur naturalist of the district, while lying out on the spacious open downs without a soul within a couple of miles of him, as he thought, and almost dozing, heard close to him the sound as of a man coughing, sneezing, and then swearing savagely to himself; and looking, beheld nothing. Yet the voice was indisputable. It continued to swear with that breadth and variety that distinguishes the swearing of a cultivated man. It grew to a climax, diminished again, and died away in the distance, going as it seemed to him in the direction of Adderdean. It lifted to a spasmodic sneeze and ended. Gibbins had heard nothing of the morning's occurrences, but the phenomenon was so striking and disturbing that his philosophical tranquillity vanished; he got up hastily, and hurried down the steepness of the hill towards the village, as fast as he could go.

CHAPTER 9

Mr Thomas Marvel

You must picture Mr Thomas Marvel* as a person of copious, flexible visage, a nose of cylindrical protrusion, a liquorish, ample, fluctuating mouth, and a beard of bristling eccentricity. His figure inclined to embonpoint;* his short limbs accentuated this inclination. He wore a furry silk hat, and the frequent substitution of twine and shoelaces for buttons, apparent at critical points of his costume, marked a man essentially bachelor.

Mr Thomas Marvel was sitting with his feet in a ditch by the roadside over the down towards Adderdean, about a mile and a half out of Iping. His feet, save for socks of irregular open-work, were bare, his big toes were broad, and pricked like the ears of a watchful dog. In a leisurely manner – he did everything in a leisurely manner – he was contemplating trying on a pair of boots. They were the soundest boots he had come across for a long time, but too large for him; whereas the ones he had were, in dry weather, a very comfortable fit, but too thin-soled for damp. Mr Thomas Marvel hated roomy shoes, but then he hated damp. He had never properly thought out which he hated most, and it was a pleasant day, and there was nothing better to do. So he put the four shoes in a graceful group on the turf and looked at them. And seeing them there among the grass and springing agrimony, it suddenly occurred to him that both pairs were exceedingly ugly to see. He was not at all startled by a voice behind him.

'They're boots, anyhow,' said the voice.

'They are – charity boots,' said Mr Thomas Marvel, with his head on one side regarding them distastefully; 'and which is the ugliest pair in the whole blessed universe, I'm darned if I know!'

'H'm,' said the voice.

'I've worn worse, in fact. I've worn none. But none so owdacious ugly, if you'll allow the expression. I've been cadging boots – in particular – for days. Because I was sick of *them*. They're sound enough, of course. But a gentleman on tramp sees such a thundering lot of his boots. And if you'll believe me, I've raised nothing in the whole blessed county, try as I would, but THEM. Look at 'em! And a good county for boots, too, in a general way. But it's just my promiscuous luck. I've got my boots in this county ten years or more. And then they treat you like this.'

'It's a beast of a county,' said the voice. 'And pigs for people.'

'Ain't it?' said Mr Thomas Marvel. 'Lord! But them boots! It beats it.'

He turned his head over his shoulder to the right, to look at the boots of his interlocutor with a view to comparisons, and lo! where the boots of his interlocutor should have been were neither legs nor boots. He turned his head over his shoulder to the left, and there also were neither legs nor boots. He was irradiated by the dawn of a great amazement. 'Where *are* yer?' said Mr Thomas Marvel over his shoulder and coming on all fours. He saw a stretch of empty downs with the wind swaying the remote green-pointed furze bushes.

'Am I drunk?' said Mr Marvel. 'Have I had visions? Was I talking to myself? What the—'

'Don't be alarmed,' said a voice.

'None of your ventriloquising *me*,' said Mr Thomas Marvel, rising sharply to his feet. 'Where *are* yer? Alarmed, indeed!'

'Don't be alarmed,' repeated the voice.

'*You'll* be alarmed in a minute, you silly fool,' said Mr Thomas Marvel. 'Where *are* yer? Lemme get my mark on yer—

'Are you *buried*?*' said Mr Thomas Marvel, after an interval.

There was no answer. Mr Thomas Marvel stood bootless and amazed, his jacket nearly thrown off.

'Peewit,' said a peewit, very remote.

'Peewit, indeed!' said Mr Thomas Marvel. 'This ain't no time for foolery.' The down was desolate, east and west, north and south; the road, with its shallow ditches and white bordering stakes, ran smooth and empty north and south, and, save for that peewit, the blue sky was empty too. 'So help me,' said Mr Thomas Marvel, shuffling his coat on to his shoulders again. 'It's the drink! I might ha' known.'

'It's not the drink,' said the voice. 'You keep your nerves steady.'

'Ow!' said Mr Marvel, and his face grew white amidst its patches. 'It's the drink,' his lips repeated noiselessly. He remained staring about him, rotating slowly backwards. 'I could have *swore* I heard a voice,' he whispered.

'Of course you did.'

'It's there again,' said Mr Marvel, closing his eyes and clapping his hand on his brow with a tragic gesture. He was suddenly taken by the collar and shaken violently, and left more dazed than ever. 'Don't be a fool,' said the voice.

'I'm – off – my – blooming – chump,' said Mr Marvel. It's no good. It's fretting about them blarsted boots. I'm off my blessed blooming chump. Or it's spirits.'

'Neither one thing nor the other,' said the voice. 'Listen!'

'Chump,' said Mr Marvel.

'One minute,' said the voice, penetratingly, tremulous with self-control.

'Well?' said Mr Thomas Marvel, with a strange feeling of having been dug in the chest by a finger.

'You think I'm just imagination? Just imagination?'

'What else *can* you be?' said Mr Thomas Marvel, rubbing the back of his neck.

'Very well,' said the voice, in a tone of relief. 'Then I'm going to throw flints at you till you think differently.'

'But where *are* yer?'

The voice made no answer. Whizz came a flint, apparently out of the air, and missed Mr Marvel's shoulder by a hair's breadth. Mr Marvel, turning, saw a flint jerk up into the air, trace a complicated path, hang for a moment, and then fling at his feet with almost invisible rapidity. He was too amazed to dodge. Whizz it came, and ricochetted from a bare toe into the ditch. Mr Thomas Marvel jumped a foot and howled aloud. Then he started to run, tripped over an unseen obstacle, and came head over heels into a sitting position.

'*Now*,' said the voice, as a third stone curved upward and hung in the air above the tramp. 'Am I imagination?'

Mr Marvel by way of reply struggled to his feet, and was immediately rolled over again. He lay quiet for a moment. 'If you struggle any more,' said the voice, 'I shall throw the flint at your head.'

'It's a fair do,' said Mr Thomas Marvel, sitting up, taking his wounded toe in hand and fixing his eye on the third missile. 'I don't understand it. Stones flinging themselves. Stones talking. Put yourself down. Rot away. I'm done.'

The third flint fell.

'It's very simple,' said the voice. 'I'm an invisible man.'

'Tell us something I don't know,' said Mr Marvel, gasping with pain. 'Where you've hid – how you do it – I *don't* know. I'm beat.'

'That's all,' said the voice. 'I'm invisible. That's what I want you to understand.'

'Any one could see that. There is no need for you to be so confounded impatient, mister. *Now* then. Give us a notion. How are you hid?'

'I'm invisible. That's the great point. And what I want you to understand is this—'

'But whereabouts?' interrupted Mr Marvel.

'Here! Six yards in front of you.'

'Oh, *come*! I ain't blind. You'll be telling me next you're just thin air. I'm not one of your ignorant tramps—'

'Yes, I am – thin air. You're looking through me.'

'What! Ain't there any stuff to you? *Vox et** – what is it? – jabber. Is it that?'

'I'm just a human being – solid, needing food and drink, needing covering too – But I'm invisible. You see? Invisible. Simple idea. Invisible.'

'What, real like?'

'Yes, real.'

'Let's have a hand of you,' said Marvel, 'if you *are* real. It won't be so darn out-of-the-way like, then – *Lord!*' he said, 'how you made me jump! – gripping me like that!'

He felt the hand that had closed round his wrist with his disengaged fingers, and his fingers went timorously up the arm, patted a muscular chest, and explored a bearded face.* Marvel's face was astonishment.

'I'm dashed!' he said. 'If this don't beat cock-fighting!* Most remarkable! And there I can see a rabbit clean through you, 'arf a mile away! Not a bit of you visible – except—'

He scrutinised the apparently empty space keenly. 'You 'aven't been eatin' bread and cheese?' he asked, holding the invisible arm.

'You're quite right, and it's not quite assimilated into the system.'*

'Ah!' said Mr Marvel. 'Sort of ghostly, though.'

'Of course, all this isn't half so wonderful as you think.'

'It's quite wonderful enough for *my* modest wants,' said Mr Thomas Marvel. 'Howjer manage it! How the dooce is it done?'

'It's too long a story. And besides—'

'I tell you, the whole business fair beats me,' said Mr Marvel.

'What I want to say at present is this: I need help. I have come to that – I came upon you suddenly. I was wandering, mad with rage, naked, impotent. I could have murdered. And I saw you—'*

'*Lord*!' said Mr Marvel.

'I came up behind you – hesitated – went on—'

Mr Marvel's expression was eloquent.

'—then stopped. "Here," I said, "is an out-cast like myself. This is the man for me." So I turned back and came to you – you. And—'

'*Lord*!' said Mr Marvel. 'But I'm all in a dizzy.* May I ask – How is it? And what you may be requiring in the way of help? Invisible!'

'I want you to help me get clothes – and shelter – and then, with other things. I've left them long enough. If you won't – well! But you *will – must.*'

'Look here,' said Mr Marvel. 'I'm too flabbergasted. Don't knock me about any more. And leave me go. I must get steady a bit. And you've pretty near broken my toe. It's all so unreasonable. Empty downs, empty sky. Nothing visible for miles except the bosom of Nature. And then comes a voice. A voice out of heaven! And stones! And a fist – Lord!'

'Pull yourself together,' said the voice, 'for you have to do the job I've chosen for you.'

Mr Marvel blew out his cheeks, and his eyes were round.

'I've chosen you,' said the voice. 'You are the only man except some of those fools down there, who knows there is such a thing as an invisible man. You have to be my helper. Help me – and I will do great things for you. An invisible man is a man of power.' He stopped for a moment to sneeze violently.

'But if you betray me,' he said, 'if you fail to do as I direct you—'

He paused and tapped Mr Marvel's shoulder smartly. Mr Marvel gave a yelp of terror at the touch. '*I* don't want to betray you,' said Mr Marvel, edging away from the direction of the fingers. 'Don't you go a-thinking that, whatever you do. All I want to do is to help you – just tell me what I got to do. (Lord!) Whatever you want done, that I'm most willing to do.'

CHAPTER 10

Mr Marvel's Visit to Iping

After the first gusty panic had spent itself Iping became argumentative. Scepticism suddenly reared its head, rather nervous scepticism, not at all assured of its back, but scepticism nevertheless. It is so much easier not to believe in an invisible man; and those who had actually seen him dissolve into air, or felt the strength of his arm, could be counted on the fingers of two hands. And of these witnesses Mr Wadgers was presently missing, having retired impregnably behind the bolts and bars of his own house, and Jaffers was lying stunned in the parlour of the Coach and Horses. Great and strange ideas transcending experience often have less effect upon men and women than smaller, more tangible considerations. Iping was gay with bunting, and everybody was in gala dress. Whit-Monday had been looked forward to for a month or more. By the afternoon even those who believed in the Unseen were beginning to resume their little amusements in a tentative fashion, on the supposition that he had quite gone away, and with the sceptics he was already a jest. But people, sceptics and believers alike, were remarkably sociable all that day.

Haysman's meadow was gay with a tent, in which Mrs Bunting and the other ladies were preparing tea, while, without, the Sunday-school children ran races and played games under the noisy guidance of the curate and the Misses Cuss and Sackbut. No doubt there was a slight uneasiness in the air, but people for the most part had the sense to conceal whatever imaginative qualms they experienced. On the village green an inclined string, down which, clinging to a pulley-swung handle, one could be hurled violently against a sack at the other end, came in for considerable favour among the adolescent, as also did the swings and the cocoanut shies. There was also promenading, and the steam organ attached to the swings filled the air with a pungent flavour of oil and with equally pungent music. Members of the Club, who had attended church in the morning, were splendid in badges of pink and green, and some of the gayer-minded had also adorned their bowler hats with brilliant-coloured favours of ribbon. Old Fletcher, whose conceptions of holiday-making were severe, was visible through the jasmine about his window or through the open door (whichever way you chose to look), poised delicately on a plank supported on two chairs, and whitewashing the ceiling of his front room.

About four o'clock a stranger entered the village from the direction of the downs. He was a short, stout person in an extraordinary shabby top hat, and he appeared to be very much out of breath. His cheeks were alternately limp and tightly puffed. His mottled face was apprehensive, and he moved with a sort of reluctant alacrity. He turned the corner by the church, and directed his way to the Coach and Horses. Among others old Fletcher remembers seeing him, and indeed the old gentleman was so struck by his peculiar agitation that he inadvertently allowed a quantity of whitewash to run down the brush into the sleeve of his coat while regarding him.

This stranger, to the perceptions of the proprietor of the cocoanut shy, appeared to be talking to himself, and Mr Huxter remarked the same thing. He stopped at the foot of the Coach and Horses steps, and, according to Mr Huxter, appeared to undergo a severe internal struggle before he could induce himself to enter the house. Finally he marched up the steps, and was seen by Mr Huxter to turn to the left and open the door of the parlour. Mr Huxter heard voices from within the room and from the bar apprising the man of his error. 'That room's private!' said Hall, and the stranger shut the door clumsily and went into the bar.

In the course of a few minutes he reappeared, wiping his lips with the back of his hand with an air of quiet satisfaction that somehow impressed Mr Huxter as assumed.* He stood looking about him for some moments, and then Mr Huxter saw him walk in an oddly furtive manner towards the gates of the yard, upon which the parlour window opened. The stranger, after some hesitation, leant against one of the gate-posts, produced a short clay pipe, and prepared to fill it. His fingers trembled while doing so. He lit it clumsily, and folding his arms began to smoke in a languid attitude, an attitude which his occasional quick glances up the yard altogether belied.

All this Mr Huxter saw over the canisters of the tobacco

window, and the singularity of the man's behaviour prompted him to maintain his observation.

Presently the stranger stood up abruptly and put his pipe in his pocket. Then he vanished into the yard. Forthwith Mr Huxter, conceiving he was witness of some petty larceny, leapt round his counter and ran out into the road to intercept the thief. As he did so, Mr Marvel reappeared, his hat askew, a big bundle in a blue table-cloth in one hand, and three books tied together – as it proved afterwards with the Vicar's braces – in the other. Directly he saw Huxter he gave a sort of gasp, and turning sharply to the left, began to run. 'Stop thief!' cried Huxter, and set off after him. Mr Huxter's sensations were vivid but brief. He saw the man just before him and spurting briskly for the church corner and the hill road. He saw the village flags and festivities beyond, and a face or so turned towards him. He bawled, 'Stop!' again. He had hardly gone ten strides before his shin was caught in some mysterious fashion, and he was no longer running, but flying with inconceivable rapidity through the air. He saw the ground suddenly close to his face. The world seemed to splash into a million whirling specks of light, and subsequent proceedings interested him no more.

CHAPTER 11

In the Coach and Horses

Now in order clearly to understand what had happened in the inn, it is necessary to go back to the moment when Mr Marvel first came into view of Mr Huxter's window. At that precise moment Mr Cuss and Mr Bunting were in the parlour. They were seriously investigating the strange occurrences of the morning, and were, with Mr Hall's permission, making a thorough examination of the Invisible Man's belongings. Jaffers had partially recovered from his fall and had gone home in the charge of his sympathetic friends. The stranger's scattered garments had been removed by Mrs Hall and the room tidied up. And on the table under the window where the stranger had been wont to work, Cuss had hit almost at once on three big books in manuscript labelled 'Diary'.

'Diary!' said Cuss, putting the three books on the table. 'Now, at any rate, we shall learn something.' The Vicar stood with his hands on the table.

'Diary,' repeated Cuss, sitting down, putting two volumes to support the third, and opening it. 'H'm – no name on the fly-leaf. Bother! cypher.* And figures.'

The Vicar came round to look over his shoulder.

Cuss turned the pages over with a face suddenly disappointed. 'I'm – dear me! It's all cypher, Bunting.'

'There are no diagrams?' asked Mr Bunting. 'No illustrations throwing light—'

'See for yourself,' said Mr Cuss. 'Some of it's mathematical and some of it's Russian or some such language (to judge by the letters), and some of it's Greek. Now the Greek I thought *you*—'

'Of course,' said Mr Bunting, taking out and wiping his spectacles and feeling suddenly very uncomfortable, for he had no Greek left in his mind worth talking about; 'yes – the Greek, of course, may furnish a clue.'

'I'll find you a place.'

'I'd rather glance through the volumes first,' said Mr Bunting, still wiping. 'A general impression first, Cuss, and *then*, you know, we can go looking for clues.'

He coughed, put on his glasses, arranged them fastidiously, coughed again, and wished something would happen to avert the seemingly inevitable exposure. Then he took the volume Cuss handed him in a leisurely manner. And then something did happen.

The door opened suddenly.

Both gentlemen started violently, looked round, and were relieved to see a sporadically rosy face beneath a furry silk hat. 'Tap?'* asked the face, and stood staring.

'No,' said both gentlemen at once.

'Over the other side, my man,' said Mr Bunting. And 'Please shut that door,' said Mr Cuss, irritably.

'All right,' said the intruder, as it seemed, in a low voice curiously different from the huskiness of its first inquiry. 'Right you are,' said the intruder in the former voice. 'Stand clear!'* and he vanished and closed the door.

'A sailor, I should judge,' said Mr Bunting. 'Amusing fellows, they are. Stand clear! indeed. A nautical term, referring to his getting back out of the room, I suppose.'

'I daresay so,' said Cuss. 'My nerves are all loose today. It quite made me jump – the door opening like that.'

Mr Bunting smiled as if he had not jumped. 'And now,' he said with a sigh, 'these books.'

'One minute,' said Cuss, and went and locked the door. 'Now I think we are safe from interruption.'

Someone sniffed as he did so.

'One thing is indisputable,' said Bunting, drawing up a chair next to that of Cuss. 'There certainly have been very strange things happen in Iping during the last few days – very strange. I cannot of course believe in this absurd invisibility story—'

'It's incredible,' said Cuss,'—incredible. But the fact remains that I saw – I certainly saw right down his sleeve—'

'But did you – are you sure? Suppose a mirror, for instance – hallucinations are so easily produced. I don't know if you have ever seen a really good conjuror—'

'I won't argue again,' said Cuss. 'We've thrashed that out, Bunting. And just now there's these books – Ah! here's some of what I take to be Greek! Greek letters certainly.'

He pointed to the middle of the page. Mr Bunting flushed slightly and brought his face nearer, apparently finding some difficulty with his glasses. Suddenly he became aware of a strange feeling at the nape of his neck. He tried to raise his head, and encountered an immovable resistance. The feeling was a curious pressure, the grip of a heavy, firm hand, and it bore his chin irresistibly to the table. '*Don't move, little men,*' whispered a voice, '*or I'll brain you both!*' He looked into the face of Cuss, close to his own, and each saw a horrified reflection of his own sickly astonishment.

'I'm sorry to handle you roughly,' said the Voice, 'but it's unavoidable.

'Since when did you learn to pry into an investigator's private memoranda?' said the Voice; and two chins struck the table simultaneously, and two sets of teeth rattled.

'Since when did you learn to invade the private rooms of a man in misfortune?' and the concussion was repeated.

'Where have they put my clothes?

'Listen,' said the Voice. 'The windows are fastened and I've taken the key out of the door. I am a fairly strong man, and I have the poker handy – besides being invisible. There's not the slightest doubt that I could kill you both and get away quite easily if I wanted to – do you understand? Very well. If I let you go will you promise not to try any nonsense and do what I tell you?'

The Vicar and the Doctor looked at one another, and the Doctor pulled a face. 'Yes,' said Mr Bunting, and the Doctor repeated it. Then the pressure on the necks relaxed, and the Doctor and the Vicar sat up, both very red in the face and wriggling their heads.

'Please keep sitting where you are,' said the Invisible Man. 'Here's the poker, you see.

'When I came into this room,' continued the Invisible Man, after presenting the poker to the tip of the nose of each of his visitors, 'I did not expect to find it occupied, and I expected to find, in addition to my books of memoranda, an outfit of clothing. Where is it? No, don't rise. I can see it's gone. Now, just at present, though the days are quite warm enough for an invisible man to run about stark, the evenings are chilly. I want clothing – and other accommodation; and I must also have those three books.'

CHAPTER 12

The Invisible Man Loses His Temper

It is unavoidable that at this point the narrative should break off again, for a certain very painful reason that will presently be apparent. And while these things were going on in the parlour, and while Mr Huxter was watching Mr Marvel smoking his pipe against the gate, not a dozen yards away were Mr Hall and Teddy Henfrey discussing in a state of cloudy puzzlement the one Iping topic.

Suddenly there came a violent thud against the door of the parlour, a sharp cry, and then – silence.

'*Hul*-lo!' said Teddy Henfrey.

'Hul-*lo*!' from the Tap.

Mr Hall took things in slowly but surely. 'That ain't right,' he said, and came round from behind the bar towards the parlour door.

He and Teddy approached the door together, with intent faces. Their eyes considered. 'Summat wrong,' said Hall, and Henfrey nodded agreement. Whiffs of an unpleasant chemical odour met them, and there was a muffled sound of conversation, very rapid and subdued.

'You all raight thur?' asked Hall, rapping.

The muttered conversation ceased abruptly, for a moment silence, then the conversation was resumed, in hissing whispers, then a sharp cry of 'No! no, you don't!' There came a sudden motion and the oversetting of a chair, a brief struggle. Silence again.

'What the dooce?'* exclaimed Henfrey, *sotto voce.**

'You – all – raight – thur?' asked Mr Hall, sharply, again.

The Vicar's voice answered with a curious jerking intonation: 'Quite ri – ight. Please don't – interrupt.'

'Odd!' said Mr Henfrey.

'Odd!' said Mr Hall.

'Says, "Don't interrupt,"' said Henfrey.

'I heerd'n,' said Hall.

'And a sniff,' said Henfrey.

They remained listening. The conversation was rapid and subdued. 'I *can't*,' said Mr Bunting, his voice rising; 'I tell you, sir, I *will* not.'

'What was that?' asked Henfrey.

'Says he wi' nart,' said Hall. 'Warn't speakin' to us, wuz he?'

'Disgraceful!' said Mr Bunting, within.

'"Disgraceful,"' said Mr Henfrey. 'I heard it – *distinct*.

'Who's that speaking now?' asked Henfrey.

'Mr Cuss, I s'pose,' said Hall. 'Can you hear – anything?'

Silence. The sounds within indistinct and perplexing.

'Sounds like throwing the table-cloth about,' said Hall.

Mrs Hall appeared behind the bar. Hall made gestures of silence and invitation. This roused Mrs Hall's wifely opposition. 'What yer listenin' there for, Hall?' she asked. 'Ain't you nothin' better to do – busy day like this?'

Hall tried to convey everything by grimaces and dumb show, but Mrs Hall was obdurate. She raised her voice. So Hall and Henfrey, rather crestfallen, tiptoed back to the bar, gesticulating to explain to her.

At first she refused to see anything in what they had heard at all. Then she insisted on Hall keeping silence, while Henfrey told her his story. She was inclined to think the whole business nonsense – perhaps they were just moving the furniture about. 'I heerd'n say "disgraceful"; *that* I did,' said Hall.

'*I* heerd that, Mis' Hall,' said Henfrey.

'Like as not—' began Mrs Hall.

'Hsh!' said Mr Teddy Henfrey. 'Didn't I hear the window?'

'What window?' asked Mrs Hall.

'Parlour window,' said Henfrey.

Everyone stood listening intently. Mrs Hall's eyes, directed straight before her, saw without seeing the brilliant oblong of the inn door, the road white and vivid, and Huxter's shop front blistering in the June sun. Abruptly Huxter's door opened and Huxter appeared, eyes staring with excitement, arms gesticulating. '*Yap!* cried Huxter. 'Stop thief!' and he ran obliquely across the oblong towards the yard gates, and vanished.

Simultaneously came a tumult from the parlour, and a sound of windows being closed.

Hall, Henfrey, and the human contents of the Tap rushed out at once pell-mell* into the street. They saw some one whisk round the corner towards the down road, and Mr Huxter executing a complicated leap in the air that ended on his face and shoulder. Down the street people were standing astonished or running towards them.

Mr Huxter was stunned. Henfrey stopped to discover this, but Hall and the two labourers from the Tap rushed at once to the corner, shouting incoherent things, and saw Mr Marvel vanishing by the corner of the church wall. They appear to have jumped to the impossible conclusion that this was the Invisible Man suddenly become visible, and set off at once along the lane in pursuit. But Hall had hardly run a dozen yards before he gave a loud shout of astonishment and went flying headlong sideways, clutching one of the labourers and bringing him to the ground. He had been charged just as one charges a man at football. The second labourer came round in a circle, stared, and conceiving that Hall had tumbled over of his own accord, turned to resume the pursuit, only to be tripped by the ankle just as Huxter had been. Then, as the first labourer struggled to his feet, he was kicked sideways by a blow that might have felled an ox.

As he went down, the rush from the direction of the village green came round the corner. The first to appear was the proprietor of the cocoanut shy, a burly man in a blue jersey. He was astonished to see the lane empty save for three men sprawling absurdly on the ground. And then something happened to his rear-most foot, and he went headlong and rolled sideways just in time to graze the feet of his brother and partner, following headlong. The two were then kicked, knelt on, fallen over, and cursed by quite a number of over-hasty people.

Now when Hall and Henfrey and the labourers ran out of the house, Mrs Hall, who had been dsciplined by years of experience, remained in the bar next the till. And suddenly the parlour door was opened, and Mr Cuss appeared, and without glancing at her rushed at once down the steps towards the corner. 'Hold him!' he cried. 'Don't let him drop that parcel! You can see him so long as he holds the parcel.' He knew nothing of the existence of Marvel. For the Invisible Man had handed over the books and bundle in the yard. The face of Mr Cuss was angry and resolute, but his costume was defective, a sort of limp white kilt that could only have passed muster in Greece. 'Hold him!' he bawled. 'He's got my trousers! And every stitch of the Vicar's clothes!'

''Tend to him in a minute!' he cried to Henfrey as he passed the prostrate Huxter, and coming round the corner to join the tumult, was promptly knocked off his feet into an indecorous sprawl. Somebody in full flight trod heavily on his finger. He yelled, struggled to regain his feet, was knocked against and thrown on all fours again, and became aware that he was involved not in a capture, but a rout. Everyone was running back to the village. He rose again and was hit severely behind the ear. He staggered and set off back to the Coach and Horses forthwith, leaping over the deserted Huxter, who was now sitting up, on his way.

Behind him as he was halfway up the inn steps he heard a sudden yell of rage, rising sharply out of the confusion of cries, and a sounding smack in someone's face. He recognised the voice as that of the Invisible Man, and the note was that of a man suddenly infuriated by a painful blow.

In another moment Mr Cuss was back in the parlour. 'He's coming back, Bunting!' he said, rushing in. 'Save yourself! He's gone mad!'

Mr Bunting was standing in the window engaged in an attempt to clothe himself in the hearth-rug and a West Surrey Gazette. 'Who's coming?' he said, so startled that his costume narrowly escaped disintegration.

'Invisible Man,' said Cuss, and rushed to the window. 'We'd better clear out from here! He's fighting mad! Mad!'

In another moment he was out in the yard.

'Good heavens!' said Mr Bunting, hesitating between two horrible alternatives. He heard a frightful struggle in the passage of the inn, and his decision was made. He clambered out of the window, adjusted his costume hastily, and fled up the village as fast as his fat little legs would carry him.

From the moment when the Invisible Man screamed with rage and Mr Bunting made his memorable flight up the village, it became impossible to give a consecutive account of affairs in Iping. Possibly the Invisible Man's original intention was simply to cover Marvel's retreat with the clothes and books. But his temper, at no time very good, seems to have gone completely at some chance blow, and forthwith he set to smiting and over-throwing, for the mere satisfaction of hurting.

You must figure the street full of running figures, of doors slamming and fights for hiding-places. You must figure the tumult suddenly striking on the unstable equilibrium of old Fletcher's planks and two chairs, with cataclysmal results. You must figure an appalled couple caught dismally in a swing. And then the whole tumultuous rush has passed and the Iping street with its gauds and flags is deserted save for the still raging Unseen, and littered with cocoanuts, overthrown canvas screens, and the scattered stock in trade of a sweetstuff stall. Everywhere there is a sound of closing shutters and shoving bolts, and the only visible humanity is an occasional flitting eye under a raised eyebrow in the corner of a window pane.

The Invisible Man amused himself for a little while by breaking all the windows in the Coach and Horses, and then he thrust a street lamp through the parlour window of Mrs Gribble. He it must have been who cut the telegraph wire to Adderdean just beyond Higgins' cottage on the Adderdean road. And after that, as his peculiar qualities allowed, he passed out of human perceptions altogether, and he was neither heard, seen, nor felt in Iping any more. He vanished absolutely.

But it was the best part of two hours before any human being ventured out again into the desolation of Iping street.

CHAPTER 13

Mr Marvel Discusses His Resignation

When the dusk was gathering and Iping was just beginning to peep timorously forth again upon the shattered wreckage of its Bank Holiday, a short, thickset man in a shabby silk hat was marching painfully through the twilight behind the beechwoods on the road to Bramblehurst. He carried three books bound together by some sort of ornamental elastic ligature, and a bundle wrapped in a blue table-cloth. His rubicund face expressed consternation and fatigue; he appeared to be in a spasmodic sort of hurry. He was accompanied by a Voice other than his own, and ever and again he winced under the touch of unseen hands.

'If you give me the slip again,' said the Voice; 'if you attempt to give me the slip again—'

'Lord!' said Mr Marvel. 'That shoulder's a mass of bruises as it is.'

'—on my honour,' said the Voice, 'I will kill you.'

'I didn't try to give you the slip,' said Marvel, in a voice that was not far remote from tears. 'I swear I didn't. I didn't know the blessed turning, that was all! How the devil was I to know the blessed turning? As it is, I've been knocked about—'

'You'll get knocked about a great deal more if you don't mind,' said the Voice, and Mr Marvel abruptly became silent. He blew out his cheeks, and his eyes were eloquent of despair.

'It's bad enough to let these floundering yokels explode my little secret, without *your* cutting off with my books. It's lucky for some of them they cut and ran when they did! Here am I – No one knew I was invisible! And now what am I to do?'

'What am *I* to do?' asked Marvel, *sotto voce*.

'It's all about. It will be in the papers! Everybody will be looking for me; everyone on their guard—' The Voice broke off into vivid curses and ceased.

The despair of Mr Marvel's face deepened, and his pace slacked.

'Go on!' said the Voice.

Mr Marvel's face assumed a greyish tint between the ruddier patches.

'Don't drop those books, stupid,' said the Voice sharply – overtaking him.

'The fact is,' said the Voice, 'I shall have to make use of you. You're a poor tool, but I must.'

'I'm a *miserable* tool,' said Marvel.

'You are,' said the Voice.

'I'm the worst possible tool you could have,' said Marvel.

'I'm not strong,' he said after a discouraging silence.

'I'm not over strong,' he repeated.

'No?'

'And my heart's weak. That little business – I pulled it through, of course – but bless you! I could have dropped.'

'Well?'

'I haven't the nerve and strength for the sort of thing you want.'

'*I'll* stimulate you.'

'I wish you wouldn't. I wouldn't like to mess up your plans, you know. But I might, out of sheer funk and misery.'

'You'd better not,' said the Voice, with quiet emphasis.

'I wish I was dead,' said Marvel.

'It ain't justice,' he said; 'you must admit – It seems to me I've a perfect right—'

'*Get* on!' said the Voice.

Mr Marvel mended his pace, and for a time they went in silence again.

'It's devilish hard,' said Mr Marvel.

This was quite ineffectual. He tried another tack.

'What do I make by it?' he began again in a tone of unendurable wrong.

'Oh! *shut up*!' said the Voice, with sudden amazing vigour. 'I'll see to you all right. You do what you're told. You'll do it all right. You're a fool and all that, but you'll do—'

'I tell you, sir, I'm not the man for it. Respectfully – but it is so—'

'If you don't shut up I shall twist your wrist again,' said the Invisible Man. 'I want to think.'

Presently two oblongs of yellow light appeared through the trees, and the square tower of a church loomed through the gloaming. 'I shall keep my hand on your shoulder,' said the Voice, 'all through the village. Go straight through and try no foolery. It will be the worse for you if you do.'

'I know that,' sighed Mr Marvel, 'I know all that.'

The unhappy-looking figure in the obsolete silk hat passed up the street of the little village with his burdens, and vanished into the gathering darkness beyond the lights of the windows.

CHAPTER 14

At Port Stowe

Ten o'clock the next morning found Mr Marvel, unshaven, dirty, and travel-stained, sitting with the books beside him and his hands deep in his pockets, looking very weary, nervous, and uncomfortable, and inflating his cheeks at frequent intervals, on the bench outside a little inn on the outskirts of Port Stowe. Beside him were the books, but now they were tied with string. The bundle had been abandoned in the pine woods beyond Bramblehurst, in accordance with a change in the plans of the Invisible Man. Mr Marvel sat on the bench, and although no one took the slightest notice of him, his agitation remained at fever heat. His hands would go ever and again to his various pockets with a curious nervous fumbling.

When he had been sitting for the best part of an hour, however, an elderly mariner, carrying a newspaper, came out of the inn and sat down beside him. 'Pleasant day,' said the mariner.

Mr Marvel glanced about him with something very like terror. 'Very,' he said.

'Just seasonable weather for the time of year,' said the mariner, taking no denial.

'Quite,' said Mr Marvel.

The mariner produced a toothpick and (saving his regard)* was engrossed thereby for some minutes. His eyes meanwhile were at liberty to examine Mr Marvel's dusty figure, and the books beside him. As he had approached Mr Marvel he had heard a sound like the dropping of coins into a pocket. He was struck by the contrast of Mr Marvel's appearance with this suggestion of opulence. Thence his mind wandered back again to a topic that had taken a curiously firm hold of his imagination.

'Books?' he said suddenly, noisily finishing with the toothpick.

Mr Marvel started and looked at them. 'Oh, yes,' he said. 'Yes, they're books.'

'There's some ex-traordinary things in books,' said the mariner.

'I believe you,' said Mr Marvel.

'And some extra-ordinary things out of 'em,' said the mariner.

'True likewise,' said Mr Marvel. He eyed his interlocutor, and then glanced about him.

'There's some extraordinary things in newspapers, for example,' said the mariner.

'There are.'

'In *this* newspaper,' said the mariner.

'Ah!' said Mr Marvel.

'There's a story,' said the mariner, fixing Mr Marvel with an eye that was firm and deliberate; 'there's a story about an Invisible Man, for instance.'

Mr Marvel pulled his mouth askew and scratched his cheek and felt his ears glowing. 'What will they be writing next?' he asked faintly. 'Ostria, or America?'

'Neither,' said the mariner. '*Here!*'

'Lord!' said Mr Marvel, starting.

'When I say *here*,' said the mariner, to Mr Marvel's intense relief, 'I don't of course mean here in this place, I mean hereabouts.'

'An Invisible Man!' said Mr Marvel. 'And what's *he* been up to?'

'Everything,' said the mariner, controlling Marvel with his eye, and then amplifying: 'Every Blessed Thing.'

'I ain't seen a paper these four days,' said Marvel.

'Iping's the place he started at,' said the mariner.

'In-*deed*!' said Mr Marvel.

'He started there. And where he came from, nobody don't seem to know. Here it is: Pe Culiar Story from Iping. And it says in this paper that the evidence is extraordinary strong – extra-ordinary.'

'Lord!' said Mr Marvel.

'But then, it's a extra-ordinary story. There is a clergyman and a medical gent witnesses – saw 'im all right and proper – or leastways, didn't see 'im. He was staying, it says, at the Coach an' Horses, and no one don't seem to have been aware of his misfortune, it says, aware of his misfortune, until in an Altera-tion* in the inn, it says, his bandages on his head was torn off. It was then ob-served that his head was invisible. Attempts were

At Once made to secure him, but casting off his garments it says, he succeeded in escaping, but not until after a desperate struggle, In Which he had inflicted serious injuries, it says, on our worthy and able constable, Mr J. A. Jaffers. Pretty straight story, eigh? Names and everything.'

'Lord!' said Mr Marvel, looking nervously about him, trying to count the money in his pockets by his unaided sense of touch, and full of a strange and novel idea. 'It sounds most astonishing.'

'Don't it? Extra-ordinary, *I* call it. Never heard tell of Invisible Men before, I haven't, but nowadays one hears such a lot of extra-ordinary things – that – '

'That all he did?' asked Marvel, trying to seem at his ease.

'It's enough, ain't it?' said the mariner.

'Didn't go Back by any chance?' asked Marvel. 'Just escaped and that's all, eh?'

'All!' said the mariner. 'Why! ain't it enough?'

'Quite enough,' said Marvel.

'I should think it was enough,' said the mariner. 'I should think it was enough.'

'He didn't have any pals – it don't say he had any pals, does it?' asked Mr Marvel, anxious.

'Ain't one of a sort enough for you?' asked the Mariner. 'No, thank Heaven, as one might say, he didn't.'

He nodded his head slowly. 'It makes me regular uncomfortable, the bare thought of that chap running about the country! He is at present At Large, and from certain evidence it is supposed that he has – taken – *took*, I suppose they mean – the road to Port Stowe. You see we're right *in* it! None of your American wonders, this time. And just think of the things he might do! Where'd you be, if he took a drop over and above,* and had a fancy to go for you? Suppose he wants to rob – who can prevent him? He can trespass, he can burgle, he could walk through a cordon of policemen as easy as me or you could give the slip to a blind man! Easier! For these here blind chaps hear uncommon sharp, I'm told. And wherever there was liquor he fancied—'

'He's got a tremenjous advantage, certainly,' said Mr Marvel. 'And – well.'

'You're right,' said the Mariner. 'He *has*.'

All this time Mr Marvel had been glancing about him intently, listening for faint footfalls, trying to detect imperceptible movements. He seemed on the point of some great resolution. He coughed behind his hand.

He looked about him again, listened, bent towards the Mariner, and lowered his voice: 'The fact of it is – I happen – to know just a thing or two about this Invisible Man. From private sources.'

'Oh!' said the Mariner, interested. '*You?*'

'Yes,' said Mr Marvel. 'Me.'

'Indeed!' said the Mariner. 'And may I ask–'

'You'll be astonished,' said Mr Marvel behind his hand. 'It's tremenjous.'

'Indeed!' said the Mariner.

'The fact is,' began Mr Marvel eagerly in a confidential undertone. Suddenly his expression changed marvellously. 'Ow!' he said. He rose stiffly in his seat. His face was eloquent of physical suffering. 'Wow!' he said.

'What's up?' said the Mariner, concerned.

'Toothache,' said Mr Marvel, and put his hand to his ear. He caught hold of his books. 'I must be getting on, I think,' he said. He edged in a curious way along the seat away from his interlocutor. 'But you was just agoing to tell me about this here Invisible Man!' protested the Mariner. Mr Marvel seemed to consult with himself. 'Hoax,' said a voice. 'It's a hoax,' said Mr Marvel.

'But it's in the paper,' said the Mariner.

'Hoax all the same,' said Marvel. 'I know the chap that started the lie. There ain't no Invisible Man whatsoever – Blimey.'

'But how 'bout this paper? D'you mean to say—?'

'Not a word of it,' said Marvel stoutly.

The Mariner stared, paper in hand. Mr Marvel jerkily faced about. 'Wait a bit,' said the Mariner, rising and speaking slowly. 'D'you mean to say—?'

'I do,' said Mr Marvel.

'Then why did you let me go on and tell you all this blarsted stuff, then? What d'yer mean by letting a man make a fool of himself like that for? Eigh?'

Mr Marvel blew out his cheeks. The Mariner was suddenly very red indeed; he clenched his hands. 'I been talking here this ten minutes,' he said; 'and you, you little pot-bellied, leathery-

faced son of an old boot, couldn't have the elementary manners—'

'Don't you come bandying words with *me*,' said Mr Marvel.

'Bandying words! I'm a jolly good mind—'

'Come up,' said a voice, and Mr Marvel was suddenly whirled
about and started marching off in a curious spasmodic manner.
'You'd better move on,' said the Mariner. '*Who's* moving on?'
said Mr Marvel. He was receding obliquely with a curious
hurrying gait, with occasional violent jerks forward. Some way
along the road he began a muttered monologue, protests and
recriminations.

'Silly devil!' said the Mariner, legs wide apart, elbows akimbo,
watching the receding figure. 'I'll show you, you silly ass,
hoaxing *me*! It's here – on the paper!'

Mr Marvel retorted incoherently and, receding, was hidden
by a bend in the road, but the Mariner still stood magnificent in
the midst of the way, until the approach of a butcher's cart
dislodged him. Then he turned himself towards Port Stowe. 'Full
of extra-ordinary asses,' he said softly to himself. 'Just to take
me down a bit – that was his silly game – It's on the paper!'

And there was another extraordinary thing he was presently
to hear, that had happened quite close to him. And that was a
vision of a 'fistful of money' (no less) travelling without visible
agency, along by the wall at the corner of St Michael's Lane. A
brother mariner had seen this wonderful sight that very morning. He had snatched at the money forthwith and had been
knocked headlong, and when he had got to his feet the butterfly
money had vanished. Our mariner was in the mood to believe
anything, he declared, but that was a bit *too* stiff. Afterwards,
however, he began to think things over.

The story of the flying money was true. And all about that
neighbourhood, even from the august London and Country
Banking Company, from the tills of shops and inns – doors
standing that sunny weather entirely open – money had been
quietly and dexterously making off that day in handfuls and
rouleaux,* floating quietly along by walls and shady places,
dodging quickly from the approaching eyes of men. And it had,
though no man had traced it, invariably ended its mysterious
flight in the pocket of that agitated gentleman in the obsolete
silk hat, sitting outside the little inn on the outskirts of Port
Stowe.

CHAPTER 15

The Man Who Was Running

In the early evening time Doctor Kemp was sitting in his study in the belvedere* on the hill overlooking Burdock. It was a pleasant little room, with three windows, north, west, and south, and bookshelves covered with books and scientific publications, and a broad writing-table, and, under the north window, a microscope, glass slips, minute instruments, some cultures, and scattered bottles of reagents. Doctor Kemp's solar lamp was lit, albeit the sky was still bright with the sunset light, and his blinds were up because there was no offence of peering outsiders to require them pulled down. Doctor Kemp was a tall and slender young man, with flaxen hair and a moustache almost white, and the work he was upon would earn him, he hoped, the fellowship of the Royal Society, so highly did he think of it.

And his eye presently wandering from his work caught the sunset blazing at the back of the hill that is over against his own. For a minute perhaps he sat, pen in mouth, admiring the rich golden colour above the crest, and then his attention was attracted by the little figure of a man, inky black, running over the hill-brow towards him. He was a shortish little man, and he wore a high hat, and he was running so fast that his legs verily twinkled.

'Another of those fools,' said Doctor Kemp. 'Like that ass who ran into me this morning round a corner, with his "'Visible Man a-coming, sir!" I can't imagine what possesses people. One might think we were in the thirteenth century.'

He got up, went to the window, and stared at the dusky hillside, and the dark little figure tearing down it. 'He seems in a confounded hurry,' said Doctor Kemp, 'but he doesn't seem to be getting on. If his pockets were full of lead, he couldn't run heavier.

'Spurted, sir,' said Doctor Kemp.

In another moment the higher of the villas that had clambered up the hill from Burdock had occulted the running figure. He was visible again for a moment, and again, and then again, three times between the three detached houses that came next, and the terrace hid him.

'Asses!' said Doctor Kemp, swinging round on his heel and walking back to his writing-table.

But those who saw the fugitive nearer, and perceived the abject terror on his perspiring face, being themselves in the open roadway, did not share in the doctor's contempt. By the man pounded, and as he ran he chinked like a well-filled purse that is tossed to and fro. He looked neither to the right nor the left, but his dilated eyes stared straight downhill to where the lamps were being lit, and the people were crowded in the street. And his ill-shaped mouth fell apart, and a glairy* foam lay on his lips, and his breath came hoarse and noisy. All he passed stopped and began staring up the road and down, and interrogating one another with an inkling of discomfort for the reason of his haste.

And then presently, far up the hill, a dog playing in the road yelped and ran under a gate, and as they still wondered something – a wind – a pad, pad, pad, a sound like a panting breathing, rushed by.

People screamed. People sprang off the pavement. It passed in shouts, it passed by instinct down the hill. They were shouting in the street before Marvel was halfway there. They were bolting into houses and slamming the doors behind them, with the news. He heard it and made one last desperate spurt. Fear came striding by, rushed ahead of him, and in a moment had seized the town.

'The Invisible Man is coming! *The Invisible Man!*'

CHAPTER 16

In the Jolly Cricketers

The Jolly Cricketers* is just at the bottom of the hill, where the tram-lines begin. The barman leant his fat red arms on the counter and talked of horses with an anaemic cabman,* while a black-bearded man in grey snapped up biscuit and cheese, drank Burton,* and conversed in American* with a policeman off duty.

'What's the shouting about!' said the anaemic cabman, going off at a tangent, trying to see up the hill over the dirty yellow blind in the low window of the inn. Somebody ran by outside, 'Fire, perhaps,' said the barman.

Footsteps approached, running heavily, the door was pushed open violently, and Marvel, weeping and dishevelled, his hat gone, the neck of his coat torn open, rushed in, made a convulsive turn, and attempted to shut the door. It was held half open by a strap.

'Coming!' he bawled, his voice shrieking with terror. 'He's coming. The 'Visible Man! After me! For Gawd's sake! Elp! Elp! Elp!'

'Shut the doors,' said the policeman. 'Who's coming? What's the row?' He went to the door, released the strap, and it slammed. The American closed the other door.

'Lemme go inside,' said Marvel, staggering and weeping, but still clutching the books. 'Lemme go inside. Lock me in – somewhere. I tell you he's after me. I give him the slip. He said he'd kill me and he will.'

'*You're* safe,' said the man with the black beard. 'The door's shut. What's it all about?'

'Lemme go inside,' said Marvel, and shrieked aloud as a blow suddenly made the fastened door shiver and was followed by a hurried rapping and a shouting outside. 'Hullo,' cried the policeman, 'who's there?' Mr Marvel began to make frantic dives at panels that looked like doors. 'He'll kill me – he's got a knife or something. For Gawd's sake!'

'Here you are,' said the barman. 'Come in here.' And he held up the flap of the bar.

Mr Marvel rushed behind the bar as the summons outside was repeated. 'Don't open the door,' he screamed. '*Please* don't open the door. *Where* shall I hide?'

'This, this Invisible Man, then?' asked the man with the black beard, with one hand behind him. 'I guess it's about time we saw him.'

The window of the inn was suddenly smashed in, and there was a screaming and running to and fro in the street. The policeman had been standing on the settee staring out, craning to see who was at the door. He got down with raised eyebrows. 'It's that,' he said. The barman stood in front of the bar-parlour door which was now locked on Mr Marvel, stared at the smashed window, and came round to the two other men.

Everything was suddenly quiet. 'I wish I had my truncheon,' said the policeman, going irresolutely to the door. 'Once we open, in he comes. There's no stopping him.'

'Don't you be in too much hurry about that door,' said the anaemic cabman, anxiously.

'Draw the bolts,' said the man with the black beard, 'and if he comes—' He showed a revolver in his hand.

'That won't do,' said the policeman; 'that's murder.'

'I know what country I'm in,' said the man with the black beard. 'I'm going to let off at his legs. Draw the bolts.'

'Not with that thing going off behind me,' said the barman, craning over the blind.

'Very well,' said the man with the black beard, and stooping down, revolver ready, drew them himself. Barman, cabman, and a policeman faced about.

'Come in,' said the bearded man in an undertone, standing back and facing the unbolted doors with his pistol behind him. No one came in, the door remained closed. Five minutes afterwards when a second cabman pushed his head in cautiously, they were still waiting, and an anxious face peered out of the bar-parlour and supplied information. 'Are all the doors of the house shut?' asked Marvel. 'He's going round – prowling round. He's as artful as the devil.'

'Good Lord!' said the burly barman. 'There's the back! Just watch them doors! I say!—' He looked about him helplessly.

The bar-parlour door slammed and they heard the key turn. 'There's the yard door and the private door. The yard door—'

He rushed out of the bar.

In a minute he reappeared with a carving-knife in his hand. 'The yard door was open!' he said, and his fat under-lip dropped. 'He may be in the house now!' said the first cabman.

'He's not in the kitchen,' said the barman. 'There's two women there, and I've stabbed every inch of it with this little beef slicer. And they don't think he's come in. They haven't noticed—'

'Have you fastened it?' said the first cabman.

'I'm out of frocks,'* said the barman.

The man with the beard replaced his revolver. And even as he did so the flap of the bar was shut down and the bolt clicked, and then with a tremendous thud the catch of the door snapped and the bar-parlour door burst open. They heard Marvel squeal like a caught leveret, and forthwith they were clambering over the bar to his rescue. The bearded man's revolver cracked and the looking-glass at the back of the parlour started and came smashing and tinkling down.

As the barman entered the room he saw Marvel, curiously crumpled up and struggling against the door that led to the yard and kitchen. The door flew open while the barman hesitated, and Marvel was dragged into the kitchen. There was a scream and a clatter of pans. Marvel, head down, and lugging back obstinately, was forced to the kitchen door, and the bolts were drawn.

Then the policeman, who had been trying to pass the barman, rushed in, followed by one of the cabmen, gripped the wrist of the invisible hand that collared Marvel, was hit in the face and went reeling back. The door opened, and Marvel made a frantic effort to obtain a lodgment behind it. Then the cabman collared something. 'I got him,' said the cabman. The barman's red hands came clawing at the unseen. 'Here he is!' said the barman.

Mr Marvel, released, suddenly dropped to the ground and made an attempt to crawl behind the legs of the fighting men. The struggle blundered round the edge of the door. The voice of the Invisible Man was heard for the first time, yelling out sharply, as the policeman trod on his foot. Then he cried out passionately and his fists flew round like flails. The cabman suddenly whooped and doubled up, kicked under the diaphragm. The door into the bar-parlour from the kitchen slammed and covered Mr Marvel's retreat. The men in the kitchen found themselves clutching at and struggling with empty air.

'Where's he gone?' cried the man with the beard. 'Out?'

'This way,' said the policeman, stepping into the yard and stopping.

A piece of tile whizzed by his head and smashed among the crockery on the kitchen table.

'I'll show him,' shouted the man with the black beard, and suddenly a steel barrel shone over the policeman's shoulder, and five bullets had followed one another into the twilight whence the missile had come. As he fired, the man with the beard moved his hand in a horizontal curve, so that his shots radiated out into the narrow yard like spokes from a wheel.

A silence followed. 'Five cartridges,' said the man with the black beard. 'That's the best of all. Four aces and the joker. Get a lantern, someone, and come and feel about for his body.'

CHAPTER 17

Doctor Kemp's Visitor

Doctor Kemp had continued writing in his study until the shots aroused him. Crack, crack, crack, they came one after the other.

'Hullo!' said Doctor Kemp, putting his pen into his mouth again and listening. 'Who's letting off revolvers in Burdock? What are the asses at now?'

He went to the south window, threw it up, and leaning out stared down on the network of windows, beaded gas-lamps and shops, with its black interstices of roofs that made up the town at night. 'Looks like a crowd down the hill,' he said, 'by the Cricketers,' and remained watching. Thence his eyes wandered over the town to far away where the ships' lights shone, and the pier glowed, a little illuminated faceted pavilion like a gem of yellow light. The moon in its first quarter hung over the western hill, and the stars were clear and almost tropically bright.

After five minutes, during which his mind had travelled into a remote speculation of social conditions of the future, and lost itself at last over the time dimension,* Doctor Kemp roused himself with a sigh, pulled down the window again, and returned to his writing-desk.

It must have been about an hour after this that the front door bell rang. He had been writing slackly, and with intervals of abstraction, since the shots. He sat listening. He heard the servant answer the door, and waited for her feet on the staircase, but she did not come. 'Wonder what that was,' said Doctor Kemp.

He tried to resume his work, failed, got up, went downstairs from his study to the landing, rang, and called over the balustrade to the housemaid as she appeared in the hall below. 'Was that a letter?' he asked.

'Only a runaway ring,* sir,' she answered.

'I'm restless tonight,' he said to himself. He went back to his study, and this time attacked his work resolutely. In a little while he was hard at work again, and the only sounds in the room were the ticking of the clock and the subdued shrillness of his quill,* hurrying in the very centre of the circle of light his lampshade threw on his table.

It was two o'clock before Doctor Kemp had finished his work for the night. He rose, yawned, and went downstairs to bed. He had already removed his coat and vest, when he noticed that he was thirsty. He took a candle and went down to the dining-room in search of a syphon and whisky.

Doctor Kemp's scientific pursuits had made him a very observant man, and as he recrossed the hall, he noticed a dark spot on the linoleum near the mat at the foot of the stairs. He went on upstairs, and then it suddenly occurred to him to ask himself what the spot on the linoleum might be. Apparently some subconscious element was at work. At any rate, he turned with his burden, went back to the hall, put down the syphon and whiskey, and bending down, touched the spot. Without any great surprise he found it had the stickiness and colour of drying blood.

He took up his burden again, and returned upstairs, looking about him and trying to account for the blood-spot. On the landing he saw something and stopped astonished. The door-handle of his own room was blood-stained.

He looked at his own hand. It was quite clean, and then he remembered that the door of his room had been open when he came down from his study, and that consequently he had not touched the handle at all. He went straight into his room, his face quite calm – perhaps a trifle more resolute than usual. His glance, wandering inquisitively, fell on the bed. On the counter-pane was a mess of blood, and the sheet had been torn. He had not noticed this before because he had walked straight to the dressing-table. On the further side the bed-clothes were depressed as if someone had been recently sitting there.

Then he had an odd impression that he had heard a loud voice say, 'Good Heavens! *Kemp!*' But Doctor Kemp was no believer in Voices.

He stood staring at the tumbled sheets. Was that really a voice? He looked about again, but noticed nothing further than the disordered and blood-stained bed. Then he distinctly heard a movement across the room, near the wash-hand stand. All men, however highly educated, retain some superstitious inklings. The feeling that is called 'eerie' came upon him. He closed the door of the room, came forward to the dressing table, and put down his burdens. Suddenly, with a start, he perceived a coiled and blood-stained bandage of linen rag hanging in mid-air, between him and the wash-hand stand.

He stared at this in amazement. It was an empty bandage, a bandage properly tied but quite empty. He would have advanced to grasp it, but a touch arrested him, and a voice speaking quite close to him.

'Kemp!' said the Voice.

'Eigh?' said Kemp, with his mouth open.

'Keep your nerve,' said the Voice. 'I'm an Invisible Man.'

Kemp made no answer for a space, simply stared at the bandage. 'Invisible Man,' he said.

'I'm an Invisible Man,' repeated the Voice.

The story he had been active to ridicule only that morning rushed through Kemp's brain. He does not appear to have been either very much frightened or very greatly surprised at the moment. Realization came later.

'I thought it was all a lie,' he said. The thought uppermost in his mind was the reiterated arguments of the morning. 'Have you a bandage on?' he asked.

'Yes,' said the Invisible Man.

'Oh!' said Kemp, and then roused himself. 'I say!' he said. 'But this is nonsense. It's some trick.' He stepped forward suddenly, and his hand, extended towards the bandage, met invisible fingers.

He recoiled at the touch and his colour changed.

'Keep steady, Kemp, for God's sake! I want help badly. Stop!'

The hand gripped his arm. He struck at it.

'Kemp!' cried the Voice. 'Kemp! Keep steady!' and the grip tightened.

A frantic desire to free himself took possession of Kemp. The hand of the bandaged arm gripped his shoulder, and he was suddenly tripped and flung backwards upon the bed. He opened his mouth to shout, and the corner of the sheet was thrust between his teeth. The Invisible Man had him down grimly, but his arms were free and he struck and tried to kick savagely.

'Listen to reason, will you?' said the Invisible Man, sticking to him in spite of a pounding in the ribs. 'By Heaven! you'll madden me in a minute!

'Lie still, you fool!' bawled the Invisible Man in Kemp's ear.

Kemp struggled for another moment and then lay still.

'If you shout I'll smash your face,' said the Invisible Man, relieving his mouth.

'I'm an Invisible Man. It's no foolishness, and no magic. I really am an Invisible Man. And I want your help. I don't want to hurt you, but if you behave like a frantic rustic, I must. Don't you remember me, Kemp? Griffin,* of University College?'*

'Let me get up,' said Kemp. 'I'll stop where I am. And let me sit quiet for a minute.'

He sat up and felt his neck.

'I am Griffin, of University College, and I have made myself invisible. I am just an ordinary man – a man you have known – made invisible.'

'Griffin?' said Kemp.

'Griffin,' answered the Voice, 'a younger student, almost an albino,* six feet high, and broad, with a pink and white face and red eyes, who won the medal for chemistry.'

'I am confused,' said Kemp. 'My brain is rioting. What has this to do with Griffin?'

'I *am* Griffin.'

Kempt thought. 'It's horrible,' he said. 'But what devilry must happen to make a man invisible?'

'It's no devilry. It's a process, sane and intelligible enough—'

'It's horrible!' said Kemp. 'How on earth—?'

'It's horrible enough. But I'm wounded and in pain, and tired – Great God! Kemp, you are a man. Take it steady. Give me some food and drink, and let me sit down here.'

Kemp stared at the bandage as it moved across the room, then saw a basket chair dragged across the floor and come to rest near the bed. It creaked, and the seat was depressed the quarter of an inch or so. He rubbed his eyes and felt his neck again. 'This beats ghosts,' he said, and laughed stupidly.

'That's better. Thank Heaven, you're getting sensible!'

'Or silly,' said Kemp, and knuckled his eyes.

'Give me some whiskey. I'm near dead.'

'It didn't feel so. Where are you? If I get up shall I run into you? *There!* all right. Whiskey? Here. Where shall I give it you?'

The chair creaked and Kemp felt the glass drawn away from him. He let go by an effort; his instinct was all against it. It came to rest poised twenty inches above the front edge of the seat of the chair. He stared at it in infinite perplexity. 'This is – this *must* be – hypnotism. You must have suggested you are invisible.'

'Nonsense,' said the Voice.

'It's frantic.'

'Listen to me.'

'I demonstrated conclusively this morning,' began Kemp, 'that invisibility—'

'Never mind what you've demonstrated! I'm starving,' said the Voice, 'and the night is – chilly to a man without clothes.'

'Food!' said Kemp.

The tumbler of whiskey tilted itself. 'Yes,' said the Invisible Man rapping it down. 'Have you got a dressing-gown?'

Kemp made some exclamation in an undertone. He walked to a wardrobe and produced a robe of dingy scarlet. 'This do?' he asked. It was taken from him. It hung limp for a moment in mid-air, fluttered weirdly, stood full and decorous buttoning itself, and sat down in his chair. 'Drawers,* socks, slippers would be a comfort,' said the Unseen, curtly. 'And food.'

'Anything. But this is the insanest thing I ever was in, in my life!'

He turned out his drawers for the articles, and then went downstairs to ransack his larder. He came back with some cold cutlets and bread, pulled up a light table, and placed them before his guest. 'Never mind knives,' said his visitor, and a cutlet hung in mid-air, with a sound of gnawing.

'Invisible!' said Kemp, and sat down on a bedroom chair.

'I always like to get something about me before I eat,'* said the Invisible Man, with a full mouth, eating greedily. 'Queer fancy!'

'I suppose that wrist is all right,' said Kemp.

'Trust me,' said the Invisible Man.

'Of *all* the strange and wonderful—'

'Exactly. But it's odd I should blunder into *your* house to get my bandaging. My first stroke of luck! Anyhow I meant to sleep in this house tonight. You must stand that! It's a filthy nuisance, my blood showing, isn't it? Quite a clot over there. Gets visible as it coagulates, I see.* I've been in the house three hours.'

'But how's it done?' began Kemp, in a tone of exasperation. 'Confound it! The whole business – it's unreasonable from beginning to end.'

'Quite reasonable,' said the Invisible Man. 'Perfectly reasonable.'

He reached over and secured the whiskey bottle. Kemp stared at the devouring dressing gown. A ray of candlelight penetrating a torn patch in the right shoulder, made a triangle of light under the left ribs. 'What were the shots?' he asked. 'How did the shooting begin?'

'There was a fool of a man – a sort of confederate of mine – curse him! who tried to steal my money. *Has* done so.'

'Is *he* invisible too?'

'No.'

'Well?'

'Can't I have some more to eat before I tell you all that? I'm hungry – in pain. And you want me to tell stories!'

Kemp got up. '*You* didn't do any shooting?' he asked.

'Not me,' said his visitor. 'Some fool I'd never seen fired at random. A lot of them got scared. They all got scared at me. Curse them! – I say – I want more to eat than this, Kemp.'

'I'll see what there is more to eat downstairs,' said Kemp. 'Not much, I'm afraid.'

After he had done eating, and he made a heavy meal, the Invisible Man demanded a cigar. He bit the end savagely before Kemp could find a knife, and cursed when the outer leaf loosened. It was strange to see him smoking; his mouth, and throat, pharynx and nares,* became visible as a sort of whirling smoke cast.

'This blessed gift of smoking!' he said, and puffed vigorously. 'I'm lucky to have fallen upon you, Kemp. You must help me. Fancy tumbling on you just now! I'm in a devilish scrape. I've been mad, I think. The things I have been through! But we will do things yet. Let me tell you—'

He helped himself to more whiskey and soda. Kemp got up, looked about him, and fetched himself a glass from his spare room. 'It's wild – but I suppose I may drink.'

'You haven't changed much, Kemp, these dozen years. You fair men don't. Cool and methodical – after the first collapse.* I must tell you. We will work together!'

'But how was it all done?' said Kemp, 'and how did you get like this?'

'For God's sake, let me smoke in peace for a little while! And then I will begin to tell you.'

But the story was not told that night. The Invisible Man's wrist was growing painful, he was feverish, exhausted, and his mind came round to brood upon his chase down the hill and the struggle about the inn. He spoke in fragments of Marvel, he smoked faster, his voice grew angry. Kemp tried to gather what he could.

'He was afraid of me, I could see he was afraid of me,' said the Invisible Man many times over. 'He meant to give me the slip – he was always casting about! What a fool I was!

'The cur!

'I should have killed him—'

'Where did you get the money?' asked Kemp, abruptly.

The Invisible Man was silent for a space. 'I can't tell you tonight,' he said.

He groaned suddenly and leant forward, supporting his invisible head on invisible hands. 'Kemp,' he said, 'I've had no sleep for near three days, except a couple of dozes of an hour or so. I must sleep soon.'

'Well, have my room – have this room.'

'But how can I sleep? If I sleep – he will get away. Ugh! What does it matter?'

'What's the shot-wound?' asked Kemp, abruptly.

'Nothing – scratch and blood. Oh, God! How I want sleep!'

'Why not?'

The Invisible Man appeared to be regarding Kemp. 'Because I've a particular objection to being caught by my fellow-men,' he said slowly.

Kemp started.

'Fool that I am!' said the Invisible Man, striking the table smartly. 'I've put the idea into your head.'

CHAPTER 18

The Invisible Man Sleeps

Exhausted and wounded as the Invisible Man was, he refused to accept Kemp's word that his freedom should be respected. He examined the two windows of the bedroom, drew up the blinds, and opened the sashes, to confirm Kemp's statement that a retreat by them would be possible. Outside the night was very quiet and still, and the new moon was setting over the down. Then he examined the keys of the bedroom and the two dressing-room doors, to satisfy himself that these also could be made an assurance of freedom. Finally he expressed himself satisfied. He stood on the hearth rug and Kemp heard the sound of a yawn.

'I'm sorry,' said the Invisible Man, 'if I cannot tell you all that I have done tonight. But I am worn out. It's grotesque, no doubt. It's horrible! But believe me, Kemp, in spite of your arguments of this morning, it is quite a possible thing. I have made a discovery. I meant to keep it to myself. I can't. I must have a partner. And you – We can do such things – But tomorrow. Now, Kemp, I feel as though I must sleep or perish.'

Kemp stood in the middle of the room staring at the headless garment. 'I suppose I must leave you,' he said. 'It's – incredible. These things happening like this, overturning all my preconceptions, would make me insane. But it's real! Is there anything more that I can get you?'

'Only bid me good-night,' said Griffin.

'Good-night,' said Kemp, and shook an invisible hand. He walked sideways to the door. Suddenly the dressing-gown walked quickly towards him. 'Understand me!' said the dressing-gown. 'No attempts to hamper me, or capture me! Or—'

Kemp's face changed a little. 'I thought I gave you my word,' he said.

Kemp closed the door softly behind him, and the key was turned upon him forthwith. Then, as he stood with an expression of passive amazement on his face, the rapid feet came to the door of the dressing-room and that too was locked. Kemp slapped his brow with his hand. 'Am I dreaming? Has the world gone mad – or have I?'*

He laughed, and put his hand to the locked door. 'Barred out of my own bedroom, by a flagrant absurdity!' he said.

He walked to the head of the staircase, turned and stared at the locked doors. 'It's fact,' he said. He put his fingers to his slightly bruised neck. 'Undeniable fact!

'But—'

He shook his head hopelessly, turned, and went downstairs.

He lit the dining-room lamp, got out a cigar, and began pacing the room, ejaculating. Now and then he would argue with himself.

'Invisible!' he said.

'Is there such a thing as an invisible animal? In the sea, yes. Thousands! millions! All the larvae, all the little nauplii and tornarias,* all the microscopic things, the jelly-fish. In the sea there are more things invisible than visible! I never thought of that before. And in the ponds too! All those little pond-life things, specks of colourless translucent jelly! But in air? No!

'It can't be.

'But after all – why not?

'If a man was made of glass he would still be visible.'

His meditation became profound. The bulk of three cigars had passed into the invisible or diffused as a white ash over the carpet before he spoke again. Then it was merely an exclamation. He turned aside, walked out of the room, and went into his little consulting-room and lit the gas there. It was a little room, because Dr Kemp did not live by practice, and in it were the day's newspapers. The morning's paper lay carelessly opened and thrown aside. He caught it up, turned it over, and read the account of a 'Strange Story from Iping' that the mariner at Port Stowe had spelt over so painfully to Mr Marvel. Kemp read it swiftly.

'Wrapped up!' said Kemp. 'Disguised! Hiding it "No one seems to have been aware of his misfortune." What the devil *is* his game?'

He dropped the paper, and his eye went seeking. 'Ah!' he said, and caught up the *St James' Gazette*, lying folded up as it arrived. 'Now we shall get at the truth,' said Dr Kemp. He rent the paper open; a couple of columns confronted him. 'An Entire Village in Sussex goes Mad' was the heading.

'Good Heavens!' said Kemp, reading eagerly an incredulous account of the events in Iping, of the previous afternoon, that have already been described. Over the leaf the report in the morning paper had been reprinted.

He re-read it. 'Ran through the streets striking right and left. Jaffers insensible. Mr Huxter in great pain – still unable to describe what he saw. Painful humiliation – vicar. Woman ill with terror! Windows smashed. This extraordinary story probably a fabrication. Too good not to print – *cum grano!*'*

He dropped the paper and stared blankly in front of him. 'Probably a fabrication!'

He caught up the paper again, and re-read the whole business. 'But when does the Tramp come in? Why the deuce was he chasing a Tramp?'

He sat down abruptly on the surgical couch. 'He's not only invisible,' he said, 'but he's mad! Homicidal!'

When dawn came to mingle its pallor with the lamplight and cigar smoke of the dining-room, Kemp was still pacing up and down, trying to grasp the incredible.

He was altogether too excited to sleep. His servants, descending sleepily, discovered him, and were inclined to think that over-study had worked this ill on him. He gave them extraordinary but quite explicit instructions to lay breakfast for two in the belvedere study – and then to confine themselves to the basement and ground-floor. Then he continued to pace the dining-room until the morning's paper came. That had much to say and little to tell, beyond the confirmation of the evening before, and a very badly written account of another remarkable tale from Port Burdock. This gave Kemp the essence of the happenings at the Jolly Cricketers, and the name of Marvel. 'He has made me keep with him twenty-four hours,' Marvel testified. Certain minor facts were added to the Iping story, notably the cutting of the village telegraph wire. But there was nothing to throw light on the connexion between the Invisible Man and the Tramp; for Mr Marvel had supplied no information about the three books, or the money with which he was lined. The incredulous tone had vanished and a shoal of reporters and inquirers were already at work elaborating the matter.

Kemp read every scrap of the report and sent his housemaid

out to get every one of the morning papers she could. These also he devoured.

'He is invisible!' he said. 'And it reads like rage growing to mania! The things he may do! The things he may do! And he's upstairs free as the air. What on earth ought I to do?

'For instance, would it be a breach of faith if—? No.'

He went to a little untidy desk in the corner, and began a note. He tore this up half written, and wrote another. He read it over and considered it. Then he took an envelope and addressed it to 'Colonel Adye, Port Burdock'.

The Invisible Man awoke even as Kemp was doing this. He awoke in an evil temper, and Kemp, alert for every sound, heard his pattering feet rush suddenly across the bedroom overhead. Then a chair was flung over and the wash-hand stand tumbler smashed. Kemp hurried upstairs and rapped eagerly.

CHAPTER 19

Certain First Principles

'What's the matter?' asked Kemp, when the Invisible Man admitted him.

'Nothing,' was the answer.

'But, confound it! The smash?'

'Fit of temper,' said the Invisible Man. 'Forgot this arm; and it's sore.'

'You're rather liable to that sort of thing.'

'I am.'

Kemp walked across the room and picked up the fragments of broken glass. 'All the facts are out about you,' said Kemp, standing up with the glass in his hand; 'all that happened in Iping, and down the hill. The world has become aware of its invisible citizen. But no one knows you are here.'

The Invisible Man swore.

'The secret's out. I gather it was a secret. I don't know what your plans are, but of course I'm anxious to help you.'

The Invisible Man sat down on the bed.

'There's breakfast upstairs,' said Kemp, speaking as easily as possible, and he was delighted to find his strange guest rose willingly. Kemp led the way up the narrow staircase to the belvedere.

'Before we can do anything else,' said Kemp, 'I must understand a little more about this invisibility of yours.' He had sat down, after one nervous glance out of the window, with the air of a man who has talking to do. His doubts of the sanity of the entire business flashed and vanished again as he looked across to where Griffin sat at the breakfast-table, a headless, handless dressing-gown, wiping unseen lips on a miraculously held *serviette*.

'It's simple enough – and credible enough,' said Griffin, putting the *serviette* aside and leaning the invisible head on an invisible hand.

'No doubt, to you, but—' Kemp laughed.

'Well, yes; to me it seemed wonderful at first, no doubt. But now, great God! But we will do great things yet! I came on the stuff first at Chesilstowe.'*

'Chesilstowe?'

'I went there after I left London. You know I dropped medicine and took up physics? *No!* – well, I did. *Light* fascinated me.'

'Ah!'

'Optical density! The whole subject is a network of riddles – a network with solutions glimmering elusively through. And being but two and twenty and full of enthusiasm, I said, "I will devote my life to this. This is worth while." You know what fools we are at two and twenty?'

'Fools then or fools now,' said Kemp.

'As though Knowing could be any satisfaction to a man!

'But I went to work – like a nigger. And I had hardly worked and thought about the matter six months before light came through one of the meshes suddenly – blindingly! I found a general principle of pigments and refraction, a formula, a geometrical expression involving four dimensions. Fools, common men, even common mathematicians, do not know anything of what some general expression may mean to the student of molecular physics. In the books – the books that Tramp has hidden – there are marvels, miracles! But this was not a method, it was an idea, that might lead to a method by which it would be possible, without changing any other property of matter – except, in some instances, colours – to lower the refractive index* of a substance, solid or liquid, to that of air – so far as all practical purposes are concerned.'

'Phew!' said Kemp. 'That's odd! But still I don't see quite – I can understand that thereby you could spoil a valuable stone,* but personal invisibility is a far cry.'

'Precisely,' said Griffin. 'But consider: Visibility depends on the action of the visible bodies on light. Either a body absorbs light, or it reflects or refracts it, or does all these things. If it neither reflects nor refracts nor absorbs light, it cannot of itself be visible. You see an opaque red box, for instance, because the colour absorbs some of the light and reflects the rest, all the red part of the light, to you. If it did not absorb any particular part of the light, but reflected it all, then it would be a shining white box. Silver! A diamond box would neither absorb much of the light nor reflect much from the general surface, but just here and there where the surfaces were favourable the light would be reflected and refracted, so that you would get a brilliant appearance of flashing reflections and translucencies, a sort of skeleton of light. A glass box would not be so brilliant, not so clearly visible, as a diamond box, because there would be less refraction and reflection. See that? From certain points of view you would see quite clearly through it. Some kinds of glass would be more visible than others, a box of flint glass would be brighter than a box of ordinary window glass. A box of very thin common glass would be hard to see in a bad light, because it would absorb hardly any light and refract and reflect very little. And if you put a sheet of common white glass in water, still more if you put it in some denser liquid than water, it would vanish almost altogether, because light passing from water to glass is only slightly refracted or reflected or indeed affected in any way. It is almost as invisible as a jet of coal gas or hydrogen is in air. And for precisely the same reason!'

'Yes,' said Kemp, 'that is pretty plain sailing.'

'And here is another fact you will know to be true. If a sheet of glass is smashed, Kemp, and beaten into a powder, it becomes much more visible while it is in the air; it becomes at last an opaque white powder. This is because the powdering multiplies the surfaces of the glass at which refraction and reflection occur. In the sheet of glass there are only two surfaces; in the powder the light is reflected or refracted by each grain it passes through, and very little gets right through the powder. But if the white powdered glass is put into water, it forthwith vanishes. The powdered glass and water have much the same refractive index; that is, the light undergoes very little refraction or reflection in passing from one to the other.

'You make the glass invisible by putting it into a liquid of nearly the same refractive index; a transparent thing becomes invisible if it is put in any medium of almost the same refractive index. And if you will consider only a second, you will see also that the powder of glass might be made to vanish in air, if its refractive index could be made the same as that of air; for then there would be no refraction or reflection as the light passed from glass to air.'

'Yes, yes,' said Kemp. 'But a man's not powdered glass!'

'No,' said Griffin. '*He's more transparent!*'

'Nonsense!'

'That from a doctor! How one forgets! Have you already forgotten your physics, in ten years? Just think of all the things that are transparent and seem not to be so. Paper, for instance, is made up of transparent fibres, and it is white and opaque only for the same reason that a powder of glass is white and opaque. Oil white paper, fill up the interstices between the particles with oil so that there is no longer refraction or reflection except at the surfaces, and it becomes as transparent as glass. And not only paper, but cotton fibre, linen fibre, wool fibre, woody fibre, and *bone*, Kemp, *flesh*, Kemp, *hair*, Kemp, *nails* and *nerves*, Kemp, in fact the whole fabric of a man except the red of his blood and the black pigment of hair, are all made up of transparent, colourless tissue. So little suffices to make us visible one to the other. For the most part the fibres of a living creature are no more opaque than water.'

'Great Heavens!' cried Kemp. 'Of course, of course! I was thinking only last night of the sea larvae and all jellyfish!'

'*Now* you have me! And all that I knew and had in mind a year after I left London – six years ago. But I kept it to myself. I had to do my work under frightful disadvantages. Oliver, my professor, was a scientific bounder, a journalist by instinct, a thief of ideas, he was always prying! And you know the knavish system of the scientific world. I simply would not publish, and let him share my credit. I went on working, I got nearer and nearer making my formula into an experiment, a reality. I told no living soul, because I meant to flash my work upon the world with crushing effect – to become famous at a blow. I took up the question of pigments to fill up certain gaps. And suddenly, not by design but by accident, I made a discovery in physiology.'

'Yes?'

'You know the red colouring matter of blood; it can be made white – colourless – and remain with all the functions it has now!'

Kemp gave a cry of incredulous amazement.

The Invisible Man rose and began pacing the little study. 'You may well exclaim. I remember that night. It was late at night – in the daytime one was bothered with the gaping, silly students – and I worked then sometimes till dawn. It came suddenly, splendid and complete into my mind. I was alone; the laboratory was still, with the tall lights burning brightly and silently. In all my great moments I have been alone. "One could make an animal – a tissue – transparent! One could make it invisible! All except the pigments – I could be invisible!" I said, suddenly realizing what it meant to be an albino with such knowledge. It was overwhelming. I left the filtering I was doing, and went and stared out of the great window at the stars. "I could be invisible!" I repeated.

'To do such a thing would be to transcend magic. And I beheld, unclouded by doubt, a magnificient vision of all that invisibility might mean to a man – the mystery, the power, the freedom. Drawbacks I saw none. You have only to think! And I, a shabby, poverty-struck, hemmed-in demonstrator, teaching fools in a provincial college, might suddenly become – this. I ask you, Kemp, if *you* – Anyone, I tell you, would have flung himself upon that research. And I worked three years, and every mountain of difficulty I toiled over showed another from its summit. The infinite details! And the exasperation – a professor, a provincial professor, always prying. "When are you going to publish this work of yours?" was his everlasting question. And the students, the cramped means! Three years I had of it—

'And after three years of secrecy and exasperation, I found that to complete it was impossible – impossible.'

'How?' asked Kemp.

'Money,' said the Invisible Man, and went again to stare out of the window.

He turned round abruptly. 'I robbed the old man – robbed my father.

'The money was not his, and he shot himself.'

CHAPTER 20

At the House in Great Portland Street

For a moment Kemp sat in silence, staring at the back of the headless figure at the window. Then he started, struck by a thought, rose, took the Invisible Man's arm, and turned him away from the outlook.

'You are tired,' he said, 'and while I sit, you walk about. Have my chair.'

He placed himself between Griffin and the nearest window.

For a space Griffin sat silent, and then he resumed abruptly:-

'I had left the Chesilstowe cottage already,' he said, 'when that happened. It was last December. I had taken a room in London, a large unfurnished room in a big ill-managed lodging-house in a slum near Great Portland Street. The room was soon full of the appliances I had bought with his money; the work was going on steadily, successfully, drawing near an end. I was like a man emerging from a thicket, and suddenly coming on some unmeaning tragedy. I went to bury him. My mind was still on this research, and I did not lift a finger to save his character. I remember the funeral, the cheap hearse, the scant ceremony, the windy frost-bitten hillside, and the old college friend of his who read the service over him, a shabby, black, bent old man with a snivelling cold.

'I remember walking back to the empty home, through the place that had once been a village and was now patched and tinkered by the jerry builders into the ugly likeness of a town. Every way the roads ran out at last into the desecrated fields and ended in rubble heaps and rank wet weeds. I remember myself as a gaunt black figure, going along the slippery, shiny pavement, and the strange sense of detachment I felt from the squalid respectability, the sordid commercialism of the place.

'I did not feel a bit sorry for my father. He seemed to me to be the victim of his own foolish sentimentality. The current cant required my attendance at his funeral, but it was really not my affair.

'But going along the High Street, my old life came back to me for a space, for I met the girl I had known ten years since. Our eyes met.

'Something moved me to turn back and talk to her. She was a very ordinary person.

'It was all like a dream, that visit to the old places. I did not feel then that I was lonely, that I had come out from the world into a desolate place. I appreciated my loss of sympathy, but I put it down to the general inanity of things. Re-entering my room seemed like the recovery of reality. There were the things I knew and loved. There stood the apparatus, the experiments arranged and waiting. And now there was scarcely a difficulty left, beyond the planning of details.

'I will tell you, Kemp, sooner or later, all the complicated processes. We need not go into that now. For the most part, saving certain gaps I chose to remember, they are written in cypher in those books that tramp has hidden. We must hunt him down. We must get those books again. But the essential phase was to place the transparent object whose refractive index was to be lowered between two radiating centres of a sort of ethereal vibration, of which I will tell you more fully later. No, not these Röntgen* vibrations – I don't know that these others of mine have been described. Yet they are obvious enough. I needed two little dynamos, and these I worked with a cheap gas engine. My first experiment was with a bit of white wool fabric. It was the strangest thing in the world to see it in the flicker of the flashes soft and white, and then to watch it fade like a wreath of smoke and vanish.

'I could scarcely believe I had done it. I put my hand into the emptiness, and there was the thing as solid as ever. I felt it awkwardly, and threw it on the floor. I had a little trouble finding it again.

'And then came a curious experience. I heard a miaow behind me, and turning, saw a lean white cat, very dirty, on the cistern cover outside the window. A thought came into my head. "Everything ready for you," I said, and went to the window, opened it, and called softly. She came in, purring – the poor beast was starving – and I gave her some milk. All my food was in a cupboard in the corner of the room. After that she went smelling round the room – evidently with the idea of making herself at home. The invisible rag upset her a bit; you should have seen her spit at it! But I made her comfortable on the pillow of my truckle-bed.* And I gave her butter to get her to wash.'*

'And you processed her?'

'I processed her. But giving drugs to a cat is no joke, Kemp! And the process failed.'

'Failed!'

'In two particulars. These were the claws and the pigment stuff – what is it? – at the back of the eye in a cat. You know?'

'*Tapetum.*'*

'Yes, the *tapetum*. It didn't go. After I'd given the stuff to bleach the blood and done certain other things to her, I gave the beast opium, and put her and the pillow she was sleeping on, on the apparatus. And after all the rest had faded and vanished, there remained two little ghosts of her eyes.'

'Odd!'

'I can't explain it. She was bandaged and clamped, of course – so I had her safe; but she woke while she was still misty, and miaowled dismally, and someone came knocking. It was an old woman from downstairs, who suspected me of vivisection – a drink-sodden old creature with only a white cat to care for in all the world. I whipped out some chloroform,* applied it, and answered the door. "Did I hear a cat?" she asked. "My cat?" "Not here," said I, very politely. She was a little doubtful and tried to peer past me into the room; strange enough to her no doubt – bare walls, uncurtained windows, truckle-bed, with the gas engine vibrating, and the seethe of the radiant points, and that faint ghastly stinging of chloroform in the air. She had to be satisfied at last and went away again.'

'How long did it take?' asked Kemp.

'Three or four hours – the cat. The bones and sinews and the fat were the last to go, and the tips of the coloured hairs. And, as I say, the back part of the eye, tough iridescent stuff it is, wouldn't go at all.

'It was night outside long before the business was over, and nothing was to be seen but the dim eyes and the claws. I stopped the gas engine, felt for and stroked the beast, which was still insensible, and then, being tired, left it sleeping on the invisible pillow and went to bed. I found it hard to sleep. I lay awake thinking weak aimless stuff, going over the experiment over and over again, or dreaming feverishly of things growing misty and vanishing about me, until everything, the ground I stood on, vanished, and so I came to that sickly falling nightmare one gets. About two, the cat began miaowling about the room. I tried to hush it by talking to it, and then I decided to turn it out. I remember the shock I had when striking a light – there were just the round eyes shining green – and nothing round them. I would have given it milk, but I hadn't any. It wouldn't be quiet, it just sat down and miaowed at the door. I tried to catch it, with an idea of putting it out of the window, but it wouldn't be caught, it vanished. Then it began miaowing in different parts of the room. At last I opened the window and made a bustle.* I suppose it went out at last. I never saw any more of it.

'Then – Heaven knows why – I fell thinking of my father's funeral again, and the dismal windy hillside, until the day had come. I found sleeping was hopeless, and, locking my door after me, wandered out into the morning streets.'

'You don't mean to say there's an invisible cat at large!' said Kemp.

'If it hasn't been killed,' said the Invisible Man. 'Why not?'

'Why not?' said Kemp. 'I didn't mean to interrupt.'

'It's very probably been killed,' said the Invisible Man. 'It was alive four days after, I know, and down a grating in Great Titchfield Street; because I saw a crowd round the place, trying to see whence the miaowing came.'

He was silent for the best part of a minute. Then he resumed abruptly:-

'I remember that morning before the change very vividly. I must have gone up Great Portland Street. I remember the barracks in Albany Street, and the horse soldiers coming out, and at last I found myself sitting in the sunshine and feeling very ill and strange, on the summit of Primrose Hill. It was a sunny day in January – one of those sunny, frosty days that came before the snow this year. My weary brain tried to formulate the position, to plot out a plan of action.

'I was surprised to find, now that my prize was within my grasp, how inconclusive its attainment seemed. As a matter of fact I was worked out; the intense stress of nearly four years' continuous work left me incapable of any strength of feeling. I was apathetic, and I tried in vain to recover the enthusiasm of my first inquiries, the passion of discovery that had enabled me to compass even the downfall of my father's grey hairs. Nothing seemed to matter. I saw pretty clearly this was a transient mood, due to overwork and want of sleep, and that either by drugs or rest it would be possible to recover my energies.

'All I could think clearly was that the thing had to be carried through; the fixed idea still ruled me. And soon, for the money I had was almost exhausted. I looked about me at the hillside, with children playing and girls watching them, and tried to think of all the fantastic advantages an invisible man would have in the world. After a time I crawled home, took some food and a strong dose of strychnine,* and went to sleep in my clothes on my unmade bed. Strychnine is a grand tonic, Kemp, to take the flabbiness out of a man.'

'It's the devil,' said Kemp. 'It's the palaeolithic* in a bottle.'

'I awoke vastly invigorated and rather irritable. You know?'

'I know the stuff.'

'And there was someone rapping at the door. It was my landlord with threats and inquiries, an old Polish Jew in a long grey coat and greasy slippers. I had been tormenting a cat in the night, he was sure – the old woman's tongue had been busy. He insisted on knowing all about it. The laws of this country against vivisection were very severe* – he might be liable. I denied the cat. Then the vibration of the little gas engine could be felt all over the house, he said. That was true, certainly. He edged round me into the room, peering about over his German-silver spectacles, and a sudden dread came into my mind that he might carry away something of my secret. I tried to keep between him and the concentrating apparatus I had arranged, and that only made him more curious. What was I doing? Why was I always alone and secretive? Was it legal? Was it dangerous? I paid nothing but the usual rent. His had always been a most respectable house – in a disreputable neighbourhood. Suddenly my temper gave way. I told him to get out. He began to protest, to jabber of his right of entry. In a moment I had him by the collar; something ripped, and he went spinning out into his own passage. I slammed and locked the door and sat down quivering.

'He made a fuss outside, which I disregarded, and after a time he went away.

'But this brought matters to a crisis. I did not know what he would do, nor even what he had power to do. To move to fresh apartments would have meant delay; all together I had barely twenty pounds left in the world – for the most part in a bank –

and I could not afford that. Vanish! It was irresistible. Then there would be an inquiry, the sacking of my room—

'At the thought of the possibility of my work being exposed or interrupted at its very climax, I became angry and active. I hurried out with my three books of notes, my cheque-book – the tramp has them now – and directed them from the nearest Post Office to a house of call for letters and parcels in Great Portland Street. I tried to go out noiselessly. Coming in, I found my landlord going quietly upstairs; he had heard the door close, I suppose. You would have laughed to see him jump aside on the landing as I came tearing after him. He glared at me as I went by him, and I made the house quiver with the slamming of my door. I heard him come shuffling up to my floor, hesitate, and go down. I set to work upon my preparations forthwith.

'It was all done that evening and night. While I was still sitting under the sickly, drowsy influence of the drugs that decolourise blood, there came a repeated knocking at the door. It ceased, footsteps went away and returned, and the knocking was resumed. There was an attempt to push something under the door – a blue paper. Then in a fit of irritation I rose and went and flung the door wide open. "Now then?" said I.

'It was my landlord, with a notice of ejectment or something. He held it out to me, saw something odd about my hands, I expect, and lifted his eyes to my face.

'For a moment he gaped. Then he gave a sort of inarticulate cry, dropped candle and writ together, and went blundering down the dark passage to the stairs. I shut the door, locked it, and went to the looking-glass. Then I understood his terror. My face was white – like white stone.

'But it was all horrible. I had not expected the suffering. A night of racking anguish, sickness and fainting. I set my teeth, though my skin was presently afire, all my body afire; but I lay there like grim death. I understood now how it was the cat had howled until I chloroformed it. Lucky it was I lived alone and untended in my room. There were times when I sobbed and groaned and talked. But I stuck to it. I became insensible and woke languid in the darkness.

'The pain had passed. I thought I was killing myself and I did not care. I shall never forget that dawn, and the strange horror of seeing that my hands had become as clouded glass, and watching them grow clearer and thinner as the day went by, until at last I could see the sickly disorder of my room through them, though I closed my transparent eyelids* My limbs became glassy, the bones and arteries faded, vanished, and the little white nerves went last. I gritted my teeth and stayed there to the end. At last only the dead tips of the fingernails remained, pallid and white, and the brown stain of some acid upon my fingers.

'I struggled up. At first I was as incapable as a swathed infant – stepping with limbs I could not see. I was weak and very hungry. I went and stared at nothing in my shaving glass, at nothing save where an attenuated pigment still remained behind the retina of my eyes, fainter than mist. I had to hang on to the table and press my forehead to the glass.

'It was only by a frantic effort of will that I dragged myself back to the apparatus and completed the process.

'I slept during the forenoon, pulling the sheet over my eyes to shut out the light, and about midday I was awakened again by a knocking. My strength had returned. I sat up and listened and heard a whispering. I sprang to my feet and as noiselessly as possible began to detach the connections of my apparatus, and to distribute it about the room, so as to destroy the suggestions of its arrangement. Presently the knocking was renewed and voices called, first my landlord's, then two others. To gain time I answered them. The invisible rag and pillow came to hand and I opened the window and pitched them out on to the cistern cover. As the window opened, a heavy crash came at the door. Someone had charged it with the idea of smashing the lock. But the stout bolts I had screwed up some days before stopped him. That startled me, made me angry. I began to tremble and do things hurriedly.

'I tossed together some loose paper, straw, packing paper and so forth, in the middle of the room, and turned on the gas. Heavy blows began to rain upon the door. I could not find the matches. I beat my hands on the wall with rage. I turned down the gas again, stepped out of the window on the cistern cover, very softly lowered the sash, and sat down, secure and invisible, but quivering with anger, to watch events. They split a panel, I saw, and in another moment they had broken away the staples of the bolts and stood in the open doorway. It was the landlord and his two step-sons, sturdy young men of three or four and twenty. Behind them fluttered the old hag of a woman from downstairs.

'You may imagine their astonishment to find the room empty. One of the younger men rushed to the window at once, flung it up and stared out. His staring eyes and thick lipped bearded face came a foot from my face. I was half minded to hit his silly countenance, but I arrested my doubled fist. He stared right through me. So did the others as they joined him. The old man went and peered under the bed, and then they all made a rush for the cupboard. They had to argue about it at length in Yiddish and Cockney English. They concluded I had not answered them, that their imagination had deceived them. A feeling of extraordinary elation took the place of my anger as I sat outside the window and watched these four people – for the old lady came in, glancing suspiciously about her like a cat, trying to understand the riddle of my behaviour.

'The old man, so far as I could understand his *patois*,* agreed with the old lady that I was a vivisectionist. The sons protested in garbled English that I was an electrician, and appealed to the dynamos and radiators. They were all nervous against* my arrival, although I found subsequently that they had bolted the front door. The old lady peered into the cupboard and under the bed, and one of the young men pushed up the register* and stared up the chimney. One of my fellow lodgers, a coster-monger* who shared the opposite room with a butcher, appeared on the landing, and he was called in and told incoherent things.

'It occurred to me that the radiators, if they fell into the hands of some acute well-educated person, would give me away too much, and watching my opportunity, I came into the room and tilted one of the little dynamos off its fellow on which it was standing, and smashed both apparatus. Then, while they were trying to explain the smash, I dodged out of the room and went softly downstairs.

'I went into one of the sitting-rooms and waited until they came down, still speculating and argumentative, all a little disappointed at finding no "horrors", and all a little puzzled how they stood with regard to me. Then I slipped up again with a box of matches, fired my heap of paper and rubbish, put the chairs and bedding thereby, led the gas to the affair, by means of an india-rubber tube, and waving a farewell to the room left it for the last time.'

'You fired the house!' exclaimed Kemp.

'Fired the house. It was the only way to cover my trail – and no doubt it was insured. I slipped the bolts of the front door quietly and went out into the street. I was invisible, and I was only just beginning to realise the extraordinary advantage my invisibility gave me. My head was already teeming with plans of all the wild and wonderful things I had now impunity to do.'

CHAPTER 21

In Oxford Street

'In going downstairs the first time I found an unexpected difficulty because I could not see my feet; indeed I stumbled twice, and there was an unaccustomed clumsiness in gripping the bolt. By not looking down, however, I managed to walk on the level passably well.

'My mood, I say was one of exaltation. I felt as a seeing man might do, with padded feet and noiseless clothes, in a city of the blind. I experienced a wild impulse to jest, to startle people, to clap men on the back, fling people's hats astray, and generally revel in my extraordinary advantage.

'But hardly had I emerged upon Great Portland Street, however (my lodging was close to the big draper's shop there), when I heard a clashing concussion and was hit violently behind, and turning saw a man carrying a basket of soda-water syphons, and looking in amazement at his burden. Although the blow had really hurt me, I found something so irresistible in his astonishment that I laughed aloud. "The devil's in the basket," I said, and suddenly twisted it out of his hand. He let go incontinently, and I swung the whole weight into the air.

'But a fool of a cabman, standing outside a public house, made a sudden rush for this, and his extending fingers took me with excruciating violence under the ear. I let the whole down with a smash on the cabman, and then, with shouts and the clatter of feet about me, people coming out of shops, vehicles pulling up, I realised what I had done for myself, and cursing my folly, backed against a shop window and prepared to dodge out of the confusion. In a moment I should be wedged into a crowd and inevitably discovered. I pushed by a butcher boy, who luckily did not turn to see the nothingness that shoved him aside, and dodged behind the cabman's four-wheeler. I do not know how they settled the business. I hurried straight across the road, which was happily clear, and hardly heeding which way I went, in the fright of detection the incident had given me, plunged into the afternoon throng of Oxford Street.

'I tried to get into the stream of people, but they were too thick for me, and in a moment my heels were being trodden upon. I took to the gutter, the roughness of which I found painful to my feet, and forthwith the shaft of a crawling hansom* dug me forcibly under the shoulder blade, reminding me that I was already bruised severely. I staggered out of the way of the cab, avoided a perambulator by a convulsive movement, and found myself behind the hansom. A happy thought saved me, and as this drove slowly along I followed in its immediate wake, trembling and astonished at the turn of my adventure. And not only trembling, but shivering. It was a bright day in January and I was stark naked and the thin slime of mud that covered the road was freezing. Foolish as it seems to me now, I had not reckoned that, transparent or not, I was still amenable to the weather and all its consequences.*

'Then suddenly a bright idea came into my head. I ran round and got into the cab. And so, shivering, scared, and sniffing with the first intimations of a cold, and with the bruises in the small of my back growing upon my attention, I drove slowly along Oxford Street and past Tottenham Court Road. My mood was as different from that in which I had sallied forth ten minutes ago as it is possible to imagine. *This* invisibility indeed! The one thought that possessed me was – how was I to get out of the scrape I was in.

'We crawled past Mudie's,* and there a tall woman with five or six yellow-labelled books hailed my cab, and I sprang out just in time to escape her, shaving a railway van narrowly in my flight. I made off up the roadway to Bloomsbury Square, intending to strike north past the Museum* and so get into the quiet district. I was now cruelly chilled, and the strangeness of my situation so unnerved me that I whimpered as I ran. At the northward corner of the Square a little white dog ran out of the Pharmaceutical Society's offices, and incontinently made for me, nose down.

'I had never realised it before, but the nose is to the mind of a dog what the eye is to the mind of a seeing man. Dogs perceive the scent of a man moving as men perceive his vision. This brute began barking and leaping, showing, as it seemed to me, only too plainly that he was aware of me. I crossed Great Russell

Street, glancing over my shoulder as I did so, and went some way along Montague Street before I realised what I was running towards.

'Then I became aware of a blare of music, and looking along the street saw a number of people advancing out of Russell Square, red shirts, and the banner of the Salvation Army* to the fore. Such a crowd, chanting in the roadway and scoffing on the pavement, I could not hope to penetrate, and dreading to go back and farther from home again, and deciding on the spur of the moment, I ran up the white steps of a house facing the museum railings and stood there until the crowd should have passed. Happily the dog stopped at the noise of the band too, hesitated, and turned tail, running back to Bloomsbury Square again.

'On came the band, bawling with unconscious irony some hymn about "When shall we see his Face?"* and it seemed an interminable time to me before the tide of the crowd washed along the pavement by me. Thud, thud, thud, came the drum with a vibrating resonance, and for the moment I did not notice two urchins stopping at the railings by me. "See 'em," said one. "See what?" said the other. "Why – them footmarks – *bare*. Like what you makes in mud."

'I looked down and saw the youngsters had stopped and were gaping at the muddy footmarks I had left behind me up the newly whitened steps. The passing people elbowed and jostled them, but their confounded intelligence was arrested. "Thud, thud, thud, When, thud, shall we see, thud, his Face, thud, thud." "There's a barefoot man gone up them steps, or I don't know nothing," said one. "And he ain't never come down again. And his foot was a-bleeding."*

'The thick of the crowd had already passed. "Looky there, Ted," quoth the younger of the detectives, with the sharpness of surprise in his voice, and pointed straight to my feet. I looked down and saw at once the dim suggestion of their outline sketched in splashes of mud. For a moment I was paralysed.

'"Why, that's rum," said the elder. "Dashed rum! It's just like the ghost of a foot, ain't it?" He hesitated and advanced with outstretched hand. A man pulled up short to see what he was catching, and then a girl. In another moment he would have touched me. Then I saw what to do. I made a step, the boy started back with an exclamation, and with a rapid movement I swung myself over into the portico of the next house. But the smaller boy was sharp-eyed enough to follow the movement, and before I was well down the steps and upon the pavement, he had recovered from his momentary astonishment and was shouting out that the feet had gone over the wall.

'They rushed round and saw my new footmarks flash into being on the lower step and upon the pavement. "What's up?" asked someone. "Feet! Look! Feet running!" Everybody in the road, except my three pursuers, was pouring along after the Salvation Army, and this blow not only impeded me but them. There was an eddy of surprise and interrogation. At the cost of bowling over one young fellow I got through, and in another moment I was rushing headlong round the circuit of Russell Square, with six or seven astonished people following my footmarks. There was no time for explanation, or else the whole host would have been after me.

'Twice I doubled round corners, thrice I crossed the road and came back on my tracks, and then, as my feet grew hot and dry, the damp impressions began to fade. At last I had a breathing space and rubbed my feet clean with my hands, and so got away altogether. The last I saw of the chase was a little group of a dozen people perhaps, studying with infinite perplexity a slowly drying footprint that had resulted from a puddle in Tavistock Square – a footprint as isolated and incomprehensible to them as Crusoe's solitary discovery.*

'This running warmed me to a certain extent, and I went on with a better courage through the maze of less frequented roads that runs hereabouts. My back had now become very stiff and sore, my tonsils were painful from the cabman's fingers, and the skin of my neck had been scratched by his nails; my feet hurt exceedingly and I was lame from a little cut on one foot. I saw in time a blind man approaching me, and fled limping, for I feared his subtle intuitions. Once or twice accidental collisions occurred and I left people amazed, with unaccountable curses ringing in their ears. Then came something silent and quiet against my face, and across the Square fell a thin veil of slowly, falling flakes of snow. I had caught a cold, and do as I would I could not avoid an occasional sneeze. And every dog that came in sight, with its pointing nose and curious sniffing, was a terror to me.

'Then came men and boys running, first one and then others,

and shouting as they ran. It was a fire. They ran in the direction of my lodging, and looking back down a street I saw a mass of black smoke streaming up above the roofs and telephone wires. It was my lodging burning; my clothes, my apparatus, all my resources indeed, except my cheque-book and the three volumes of memoranda that awaited me in Great Portland Street, were there. Burning! I had burnt my boats – if ever a man did! The place was blazing.'

The Invisible Man paused and thought. Kemp glanced nervously out of the window. 'Yes?' he said. 'Go on.'

CHAPTER 22

In the Emporium

'So last January, with the beginnings of a snowstorm in the air about me – and if it settled on me it would betray me! – weary, cold, painful, inexpressibly wretched, and still but half convinced of my invisible quality, I began this new life to which I am committed. I had no refuge, no appliances, no human being in the world in whom I could confide. To have told my secret would have given me away – made a mere show and rarity of me. Nevertheless, I was half minded to accost some passer-by and throw myself upon his mercy. But I knew too clearly the terror and brutal cruelty my advances would evoke. I made no plans in the street. My sole object was to get shelter from the snow, to get myself covered and warm; then I might hope to plan. But even to me, an Invisible Man, the rows of London houses stood latched, barred, and bolted impregnably.

'Only one thing could I see clearly before me, the cold exposure and misery of the snowstorm and the night.

'And then I had a brilliant idea. I turned down one of the roads leading from Gower Street to Tottenham Court Road, and found myself outside Omniums, the big establishment where everything is to be bought – you know the place – meat, grocery, linen, furniture, clothing, oil paintings even, a huge meandering collection of shops rather than a shop. I had thought I should find the doors open, but they were closed, and as I stood in the wide entrance a carriage stopped outside, and a man in uniform – you know the kind of personage with "*Omnium*" on his cap – flung open the door. I contrived to enter, and walking down the shop – it was a department where they were selling ribbons and gloves and stockings and that kind of thing – came to a more spacious region devoted to picnic baskets and wicker furniture.

'I did not feel safe there, however; people were going to and fro, and I prowled restlessly about until I came upon a huge section in an upper floor containing multitudes of bedsteads, and this I clambered, and found a resting-place at last among a huge pile of folded flock mattresses. The place was already lit up and agreeably warm, and I decided to remain where I was, keeping a cautious eye on the two or three sets of shopmen and customers who were meandering through the place, until closing time came. Then I should be able, I thought, to rob the place for food and clothing, and disguised, prowl through it and examine its resources, perhaps sleep on some of the bedding. That seemed an acceptable plan. My idea was to procure clothing to make myself a muffled but acceptable figure, to get money, and then to recover my books and parcels where they awaited me, take a lodging somewhere and elaborate plans for the complete realisation of the advantages my invisibility gave me (as I still imagined) over my fellow-men.

'Closing time arrived quickly enough; it could not have been more than an hour after I took up my position on the mattresses before I noticed the blinds of the windows being drawn, and customers being marched doorward. And then a number of brisk young men began with remarkable alacrity to tidy up the goods that remained disturbed. I left my lair as the crowds diminished, and prowled cautiously out into the less desolate parts of the shop. I was really surprised to observe how rapidly the young men and women whipped away the goods displayed for sale during the day. All the boxes of goods, the hanging fabrics, the festoons of lace, the boxes of sweets in the grocery section, the displays of this and that, were being whipped down, folded up, slapped into tidy receptacles, and everything that could not be taken down and put away had sheets of some coarse stuff like sacking flung over them. Finally all the chairs were turned up on to the counters, leaving the floor clear. Directly each of these young people had done, he or she made promptly for the door with such an expression of animation as I have rarely observed in a shop assistant before. Then came a lot of youngsters scattering sawdust and carrying pails and brooms. I had to dodge to get out of the way, and as it was, my ankle got stung with the sawdust. For some time, wandering through the swathed and darkened departments, I could hear the brooms at work. And at last a good hour or more after the shop had been closed, came a noise of locking doors. Silence came upon the place, and I found myself wandering through the vast and intricate shops, galleries, showrooms of the place,

alone. It was very still; in one place I remember passing near one
of the Tottenham Court Road entrances and listening to the
tapping of boot-heels of the passers-by.

'My first visit was to the place where I had seen stockings and
gloves for sale. It was dark, and I had the devil of a hunt after
matches, which I found at last in the drawer of the little cash
desk. Then I had to get a candle. I had to tear down wrappings
and ransack a number of boxes and drawers, but at last I
managed to turn out what I sought; the box label called them
lambswool pants, and lambswool vests. Then socks, a thick
comforter,* and then I went to the clothing place and got
trousers, a lounge jacket, an overcoat and a slouch hat* – a
clerical sort of hat with the brim turned down. I began to feel a
human being again, and my next thought was food.

'Upstairs was a refreshment department, and there I got cold
meat. There was coffee still in the urn, and I lit the gas and
warmed it up again, and altogether I did not do badly. Afterwards, prowling through the place in search of blankets – I had
to put up at last with a heap of down quilts – I came upon a
grocery section with a lot of chocolate and candied fruits, more
than was good for me indeed – and some white burgundy. And
near that was a toy department, and I had a brilliant idea. I
found some artifical noses – dummy noses, you know, and I
thought of dark spectacles. But Omniums had no optical department. My nose had been a difficulty indeed – I had thought of
paint. But the discovery set my mind running on wigs and masks
and the like. Finally I went to sleep in a heap of down quilts,
very warm and comfortable.

'My last thoughts before sleeping were the most agreeable I
had had since the change. I was in a state of physical serenity,
and that was reflected in my mind. I thought that I should be
able to slip out unobserved in the morning with my clothes upon
me, muffling my face with a white wrapper I had taken,
purchase, with the money I had taken, spectacles and so forth,
and so complete my disguise. I lapsed into disorderly dreams of
all the fantastic things that had happened during the last few
days. I saw the ugly little landlord vociferating in his rooms; I
saw his two sons marvelling, and the wrinkled old woman's
gnarled face as she asked for her cat. I experienced again the
strange sensation of seeing the cloth disappear, and so I came
round to the windy hillside and the sniffing old clergyman

mumbling "Dust to dust, earth to earth,"* and my father's open grave.

'"You also," said a voice, and suddenly I was being forced towards the grave. I struggled, shouted, appealed to the mourners, but they continued stonily following the service; the old clergyman, too, never faltered droning and sniffing through the ritual. I realised I was invisible and inaudible, that overwhelming forces had their grip on me. I struggled in vain, I was forced over the brink, the coffin rang hollow as I fell upon it, and the gravel came flying after me in spadefuls. Nobody heeded me, nobody was aware of me. I made convulsive struggles and awoke.

'The pale London dawn had come, the place was full of a chilly grey light that filtered round the edges of the window blinds. I sat up, and for a time I could not think where this ample apartment, with its counters, its piles of rolled stuff, its heap of quilts and cushions, its iron pillars, might be. Then, as recollection came back to me, I heard voices in conversation.

'Then far down the place, in the brighter light of some department which had already raised its blinds, I saw two men approaching. I scrambled to my feet, looking about me for some way of escape, and even as I did so the sound of my movement made them aware of me. I suppose they saw merely a figure moving quietly and quickly away. "Who's that?" cried one, and "Stop there!" shouted the other. I dashed round a corner and came full tilt – a faceless figure, mind you! – on a lanky lad of fifteen. He yelled and I bowled him over, rushed past him, turned another corner, and by a happy inspiration threw myself flat behind a counter. In another moment feet went running past and I heard voices shouting, "All hands to the doors!" asking what was "up", and giving one another advice how to catch me.

'Lying on the ground, I felt scared out of my wits. But – odd as it may seem – it did not occur to me at the moment to take off my clothes as I should have done. I had made up my mind, I suppose, to get away in them, and that ruled me. And then down the vista of the counters came a bawling of "Here he is!"

'I sprang to my feet, whipped a chair off the counter, and sent it whirling at the fool who had shouted, turned, came into another round a corner, sent him spinning, and rushed up the stairs. He kept his footing, gave a view hallo! and came up the staircase hot after me. Up the staircase were piled a multitude of those bright-coloured pot things – what are they?'

'Art pots,' suggested Kemp.

'That's it! Art pots. Well, I turned at the top step and swung round, plucked one out of a pile and smashed it on his silly head as he came at me. The whole pile of pots went headlong, and I heard shouting and footsteps running from all parts. I made a mad rush for the refreshment place, and there was a man in white like a man cook, who took up the chase. I made one last desperate turn and found myself among lamps and ironmongery. I went behind the counter of this, and waited for my cook, and as he bolted in at the head of the chase, I doubled him up with a lamp. Down he went, and I crouched down behind the counter and began whipping off my clothes as fast as I could. Coat, jacket, trousers, shoes were all right, but a lambswool vest fits a man like a skin. I heard more men coming, my cook was lying quiet on the other side of the counter, stunned or scared speechless, and I had to make another dash for it, like a rabbit hunted out of a wood-pile.

'"This way, policeman!" I heard someone shouting. I found myself in my bedstead storeroom again, and at the end a wilderness of wardrobes. I rushed among them, went flat, got rid of my vest after infinite wriggling, and stood a free man again, panting and scared, as the policeman and three of the shopmen came round the corner. They made a rush for the vest and pants, and collared the trousers. "He's dropping his plunder," said one of the young men. "He *must* be somewhere here."

'But they did not find me all the same.

'I stood watching them hunt for me for a time, and cursing my ill-luck in losing the clothes. Then I went into the refreshment-room, drank a little milk I found there, and sat down by the fire to consider my position.

'In a little while two assistants came in and began to talk over the business very excitedly and like the fools they were. I heard a magnified account of my depredations, and other speculations as to my whereabouts. Then I fell to scheming again. The insurmountable difficulty of the place, especially now it was alarmed, was to get any plunder out of it. I went down into the warehouse to see if there was any chance of packing and addressing a parcel, but I could not understand the system of checking. About eleven o'clock, the snow having thawed as it fell, and the day being finer and a little warmer than the previous one, I decided that the Emporium was hopeless, and went out again, exasperated at my want of success, with only the vaguest plans of action in my mind.'

CHAPTER 23

In Drury Lane

'But you begin now to realise,' said the Invisible Man, 'the full disadvantage of my condition. I had no shelter, no covering – to get clothing, was to forego all my advantage, to make of myself a strange and terrible thing. I was fasting; for to eat, to fill myself with unassimilated matter, would be to become grotesquely visible again.'

'I never thought of that,' said Kemp.

'Nor had I. And the snow had warned me of other dangers. I could not go abroad in snow – it would settle on me and expose me. Rain, too, would make me a watery outline, a glistening surface of a man – a bubble. And fog – I should be like a fainter bubble in a fog, a surface, a greasy glimmer of humanity. Moreover, as I went abroad – in the London air – I gathered dirt about my ankles, floating smuts and dust upon my skin. I did not know how long it would be before I should become visible from that cause also. But I saw clearly it could not be for long.

'Not in London at any rate.

'I went into the slums towards Great Portland Street, and found myself at the end of the street in which I had lodged. I did not go that way, because of the crowd halfway down it opposite to the still smoking ruins of the house I had fired. My most immediate problem was to get clothing. What to do with my face puzzled me. Then I saw in one of those little miscellaneous shops – news, sweets, toys, stationery, belated Christmas tomfoolery, and so forth – an array of masks and noses. I realised that problem was solved. In a flash I saw my course. I turned about, no longer aimless, and went – circuitously in order to avoid the busy ways, towards the back streets north of the Strand; for I remembered, though not very distinctly where, that some theatrical costumiers had shops in that district.

'The day was cold, with a nipping wind down the northward running streets. I walked fast to avoid being overtaken. Every crossing was a danger, every passenger a thing to watch alertly. One man as I was about to pass him at the top of Bedford Street, turned upon me abruptly and came into me, sending me into the road and almost under the wheel of a passing hansom. The verdict of the cab-rank was that he had had some sort of stroke. I was so unnerved by this encounter that I went into Covent Garden Market and sat down for some time in a quiet corner by a stall of violets, panting and trembling. I found I had caught a fresh cold, and had to turn out after a time lest my sneezes should attract attention.

'At last I reached the object of my quest, a dirty fly-blown little shop in a byway near Drury Lane,* with a window full of tinsel robes, sham jewels, wigs, slippers, dominoes and theatrical photographs. The shop was old-fashioned and low and dark, and the house rose above it for four storeys, dark and dismal. I peered through the window and, seeing no one within, entered. The opening of the door set a clanking bell ringing. I left it open, and walked round a bare costume stand, into a corner behind a cheval glass.* For a minute or so no one came. Then I heard heavy feet striding across a room, and a man appeared down the shop.

'My plans were now perfectly definite. I proposed to make my way into the house, secrete myself upstairs, watch my opportunity, and when everything was quiet, rummage out a wig, mask, spectacles, and costume, and go into the world, perhaps a grotesque but still a credible figure. And incidentally of course I could rob the house of any available money.

'The man who had entered the shop was a short, slight, hunched, beetle-browed man, with long arms and very short bandy legs. Apparently I had interrupted a meal. He stared about the shop with an expression of expectation. This gave way to surprise, and then anger, as he saw the shop empty. "Damn the boys!"* he said. He went to stare up and down the street. He came in again in a minute, kicked the door to with his foot spitefully, and went muttering back to the house door.

'I came forward to follow him, and at the noise of my movement he stopped dead. I did so too, startled by his quickness of ear. He slammed the house door in my face.

'I stood hesitating. Suddenly I heard his quick footsteps returning, and the door reopened. He stood looking about the shop like one who was still not satisfied. Then, murmuring to himself, he examined the back of the counter and peered behind some fixtures. Then he stood doubtful. He had left the house door open and I slipped into the inner room.

'It was a queer little room, poorly furnished and with a number of big masks in the corner. On the table was his belated breakfast, and it was a confoundedly exasperating thing for me, Kemp, to have to sniff his coffee and stand watching while he came in and resumed his meal. And his table manners were irritating. Three doors opened into the little room, one going upstairs and one down, but they were all shut. I could not get out of the room while he was there, I could scarcely move because of his alertness, and there was a draught down my back. Twice I strangled a sneeze just in time.

'The spectacular quality of my sensations was curious and novel, but for all that I was heartily tired and angry long before he had done his eating. But at last he made an end and putting his beggarly crockery on the black tin tray upon which he had had his teapot, and gathering all the crumbs up on the mustard stained cloth, he took the whole lot of things after him. His burden prevented his shutting the door behind him – as he would have done; I never saw such a man for shutting doors – and I followed him into a very dirty underground kitchen and scullery. I had the pleasure of seeing him begin to wash up, and then, finding no good in keeping down there, and the brick floor being cold to my feet, I returned upstairs and sat in his chair by the fire. It was burning low, and scarcely thinking, I put on a little coal. The noise of this brought him up at once, and he stood aglare. He peered about the room and was within an ace of touching me. Even after that examination, he scarcely seemed satisfied. He stopped in the doorway and took a final inspection before he went down.

'I waited in the little parlour for an age, and at last he came up and opened the upstairs door. I just managed to get by him.

'On the staircase he stopped suddenly, so that I very nearly blundered into him. He stood looking back right into my face and listening. "I could have sworn," he said. His long hairy hand pulled at his lower lip. His eye went up and down the staircase. Then he grunted and went on up again.

'His hand was on the handle of a door, and then he stopped again with the same puzzled anger on his face. He was becoming aware of the faint sounds of my movements about him. The man must have had diabolically acute hearing. He suddenly flashed into rage. "If there's anyone in this house," he cried with an oath, and left the threat unfinished. He put his hand in his pocket, failed to find what he wanted, and rushing past me went blundering noisily and pugnaciously downstairs. But I did not follow him. I sat on the head of the staircase until his return.

'Presently he came up again, still muttering. He opened the door of the room, and before I could enter, slammed it in my face.

'I resolved to explore the house, and spent some time in doing so as noiselessly as possible. The house was very old and tumble-down, damp so that the paper in the attics was peeling from the walls, and rat infested. Some of the door handles were stiff and I was afraid to turn them. Several rooms I did inspect were unfurnished, and others were littered with theatrical lumber, bought second-hand, I judged, from its appearance. In one room next to his I found a lot of old clothes. I began routing among these, and in my eagerness forgot again the evident sharpness of his ears. I heard a stealthy footstep and, looking up just in time, saw him peering in at the tumbled heap and holding an old-fashioned revolver in his hand. I stood perfectly still while he stared about open-mouthed and suspicious. "It must have been her," he said slowly. "Damn her!"

'He shut the door quietly, and immediately I heard the key turn in the lock. Then his footsteps retreated. I realised abruptly that I was locked in. For a minute I did not know what to do. I walked from door to window and back, and stood perplexed. A gust of anger came upon me. But I decided to inspect the clothes before I did anything further, and my first attempt brought down a pile from an upper shelf. This brought him back, more sinister than ever. That time he actually touched me, jumped back with amazement and stood astonished in the middle of the room.

'Presently he calmed a little. "Rats," he said in an undertone, fingers on lip. He was evidently a little scared. I edged quietly out of the room, but a plank creaked. Then the infernal little brute started going all over the house, revolver in hand and locking door after door and pocketing the keys. When I realised what he was up to I had a fit of rage – I could hardly control myself sufficiently to watch my opportunity. By this time I knew he was alone in the house, and so I made no more ado, but knocked him on the head.'

'Knocked him on the head!' exclaimed Kemp.

'Yes – stunned him – as he was going downstairs. Hit him from behind with a stool that stood on the landing. He went downstairs like a bag of old boots.'

'But—! I say! The common conventions of humanity—'

'Are all very well for common people. But the point was, Kemp, that I had to get out of that house in a disguise without his seeing me. I couldn't think of any other way of doing it. And then I gagged him with a Louis Quatorze vest* and tied him up in a sheet.'

'Tied him up in a sheet!'

'Made a sort of bag of it. It was rather a good idea to keep the idiot scared and quiet, and a devilish hard thing to get out of – head away from the string. My dear Kemp, it's no good your sitting and glaring as though I was a murderer. It had to be done. He had his revolver. If once he saw me he would be able to describe me—'

'But still,' said Kemp, 'in England – today. And the man was in his own house, and you were – well, robbing.'

'Robbing! Confound it! You'll call me a thief next! Surely, Kemp, you're not fool enough to dance on the old strings. Can't you see my position?'

'And his too,' said Kemp.

The Invisible Man stood up sharply. 'What do you mean to say?'

Kemp's face grew a trifle hard. He was about to speak and checked himself. 'I suppose, after all,' he said with a sudden change of manner, 'the thing had to be done. You were in a fix. But still—'

'Of course I was in a fix – an infernal fix. And he made me wild too – hunting me about the house, fooling about with his revolver, locking and unlocking doors. He was simply exasperating. You don't blame me, do you? You don't blame me?'

'I never blame anyone,' said Kemp. 'It's quite out of fashion. What did you do next?'

'I was hungry. Downstairs I found a loaf and some rank cheese – more than sufficient to satisfy my hunger. I took some brandy and water, and then went up past my impromptu bag – he was lying quite still – to the room containing the old clothes.

This looked out upon the street, two lace curtains brown with
dirt guarding the window. I went and peered out through their
interstices. Outside the day was bright – by contrast with the
brown shadows of the dismal house in which I found myself,
dazzlingly bright. A brisk traffic was going by, fruit carts, a
hansom, a four-wheeler with a pile of boxes, a fishmonger's
cart. I turned with spots of colour swimming before my eyes to
the shadowy fixtures behind me. My excitement was giving
place to a clear apprehension of my position again. The room
was full of a faint scent of benzoline,* used, I suppose, in
cleaning the garments.

'I began a systematic search of the place. I should judge the
hunchback had been alone in the house for some time. He was
a curious person. Everything that could possibly be of service to
me I collected in the clothes store-room, and then I made a
deliberate selection. I found a handbag I thought a suitable
possession, and some powder, rouge, and sticking plaster.

'I had thought of painting and powdering my face and all that
there was to show of me, in order to render myself visible, but
the disadvantage of this lay in the fact that I should require
turpentine* and other appliances and a considerable amount of
time before I could vanish again. Finally I chose a mask of the
better type, slightly grotesque but not more so than many human
beings, dark glasses, greyish whiskers, and a wig. I could find no
underclothing, but that I could buy subsequently, and for the
time I swathed myself in calico dominoes* and some white
cashmere scarfs.* I could find no socks, but the hunchback's
boots were rather a loose fit and sufficed. In a desk in the shop
were three sovereigns and about thirty shillings' worth of silver,
and in a locked cupboard I burst in the inner room were eight
pounds in gold. I could go forth into the world again, equipped.

'Then came a curious hesitation. Was my appearance really –
credible? I tried myself with a little bedroom looking-glass,
inspecting myself from every point of view to discover any
forgotten chink, but it all seemed sound. I was grotesque to the
theatrical pitch, a stage miser, but I was certainly not a physical
impossibility. Gathering confidence, I took my looking-glass
down into the shop, pulled down the shop blinds, and surveyed
myself from every point of view with the help of the cheval glass
in the corner.

'I spent some minutes screwing up my courage and then

unlocked the shop door and marched out into the street, leaving the little man to get out of his sheet again when he liked. In five minutes a dozen turnings intervened between me and the costumier's shop. No one appeared to notice me very pointedly. My last difficulty seemed overcome.'

He stopped again.

'And you troubled no more about the hunchback?' said Kemp.

'No,' said the Invisible Man. 'Nor have I heard what became of him. I suppose he untied himself or kicked himself out. The knots were pretty tight.'

He became silent and went to the window and stared out.

'What happened when you went out into the Strand?'

'Oh! – disillusionment again. I thought my troubles were over. Practically I thought I had impunity to do whatever I chose, everything – save to give away my secret. So I thought. Whatever I did, whatever the consequences might be, was nothing to me. I had merely to fling aside my garments and vanish. No person could hold me. I could take my money where I found it. I decided to treat myself to a sumptuous feast, and then put up at a good hotel, and accumulate a new outfit of property. I felt amazingly confident – it's not particularly pleasant recalling that I was an ass. I went into a place and was already ordering a lunch, when it occurred to me that I could not eat unless I exposed my invisible face. I finished ordering the lunch, told the man I should be back in ten minutes, and went out exasperated. I don't know if you have ever been disappointed in your appetite.'

'Not quite so badly,' said Kemp, 'but I can imagine it.'

'I could have smashed the silly devils. At last, faint with the desire for tasteful food, I went into another place and demanded a private room. "I am disfigured," I said. "Badly." They looked at me curiously, but of course it was not their affair – and so at last I got my lunch. It was not particularly well served, but it sufficed; and when I had had it, I sat over a cigar, trying to plan my line of action. And outside a snowstorm was beginning.

'The more I thought it over, Kemp, the more I realised what a helpless absurdity an Invisible Man was – in a cold and dirty climate and a crowded civilised city. Before I made this mad experiment I had dreamt of a thousand advantages. That afternoon it seemed all disappointment. I went over the heads of the things a man reckons desirable. No doubt invisibility made it possible to get them, but it made it impossible to enjoy them when they were got. Ambition – what is the good of pride of place when you cannot appear there? What is the good of the love of woman when her name must needs be Delilah?* I have no taste for politics, for the blackguardisms of fame, for philanthropy, for sport. What was I to do? And for this I had become a wrapped-up mystery, a swathed and bandaged caricature of a man!'

He paused, and his attitude suggested a roving glance at the window.

'But how did you get to Iping?' said Kemp, anxious to keep his guest busy talking.

'I went there to work. I had one hope. It was a half idea! I have it still. It is a full blown idea now. A way of getting back! Of restoring what I have done. When I choose. When I have done all I mean to do invisibly. And that is what I chiefly want to talk to you about now.'

'You went straight to Iping?'

'Yes. I had simply to get my three volumes of memoranda and my cheque-book, my luggage and underclothing, order a quantity of chemicals to work out this idea of mine – I will show you the calculations as soon as I get my books – and then I started. Jove! I remember the snowstorm now, and the accursed bother it was to keep the snow from damping my pasteboard nose.'

'At the end,' said Kemp, 'the day before yesterday, when they found you out, you rather – to judge by the papers—'

'I did. Rather. Did I kill that fool of a constable?'

'No,' said Kemp. 'He's expected to recover.'

'That's his luck, then. I clean lost my temper, the fools! Why couldn't they leave me alone? And that grocer lout?'

'There are no deaths expected,' said Kemp.

'I don't know about that tramp of mine,' said the Invisible Man, with an unpleasant laugh.

'By Heaven, Kemp, you don't know what rage *is*! To have worked for years, to have planned and plotted, and then to get some fumbling purblind idiot messing across your course! Every conceivable sort of silly creature that has ever been created has been sent to cross me.

'If I have much more of it, I shall go wild – I shall start mowing 'em.

'As it is, they've made things a thousand times more difficult.'

'No doubt it's exasperating,' said Kemp, drily.

CHAPTER 24

The Plan That Failed

'But now,' said Kemp, with a side glance out of the window, 'what are we to do?'

He moved nearer his guest as he spoke in such a manner as to prevent the possibility of a sudden glimpse of the three men who were advancing up the hill road – with an intolerable slowness, as it seemed to Kemp.

'What were you planning to do when you were heading for Port Burdock? *Had* you any plan?'

'I was going to clear out of the country. But I have altered that plan rather since seeing you. I thought it would be wise, now the weather is hot and invisibility possible, to make for the South. Especially as my secret was known, and everyone would be on the lookout for a masked and muffled man. You have a line of steamers from here to France. My idea was to get aboard one and run the risks of the passage. Thence I could go by train into Spain, or else get to Algiers. It would not be difficult. There a man might always be invisible – and yet live. And do things. I was using that tramp as a money box and luggage carrier, until I decided how to get my books and things sent over to meet me.'

'That's clear.'

'And then the filthy brute must needs try and rob me! He has hidden my books, Kemp. Hidden my books! If I can lay my hands on him!'

'Best plan to get the books out of him first.'

'But where is he? Do you know?'

'He's in the town police station, locked up, by his own request, in the strongest cell in the place.'

'Cur!' said the Invisible Man.

'But that hangs up your plans a little.'

'We must get those books; those books are vital.'

'Certainly,' said Kemp, a little nervously, wondering if he heard footsteps outside. 'Certainly we must get those books. But that won't be difficult, if he doesn't know they're for you.'

'No,' said the Invisible Man, and thought.

Kemp tried to think of something to keep the talk going, but the Invisible Man resumed of his own accord.

'Blundering into your house, Kemp,' he said, 'changes all my plans. For you are a man that can understand. In spite of all that has happened, in spite of this publicity, of the loss of my books, of what I have suffered, there still remain great possibilities, huge possibilities—

'You have told no one I am here?' he asked abruptly.

Kemp hesitated. 'That was implied,' he said.

'No one?' insisted Griffin.

'Not a soul.'

'Ah! Now—' The Invisible Man stood up, and sticking his arms akimbo began to pace the study.

'I made a mistake, Kemp, a huge mistake, in carrying this thing through alone. I have wasted strength, time, opportunities. Alone – it is wonderful how little a man can do alone! To rob a little, to hurt a little, and there is the end.

'What I want, Kemp, is a goal-keeper, a helper, and a hiding-place, an arrangement whereby I can sleep and eat and rest in peace, and unsuspected. I must have a confederate. With a confederate, with food and rest – a thousand things are possible.

'Hitherto I have gone on vague lines. We have to consider all that invisibility means, all that it does not mean. It means little advantage for eavesdropping and so forth – one makes sounds. It's of little help, a little help perhaps – in housebreaking and so forth. Once you've caught me you could easily imprison me. But on the other hand I am hard to catch. This invisibility, in fact, is only good in two cases: It's useful in getting away, it's useful in approaching. It's particularly useful, therefore, in killing. I can walk round a man, whatever weapon he has, choose my point, strike as I like. Dodge as I like. Escape as I like.'

Kemp's hand went to his moustache. Was that a movement downstairs?

'And it is killing we must do, Kemp.'

'It is killing we must do,' repeated Kemp. 'I'm listening to your plan, Griffin, but I'm not agreeing, mind. *Why* killing?'

'Not wanton killing, but a judicious slaying. The point is, they know there is an Invisible Man. And that Invisible Man, Kemp, must now establish a Reign of Terror. Yes – no doubt it's startling. But I mean it. A Reign of Terror. He must take some town like your Burdock and terrify and dominate it. He must issue his orders. He can do that in a thousand ways – scraps of paper thrust under doors would suffice. And all who disobey his orders he must kill, and kill all who would defend them.'

'Humph!' said Kemp, no longer listening to Griffin but to the sound of his front door opening and closing.

'It seems to me, Griffin,' he said, to cover his wandering attention, 'that your confederate would be in a difficult position.'

'No one would know he was a confederate,' said the Invisible Man, eagerly. And then suddenly, '*Hush!* What's that downstairs?'

'Nothing,' said Kemp, and suddenly began to speak loud and fast. 'I don't agree to this, Griffin,' he said. 'Understand me, I don't agree to this. Why dream of playing a game against the race? How can you hope to gain happiness? Don't be a lone wolf. Publish your results; take the world – take the nation at least – into your confidence. Think what you might do with a million helpers—'

The Invisible Man interrupted Kemp – arms extended. 'There are footsteps coming upstairs,' he said in a low voice.

'Nonsense,' said Kemp.

'Let me see,' said the Invisible Man, and advanced, arm extended, to the door.

And then things happened very swiftly. Kemp hesitated for a second and then moved to intercept him. The Invisible Man started and stood still. 'Traitor!' cried the Voice, and suddenly the dressing-gown opened, and sitting down the Unseen began to disrobe. Kemp made three swift steps to the door, and forthwith the Invisible Man – his legs had vanished – sprang to his feet with a shout. Kemp flung the door open.

As it opened, there came a sound of hurrying feet downstairs and voices.

With a quick movement Kemp thrust the Invisible Man back, sprang aside, and slammed the door. The key was outside and ready. In another moment Griffin would have been alone in the belvedere study, a prisoner. Save for one little thing. The key had been slipped in hastily that morning. As Kemp slammed the door it fell noisily upon the carpet.

Kemp's face became white. He tried to grip the door handle with both hands. For a moment he stood lugging. Then the door gave six inches. But he got it closed again. The second time it was jerked a foot wide, and the dressing-gown came wedging itself into the opening. His throat was gripped by invisible fingers, and he left his hold on the handle to defend himself. He was forced back, tripped and pitched heavily into the corner of the landing. The empty dressing-gown was flung on the top of him.

Halfway up the staircase was Colonel Adye, the recipient of Kemp's letter, the chief of the Burdock police. He was staring aghast at the sudden appearance of Kemp, followed by the extraordinary sight of clothing tossing empty in the air. He saw Kemp felled, and struggling to his feet. He saw him rush forward, and go down again, felled like an ox.

Then suddenly he was struck violently. By nothing! A vast weight, it seemed, leapt upon him, and he was hurled headlong down the staircase, with the grip at his throat and a knee in his groin. An invisible foot trod on his back, a ghostly patter passed downstairs, he heard the two police officers in the hall shout and run, and the front door of the house slammed violently.

He rolled over and sat up staring. He saw, staggering down the staircase, Kemp, dusty and dishevelled, one side of his face white from a blow, his lip bleeding, and a pink dressing-gown and some underclothing held in his arms.

'My God!' cried Kemp, 'the game's up! He's gone!'

CHAPTER 25

The Hunting of the Invisible Man

For a space Kemp was too inarticulate to make Adye understand the swift things that had just happened. They stood on the landing, Kemp speaking swiftly, the grotesque swathings of Griffin still on his arm. But presently Adye began to grasp something of the situation.

'He is mad,' said Kemp; 'inhuman. He is pure selfishness. He thinks of nothing but his own advantage, his own safety. I have listened to such a story this morning of brutal self-seeking! He has wounded men. He will kill them unless we can prevent him. He will create a panic. Nothing can stop him. He is going out now – furious!'

'He must be caught,' said Adye. 'That is certain.'

'But how?' cried Kemp, and suddenly became full of ideas. 'You must begin at once. You must set every available man to work. You must prevent his leaving this district. Once he gets away, he may go through the countryside as he wills, killing and maiming. He dreams of a reign of terror! A reign of terror, I tell you. You must set a watch on trains and roads and shipping. The garrison must help. You must wire for help. The only thing that may keep him here is the thought of recovering some books of notes he counts of value. I will tell you of that! There is a man in your police station – Marvel.'

'I know,' said Adye, 'I know. Those books – yes.'

'And you must prevent him from eating or sleeping; day and night the country must be astir for him. Food must be locked up and secured, all food, so that he will have to break his way to it. The houses everywhere must be barred against him. Heaven send us cold nights and rain! The whole countryside must begin hunting and keep hunting. I tell you, Adye, he is a danger, a disaster; unless he is pinned and secured, it is frightful to think of the things that may happen.'

'What else can we do?' said Adye. 'I must go down at once and begin organising. But why not come? Yes – you come too!

Come, and we must hold a sort of council of war – get Hopps to help – and the railway managers. By Jove! it's urgent. Come along – tell me as we go. What else is there we can do? Put that stuff down.'

In another moment Adye was leading the way downstairs. They found the front door open and the policemen standing outside staring at empty air. 'He's got away, sir,' said one.

'We must go to the central station at once,' said Adye. 'One of you go on down and get a cab to come up and meet us – quickly. And now, Kemp, what else?'

'Dogs,' said Kemp. 'Get dogs. They don't see him, but they wind him. Get dogs.'

'Good,' said Adye. 'It's not generally known, but the prison officials over at Halstead* know a man with bloodhounds. Dogs. What else?'

'Bear in mind,' said Kemp, 'his food shows. After eating, his food shows until it is assimilated. So that he has to hide after eating. You must keep on beating – every thicket, every quiet corner. And put all weapons, all implements that might be weapons, away. He can't carry such things for long. And what he can snatch up and strike men with must be hidden away.'

'Good again,' said Adye. 'We shall have him yet!'

'And on the roads,' said Kemp, and hesitated.

'Yes?' said Adye.

'Powdered glass,'* said Kemp. 'It's cruel, I know. But think of what he may do!'

Adye drew the air in sharply between his teeth. 'It's unsportsmanlike. I don't know. But I'll have powdered glass got ready. If he goes too far—'

'The man's become inhuman, I tell you,' said Kemp. 'I am as sure he will establish a reign of terror – so soon as he has got over the emotions of this escape – as I am sure I am talking to you. Our only chance is to be ahead. He has cut himself off from his kind. His blood be upon his own head.'

CHAPTER 26

The Wicksteed Murder

The Invisible Man seems to have rushed out of Kemp's house in a state of blind fury. A little child playing near Kemp's gateway was violently caught up and thrown aside, so that its ankle was broken, and thereafter for some hours the Invisible Man passed out of human perceptions. No one knows where he went nor what he did. But one can imagine him hurrying through the hot June forenoon, up the hill and on to the open downland behind Port Burdock, raging and despairing at his intolerable fate, and sheltering at last, heated and weary, amid the thickets of Hintondean, to piece together again his shattered schemes against his species. That seems the most probable refuge for him, for there it was he re-asserted himself in a grimly tragical manner about two in the afternoon.

One wonders what his state of mind may have been during that time, and what plans he devised. No doubt he was almost ecstatically exasperated by Kemp's treachery, and though we may be able to understand the motives that led to that deceit, we may still imagine and even sympathise a little with the fury the attempted surprise must have occasioned. Perhaps something of the stunned astonishment of his Oxford Street experiences may have returned to him, for he had evidently counted on Kemp's co-operation in his brutal dream of a terrorised world. At any rate he vanished from human ken* about midday, and no living witness can tell what he did until about half-past two. It was a fortunate thing, perhaps, for humanity, but for him it was a fatal inaction.

During that time a growing multitude of men scattered over the countryside were busy. In the morning he had still been simply a legend, a terror; in the afternoon, by virtue chiefly of Kemp's drily worded proclamation, he was presented as a tangible antagonist, to be wounded, captured, or overcome, and the countryside began organising itself with inconceivable rapidity. By two o'clock even he might still have removed himself out of the district by getting aboard a train, but after two that became impossible. Every passenger train along the lines on a great parallelogram between Southampton, Manchester, Brighton, and Horsham, travelled with locked doors, and the goods traffic was almost entirely suspended. And in a great circle of twenty miles round Port Burdock, men armed with guns and bludgeons were presently setting out in groups of three and four with dogs, to beat the roads and fields.

Mounted policemen rode along the country lanes, stopping at every cottage and warning the people to lock up their houses and keep indoors unless they were armed, and all the elementary schools had broken up by three o'clock, and the children, scared and keeping together in groups, were hurrying home. Kemp's proclamation – signed indeed by Adye – was posted over almost the whole district by four or five o'clock in the afternoon. It gave briefly but clearly all the conditions of the struggle, the necessity of keeping the Invisible Man from food and sleep, the necessity for incessant watchfulness and for a prompt attention to any evidence of his movements. And so swift and decided was the action of the authorities, so prompt and universal was the belief in this strange being, that before nightfall an area of several hundred square miles was in a stringent state of siege. And before nightfall, too, a thrill of horror went through the whole watching nervous countryside. Going from whispering mouth to mouth, swift and certain over the length and breadth of the county, passed the story of the murder of Mr Wicksteed.

If our supposition that the Invisible Man's refuge was the Hintondean thickets is correct, then we must suppose that in the early afternoon he sallied out again bent upon some project that involved the use of a weapon. We cannot know what the project was, but the evidence that he had the iron rod in hand before he met Wicksteed is to me at least overwhelming.

Of course we can know nothing of the details of the encounter.* It occurred on the edge of a gravel pit, not two hundred yards from Lord Burdock's Lodge gate. Everything points to a desperate struggle – the trampled ground, the numerous wounds Mr Wicksteed received, his splintered walking-stick; but why the attack was made – save in a murderous frenzy – it is impossible to imagine. Indeed the theory of madness is almost unavoidable. Mr Wicksteed was a man of forty-five or forty-six, steward to Lord Burdock, of inoffensive habits and appearance, the very last person in the world to provoke such a terrible antagonist. Against him it would seem the Invisible Man used an iron rod dragged from a broken piece of fence. He stopped this quiet man, going quietly home to his midday meal, attacked him, beat down his feeble defences, broke his arm, felled him, and smashed his head to a jelly.

Of course he must have dragged this rod out of the fencing before he met his victim; he must have been carrying it ready in his hand. Only two details beyond what has already been stated seem to bear on the matter. One is the circumstance that the gravel pit was not in Mr Wicksteed's direct path home, but nearly a couple of hundred yards out of his way. The other is the assertion of a little girl to the effect that, going to her afternoon school, she saw the murdered man 'trotting' in a peculiar manner across a field towards the gravel pit. Her pantomime of his action suggests a man pursuing something on the ground before him and striking at it ever and again with his walking-stick. She was the last person to see him alive. He passed out of her sight to his death, the struggle being hidden from her only by a clump of beech trees and a slight depression in the ground.

Now this, to the present writer's mind at least, lifts the murder out of the realm of the absolutely wanton. We may imagine that Griffin had taken the rod as a weapon indeed, but without any deliberate intention of using it in murder. Wicksteed may then have come by and noticed this rod inexplicably moving through the air. Without any thought of the Invisible Man – for Port Burdock is ten miles away – he may have pursued it. It is quite conceivable that he may not even have heard of the Invisible Man. One can then imagine the Invisible Man making off – quietly in order to avoid discovering his presence in the neighbourhood, and Wicksteed, excited and curious, pursuing this unaccountably locomotive object – finally striking at it.

No doubt the Invisible Man could easily have distanced his middle-age pursuer under ordinary circumstances, but the position in which Wicksteed's body was found suggests that he had the ill luck to drive his quarry into a corner between a drift of stinging nettles and the gravel pit. To those who appreciate the extraordinary irascibility of the Invisible Man, the rest of the encounter will be easy to imagine.

But this is pure hypothesis. The only undeniable facts – for stories of children are often unreliable – are the discovery of Wicksteed's body, done to death, and of the blood-stained iron rod flung among the nettles. The abandonment of the rod by Griffin, suggests that in the emotional excitement of the affair, the purpose for which he took it – if he had a purpose – was abandoned. He was certainly an intensely egotistical and unfeeling man, but the sight of his victim, his first victim, bloody and pitiful at his feet, may have released some long pent fountain of remorse which for a time may have flooded whatever scheme of action he had contrived.

After the murder of Mr Wicksteed, he would seem to have struck across the country towards the downland. There is a story of a voice heard about sunset by a couple of men in a field near Fern Bottom. It was wailing and laughing, sobbing and groaning, and ever and again it shouted. It must have been queer hearing. It drove up across the middle of a clover field and died away towards the hills.

That afternoon the Invisible Man must have learnt something of the rapid use Kemp had made of his confidences. He must have found houses locked and secured; he may have loitered about railway stations and prowled about inns, and no doubt he read the proclamations and realised something of the nature of the campaign against him. And as the evening advanced, the fields became dotted here and there with groups of three or four men, and noisy with the yelping of dogs. These men-hunters had particular instructions in the case of an encounter as to the way they should support one another. He avoided them all. We may understand something of his exasperation, and it could have been none the less because he himself had supplied the information that was being used so remorselessly against him. For that day at least he lost heart; for nearly twenty-four hours, save when he turned on Wicksteed, he was a hunted man. In the night, he must have eaten and slept; for in the morning he was himself again, active, powerful, angry, and malignant, prepared for his last great struggle against the world.

The Siege of Kemp's House

Kemp read a strange missive, written in pencil on a greasy sheet of paper.

'You have been amazingly energetic and clever,' this letter ran, 'though what you stand to gain by it I cannot imagine. You are against me. For a whole day you have chased me; you have tried to rob me of a night's rest. But I have had food in spite of you, I have slept in spite of you, and the game is only beginning. The game is only beginning. There is nothing for it, but to start the Terror. This announces the first day of the Terror. Port Burdock is no longer under the Queen, tell your Colonel of Police, and the rest of them; it is under me – the Terror! This is day one of year one of the new epoch – the Epoch of the Invisible Man. I am Invisible Man the First. To begin with the rule will be easy. The first day there will be one execution for the sake of example – a man named Kemp. Death starts for him today. He may lock himself away, hide himself away, get guards about him, put on armour if he likes; Death, the unseen Death, is coming. Let him take precautions; it will impress my people. Death starts from the pillar box* by midday. The letter will fall in as the postman comes along, then off! The game begins. Death starts. Help him not, my people, lest Death fall upon you also. Today Kemp is to die.'

When Kemp read this letter twice, 'It's no hoax,' he said. 'That's his voice! And he means it.'

He turned the folded sheet over and saw on the addressed side of it the postmark Hintondean, and the prosaic detail '2d. to pay.'*

He got up slowly, leaving his lunch unfinished – the letter had come by the one o'clock post* – and went into his study. He rang for his housekeeper, and told her to go round the house at once, examine all the fastenings of the windows, and close all the shutters. He closed the shutters of his study himself. From a locked drawer in his bedroom he took a little revolver, examined it carefully, and put it into the pocket of his lounge jacket. He wrote a number of brief notes, one to Colonel Adye, gave them to his servant to take, with explicit instructions as to her way of leaving the house. 'There is no danger,' he said, and added a mental reservation, 'to you.' He remained meditative for a space after doing this, and then returned to his cooling lunch.

He ate with gaps of thought. Finally he struck the table sharply. 'We will have him!' he said; 'and I am the bait. He will come too far.'

He went up to the belvedère, carefully shutting every door after him. 'It's a game,' he said, 'an odd game – but the chances are all for me, Mr Griffin, in spite of your invisibility. Griffin *contra mundum** – with a vengeance.'

He stood at the window staring at the hot hillside. 'He must get food every day – and I don't envy him. Did he really sleep last night? Out in the open somewhere – secure from collisions. I wish we could get some good cold wet weather instead of the heat.'

'He may be watching me now.'

He went close to the window. Something rapped smartly against the brickwork over the frame, and made him start violently back.

'I'm getting nervous,' said Kemp. But it was five minutes before he went to the window again. 'It must have been a sparrow,' he said.

Presently he heard the front-door bell ringing, and hurried downstairs. He unbolted and unlocked the door, examined the chain, put it up, and opened cautiously without showing himself. A familiar voice hailed him. It was Adye.

'Your servant's been assaulted, Kemp,' he said round the door.

'What!' exclaimed Kemp.

'Had that note of yours taken away from her. He's close about here. Let me in.'

Kemp released the chain, and Adye entered through as narrow an opening as possible. He stood in the hall looking with infinite relief at Kemp refastening the door. 'Note was snatched out of her hand. Scared her horribly. She's down at the station. Hysterics. He's close here. What was it about?'

Kemp swore.

'What a fool I was,' said Kemp, 'I might have known. It's not an hour's walk from Hintondean. Already!'

'What's up?' said Adye.

'Look here!' said Kemp, and led the way into his study. He handed Adye the Invisible Man's letter. Adye read it and whistled softly. 'And you—?' said Adye.

'Proposed a trap – like a fool,' said Kemp, 'and sent my proposal out by a maid servant. To him.'

Adye followed Kemp's profanity.

'He'll clear out,' said Adye.

'Not he,' said Kemp.

A resounding smash of glass came from upstairs. Adye had a silvery glimpse of a little revolver half out of Kemp's pocket. 'It's the window, upstairs!' said Kemp, and led the way up. There came a second smash while they were still on the staircase. When they reached the study they found two of the three windows smashed, half the room littered with splintered glass, and one big flint lying on the writing table. The two men stopped in the doorway, contemplating the wreckage. Kemp swore again, and as he did so the third window went with a snap like a pistol, hung starred for a moment, and collapsed in jagged, shivering triangles into the room.

'What's this for?' said Adye.

'It's a beginning,' said Kemp.

'There's no way of climbing up here?'

'Not for a cat,' said Kemp.

'No shutters?'

'Not here. All the downstairs rooms – Hullo!'

Smash, and then whack of boards hit hard came from downstairs. 'Confound him!' said Kemp. 'That must be – yes – it's one of the bedrooms. He's going to do all the house. But he's a fool. The shutters are up, and the glass will fall outside. He'll cut his feet.'

Another window proclaimed its destruction. The two men stood on the landing perplexed. 'I have it!' said Adye. 'Let me have a stick or something, and I'll go down to the station and get the bloodhounds put on. That ought to settle him! They're hard by* – not ten minutes—'

Another window went the way of its fellows.

'You haven't a revolver?' asked Adye.

Kemp's hand went to his pocket. Then he hesitated. 'I haven't one – at least to spare.'

'I'll bring it back,' said Adye, 'you'll be safe here.'

Kemp, ashamed of his momentary lapse from truthfulness, handed him the weapon.

'Now for the door,' said Adye.

As they stood hesitating in the hall, they heard one of the first-floor bedroom windows crack and clash. Kemp went to the door and began to slip the bolts as silently as possible. His face was a little paler than usual. 'You must step straight out,' said Kemp. In another moment Adye was on the doorstep and the bolts were dropping back into the staples. He hesitated for a moment, feeling more comfortable with his back against the door. Then he marched, upright and square, down the steps. He crossed the lawn and approached the gate. A little breeze seemed to ripple over the grass. Something moved near him. 'Stop a bit,' said a Voice, and Adye stopped dead and his hand tightened on the revolver.

'Well?' said Adye, white and grim, and every nerve tense.

'Oblige me by going back to the house,' said the Voice, as tense and grim as Adye's.

'Sorry,' said Adye a little hoarsely, and moistened his lips with his tongue. The Voice was on his left front, he thought. Suppose he were to take his luck with a shot?

'What are you going for?' said the Voice, and there was a quick movement of the two, and a flash of sunlight from the open lip of Adye's pocket.

Adye desisted and thought. 'Where I go,' he said slowly, 'is my own business.' The words were still on his lips, when an arm came round his neck, his back felt a knee, and he was sprawling backward. He drew clumsily and fired absurdly, and in another moment he was struck in the mouth and the revolver wrested from his grip. He made a vain clutch at a slippery limb, tried to struggle up and fell back. 'Damn!' said Adye. The Voice laughed. 'I'd kill you now if it wasn't the waste of a bullet,' it said. He saw the revolver in mid-air, six feet off, covering him.

'Well?' said Adye, sitting up.

'Get up,' said the Voice.

Adye stood up.

'Attention,' said the Voice, and then fiercely, 'Don't try any games. Remember I can see your face if you can't see mine. You've got to go back to the house.'

'He won't let me in,' said Adye.

'That's a pity,' said the Invisible Man. 'I've got no quarrel with you.'

Adye moistened his lips again. He glanced away from the barrel of the revolver and saw the sea far off very blue and dark under the midday sun, the smooth green down, the white cliff of the Head, and the multitudinous town, and suddenly he knew that life was very sweet. His eyes came back to this little metal thing hanging between heaven and earth, six feet away. 'What am I to do?' he said sullenly.

'What am I to do?' asked the Invisible Man. 'You will get help. The only thing is for you to go back.'

'I will try. If he lets me in will you promise not to rush the door?'

'I've got no quarrel with you,' said the Voice.

Kemp had hurried upstairs after letting Adye out, and now crouching among the broken glass and peering cautiously over the edge of the study window sill, he saw Adye stand parleying with the Unseen. 'Why doesn't he fire?' whispered Kemp to himself. Then the revolver moved a little and the glint of the sunlight flashed in Kemp's eyes. He shaded his eyes and tried to see the source of the blinding beam.

'Surely!' he said, 'Adye has given up the revolver.'

'Promise not to rush the door,' Adye was saying. 'Don't push a winning game too far. Give a man a chance.'

'You go back to the house. I tell you flatly I will not promise anything.'

Adye's decision seemed suddenly made. He turned towards the house, walking slowly with his hands behind him. Kemp watched him – puzzled. The revolver vanished, flashed again into sight, vanished again, and became evident on a closer scrutiny as a little dark object following Adye. Then things happened very quickly. Adye leapt backwards, swung round, clutched at this little object, missed it, threw up his hands and fell forward on his face, leaving a little puff of blue in the air. Kemp did not hear the sound of the shot. Adye writhed, raised himself on one arm, fell forward, and lay still.

For a space Kemp remained staring at the quiet carelessness of Adye's attitude. The afternoon was very hot and still, nothing

seemed stirring in all the world save a couple of yellow butter-
flies chasing each other through the shrubbery between the
house and the road gate. Adye lay on the lawn near the gate.
The blinds of all the villas down the hill road were drawn, but
in one little green summer-house was a white figure, apparently
an old man asleep. Kemp scrutinised the surroundings of the
house for a glimpse of the revolver, but it had vanished. His eyes
came back to Adye. The game was opening well.

Then came a ringing and knocking at the front door, that
grew at last tumultuous, but pursuant to Kemp's instructions
the servants had locked themselves into their rooms. This was
followed by a silence. Kemp sat listening and then began peering
cautiously out of the three windows, one after another. He went
to the staircase head and stood listening uneasily. He armed
himself with his bedroom poker, and went to examine the
interior fastenings of the ground-floor windows again. Everything was safe and quiet. He returned to the belvedere. Adye lay
motionless over the edge of the gravel just as he had fallen.
Coming along the road by the villas were the housemaid and
two policemen.

Everything was deadly still. The three people seemed very
slow in approaching. He wondered what his antagonist was
doing.

He started. There was a smash from below. He hesitated and
went downstairs again. Suddenly the house resounded with
heavy blows and the splintering of wood. He heard a smash and
the destructive clang of the iron fastenings of the shutters. He
turned the key and opened the kitchen door. As he did so, the
shutters, split and splintering, came flying inward. He stood
aghast. The window frame, save for one cross bar, was still
intact, but only little teeth of glass remained in the frame. The
shutters had been driven in with an axe, and now the axe was
descending in sweeping blows upon the window frame and the
iron bars defending it. Then suddenly it leapt aside and vanished.
He saw the revolver lying on the path outside, and then the little
weapon sprang into the air. He dodged back. The revolver
cracked just too late, and a splinter from the edge of the closing
door flashed over his head. He slammed and locked the door,
and as he stood outside he heard Griffin shouting and laughing.
Then the blows of the axe with its splitting and smashing
consequences, were resumed.

Kemp stood in the passage trying to think. In a moment the Invisible Man would be in the kitchen. This door would not keep him a moment, and then—

A ringing came at the front door again. It would be the policemen. He ran into the hall, put up the chain, and drew the bolts. He made the girl speak before he dropped the chain, and the three people blundered into the house in a heap, and Kemp slammed the door again.

'The Invisible Man!' said Kemp. 'He has a revolver, with two shots – left. He's killed Adye. Shot him anyhow.* Didn't you see him on the lawn? He's lying there.'

'Who?' said one of the policemen.

'Adye,' said Kemp.

'We came in the back way,' said the girl.

'What's that smashing?' asked one of the policemen.

'He's in the kitchen – or will be. He has found an axe—'

Suddenly the house was full of the Invisible Man's resounding blows on the kitchen door. The girl stared towards the kitchen, shuddered, and retreated into the dining-room. Kemp tried to explain in broken sentences. They heard the kitchen door give.

'This way,' cried Kemp, starting into activity, and bundled the policemen into the dining-room doorway.

'Poker,' said Kemp, and rushed to the fender. He handed the poker he had carried to the policeman and the dining-room one to the other. He suddenly flung himself backward.

'Whup!' said one policeman, ducked, and caught the axe on his poker. The pistol snapped its penultimate shot and ripped a valuable Sidney Cooper.* The second policeman brought his poker down on the little weapon, as one might knock down a wasp, and sent it rattling to the floor.

At the first clash the girl screamed, stood screaming for a moment by the fireplace, and then ran to open the shutters – possibly with an idea of escaping by the shattered window.

The axe receded into the passage, and fell to a position about two feet from the ground. They could hear the Invisible Man breathing. 'Stand away, you two,' he said. 'I want that man Kemp.'

'We want you,' said the first policeman, making a quick step forward and wiping with his poker at the Voice. The Invisible Man must have started back, and he blundered into the umbrella stand. Then, as the policeman staggered with the swing of the blow he had aimed, the Invisible Man countered with the axe, the helmet crumpled like paper, and the blow sent the man spinning to the floor at the head of the kitchen stairs. But the second policeman, aiming behind the axe with his poker, hit something soft that snapped. There was a sharp exclamation of pain and then the axe fell to the ground. The policeman wiped again at vacancy and hit nothing; he put his foot on the axe, and struck again. Then he stood, poker clubbed,* listening intent for the slightest movement.

He heard the dining-room window open, and a quick rush of feet within. His companion rolled over and sat up, with the blood running down between his eye and ear. 'Where is he?' asked the man on the floor.

'Don't know. I've hit him. He's standing somewhere in the hall. Unless he's slipped past you. Doctor Kemp – sir.'

Pause.

'Doctor Kemp,' cried the policeman again.

The second policeman began struggling to his feet. He stood up. Suddenly the faint pad of bare feet on the kitchen stairs could be heard. 'Yap!' cried the first policeman, and incontinently flung his poker. It smashed a little gas bracket.

He made as if he would pursue the Invisible Man downstairs. Then he thought better of it and stepped into the dining-room.

'Doctor Kemp,' he began, and stopped short—

'Doctor Kemp's a hero,'* he said, as his companion looked over his shoulder.

The dining-room window was wide open, and neither house-maid nor Kemp was to be seen.

The second policeman's opinion of Kemp was terse and vivid.

CHAPTER 28

The Hunter Hunted

Mr Heelas, Dr Kemp's nearest neighbour among the villa holders, was asleep in his summer-house when the siege of Kemp's house began. Mr Heelas was one of the sturdy minority who refused to believe 'in all this nonsense' about an Invisible Man. His wife, however, as he was subsequently to be reminded, did. He insisted upon walking about his garden just as if nothing was the matter, and he went to sleep in the afternoon in accordance with the custom of years. He slept through the smashing of the windows, and then woke up suddenly with a curious persuasion of something wrong. He looked across at Kemp's house, rubbed his eyes and looked again. Then he put his feet to the ground, and sat listening. He said he was damned, and still the strange thing was visible. The house looked as though it had been deserted for weeks – after a violent riot. Every window was broken, and every window, save those of the belvedere study, was blinded by the internal shutters.

'I could have sworn it was all right' – he looked at his watch – 'twenty minutes ago.'

He became aware of a measured concussion and the clash of glass, far away in the distance. And then, as he sat open mouthed, came a still more wonderful thing. The shutters of the dining-room window were flung open violently, and the house-maid in her outdoor hat and garments, appeared struggling in a frantic manner to throw up the sash. Suddenly a man appeared beside her, helping her – Dr Kemp! In another moment the window was open, and the housemaid was struggling out; she pitched forward and vanished among the shrubs. Mr Heelas stood up, exclaiming vaguely and vehemently at all these wonderful things. He saw Kemp stand on the sill, spring from the window, and reappear almost instantaneously running along a path in the shrubbery and stooping as he ran, like a man who evades observation. He vanished behind a laburnum, and appeared again clambering a fence that abutted on the open down. In a second he had tumbled over and was running at a tremendous pace down the slope towards Mr Heelas.

'Lord!' cried Mr Heelas, struck with an idea; 'it's that Invisible Man brute! It's right, after all!'

With Mr Heelas to think things like that was to act, and his cook watching him from the top window was amazed to see him come pelting towards the house at a good nine miles an hour. 'Thought he wasn't afraid,' said the cook. 'Mary, just come here!' There was a slamming of doors, a ringing of bells, and the voice of Mr Heelas bellowing like a bull. 'Shut the doors, shut the windows, shut everything! the Invisible Man is coming!' Instantly the house was full of screams and directions, and scurrying feet. He ran himself to shut the French windows* that opened on the veranda; as he did so Kemp's head and shoulders and knee appeared over the edge of the garden fence. In another moment Kemp had ploughed through the asparagus, and was running across the tennis lawn to the house.

'You can't come in,' said Mr Heelas, shutting the bolts. 'I'm very sorry if he's after you, but you can't come in!'

Kemp appeared with a face of terror close to the glass, rapping and then shaking frantically at the French window. Then, seeing his efforts were useless, he ran along the veranda, vaulted the end, and went to hammer at the side door. Then he ran around by the side gate to the front of the house, and so into the hill-road. And Mr Heelas staring from his window – a face of horror – had scarcely witnessed Kemp vanish, ere the asparagus was being trampled this way and that by feet unseen. At that Mr Heelas fled precipitately upstairs, and the rest of the chase is beyond his purview. But as he passed the staircase window, he heard the side gate slam.

Emerging into the hill-road, Kemp naturally took the downward direction, and so it was he came to run in his own person the very race he had watched with such a critical eye from the belvedere study only four days ago. He ran it well, for a man out of training, and though his face was white and wet, his wits were cool to the last. He ran with wide strides, and wherever a patch of rough ground intervened, wherever there came a patch of raw flints, or a bit of broken glass shone dazzling, he crossed it and left the bare invisible feet that followed to take what line they would.

For the first time in his life Kemp discovered that the hill-road was indescribably vast and desolate, and that the beginnings of the town far below at the hill foot were strangely remote. Never had there been a slower or more painful method of progression than running. All the gaunt villas, sleeping in the afternoon sun, looked locked and barred; no doubt they were locked and barred – by his own orders. But at any rate they might have kept a lookout for an eventuality like this! The town was rising up now, the sea had dropped out of sight behind it, and people down below were stirring. A tram was just arriving at the hill foot. Beyond that was the police station. Was that footsteps he heard behind him? Spurt.

The people below were staring at him, one or two were running, and his breath was beginning to saw in his throat. The tram was quite near now, and the Jolly Cricketers was noisily barring its doors. Beyond the tram were posts and heaps of gravel – the drainage works. He had a transitory idea of jumping into the train and slamming the doors, and then he resolved to go for the police station. In another moment he had passed the door of the Jolly Cricketers, and was in the blistering fag end* of the street, with human beings about him. The tram driver and his helper – arrested by the sight of his furious haste – stood staring with the tram horses* unhitched. Further on the astonished features of navvies appeared above the mounds of gravel.

His pace broke a little, and then he heard the swift pad of his pursuer, and leapt forward again. 'The Invisible Man!' he cried to the navvies, with a vague indicative gesture, and by an inspiration leapt the excavation and placed a burly group between him and the chase. Then abandoning the idea of the police station he turned into a little side street, rushed by a greengrocer's cart, hesitated for the tenth of a second at the door of a sweetstuff shop, and then made for the mouth of an alley that ran back into the main Hill Street again. Two or three little children were playing here, and shrieked and scattered running at his apparition, and forthwith doors and windows opened and excited mothers revealed their hearts. Out he shot into Hill Street again, three hundred yards from the tram-line end, and immediately he became aware of a tumultuous vociferation and running people.

He glanced up the street towards the hill. Hardly a dozen yards off ran a huge navvy, cursing in fragments and slashing viciously with a spade, and hard behind him came the tram conductor with his fists clenched. Up the street others followed these two, striking and shouting. Down towards the town, men and women were running, and he noticed clearly one man coming out of a shop-door with a stick in his hand. 'Spread out! Spread out!' cried some one. Kemp suddenly grasped the altered condition of the chase. He stopped, and looked round, panting. 'He's close here!' he cried. 'Form a line across—'

'Aha!' shouted a voice.

He was hit hard under the ear, and went reeling, trying to face round towards his unseen antagonist. He just managed to keep his feet, and he struck a vain counter in the air. Then he was hit again under the jaw, and sprawled headlong on the ground. In another moment a knee compressed his diaphragm, and a couple of eager hands gripped his throat, but the grip of one was weaker than the other; he grasped the wrists, heard a cry of pain from his assailant, and then the spade of the navvy came whirling through the air above him, and struck something with a dull thud. He felt a drop of moisture on his face. The grip at his throat suddenly relaxed, and with a convulsive effort, Kemp loosed himself, grasped a limp shoulder, and rolled uppermost. He gripped the unseen elbows near the ground. 'I've got him!' screamed Kemp. 'Help! Help hold! He's down! Hold his feet!'

In another second there was a simultaneous rush upon the struggle, and a stranger coming into the road suddenly might have thought an exceptionally savage game of Rugby football* was in progress. And there was no shouting after Kemp's cry – only a sound of blows and feet and a heavy breathing.

Then came a mighty effort, and the Invisible Man threw off a couple of his antagonists and rose to his knees. Kemp clung to him in front like a hound to a stag, and a dozen hands gripped, clutched, and tore at the Unseen. The tram conductor suddenly got the neck and shoulders and lugged him back.

Down went the heap of struggling men again and rolled over. There was, I am afraid, some savage kicking. Then suddenly a wild scream of 'Mercy! Mercy!' that died down swiftly to a sound like choking.

'Get back, you fools!' cried the muffled voice of Kemp, and there was a vigorous shoving back of stalwart forms. 'He's hurt, I tell you. Stand back!'

There was a brief struggle to clear a space, and then the circle of eager faces saw the doctor kneeling, as it seemed, fifteen inches in the air, and holding invisible arms to the ground. Behind him a constable gripped invisible ankles.

'Don't you leave go of en,' cried the big navvy, holding a bloodstained spade: 'he's shamming.'*

'He's not shamming,' said the doctor, cautiously raising his knee; 'and I'll hold him.' His face was bruised and already going red; he spoke thickly because of a bleeding lip. He released one hand and seemed to be feeling at the face. 'The mouth's all wet,' he said. And then, 'Good God!'

He stood up abruptly and then knelt down on the ground by the side of the thing unseen. There was a pushing and shuffling, a sound of heavy feet as fresh people turned up to increase the pressure of the crowd. People now were coming out of the houses. The doors of the Jolly Cricketers were suddenly wide open. Very little was said.

Kemp felt about, his hand seeming to pass through empty air. 'He's not breathing,' he said, and then, 'I can't feel his heart. His side – ugh!'

Suddenly an old woman, peering under the arm of the big navvy, screamed sharply. 'Looky there!' she said, and thrust out a wrinkled finger.

And looking where she pointed, everyone saw, faint and transparent as though it was made of glass, so that veins and arteries and bones and nerves could be distinguished, the outline of a hand, a hand limp and prone. It grew clouded and opaque even as they stared.

'Hullo!' cried the constable. 'Here's his feet a-showing!'

And so, slowly, beginning at his hands and feet and creeping along his limbs to the vital centres of his body, that strange change continued. It was like the slow spreading of a poison. First came the little white nerves, a hazy grey sketch of a limb, then the glassy bones and intricate arteries, then the flesh and skin, first a faint fogginess, and then growing rapidly dense and opaque. Presently they could see his crushed chest and his shoulders, and the dim outline of his drawn and battered features.

When at last the crowd made way for Kemp to stand erect, there lay, naked and pitiful on the ground, the bruised and broken body of a young man about thirty. His hair and beard were white – not grey with age, but white with the whiteness of albinism, and his eyes were like garnets.* His hands were clenched, his eyes wide open, and his expression was one of anger and dismay.

'Cover his face!' said a man. 'For Gawd's sake, cover that face!' and three little children, pushing forward through the crowd, were suddenly twisted round and sent packing off again.

Someone brought a sheet from the Jolly Cricketers, and having covered him, they carried him into that house.*

The Epilogue

So ends the story of the strange and evil experiment of the Invisible Man. And if you would learn more of him you must go to a little inn near Port Stowe and talk to the landlord. The sign of the inn is an empty board save for a hat and boots, and the name is the title of this story. The landlord is a short and corpulent little man with a nose of cylindrical protrusion, wiry hair, and a sporadic rosiness of visage. Drink generously, and he will tell you generously of all the things that happened to him after that time, and of how the lawyers tried to do him out of the treasure found upon him.

'When they found they couldn't prove whose money was which, I'm blessed,' he says, 'if they didn't try to make me out a blooming treasure trove!* Do I *look* like a Treasure Trove? And then a gentleman gave me a guinea a night to tell the story at the Empire Music 'all – just tell 'em in my own words – barring one.'

And if you want to cut off the flow of his reminiscences abruptly, you can always do so by asking if there weren't three manuscript books in the story. He admits there were and proceeds to explain, with asseverations that everybody thinks *he* has 'em! But bless you! he hasn't. 'The Invisible Man it was took 'em off to hide 'em when I cut and ran for Port Stowe. It's that Dr Kemp put people on with the idea of *my* having 'em.'

And then he subsides into a pensive state, watches you furtively, bustles nervously with glasses, and presently leaves the bar.

He is a bachelor man – his tastes were ever bachelor, and there are no women folk in the house. Outwardly he buttons – it is expected of him – but in his more vital privacies, in the matter of braces for example, he still turns to string. He conducts his house without enterprise, but with eminent decorum. His movements are slow, and he is a great thinker. But he has a reputation for wisdom and for a respectable parsimony in the village, and his knowledge of the roads of the South of England would beat Cobbett.*

And on Sunday mornings, every Sunday morning, all the year round, while he is closed to the outer world, and every night after ten, he goes into his bar parlour, bearing a glass of gin faintly tinged with water, and having placed this down, he locks the door and examines the blinds, and even looks under the table. And then, being satisfied of his solitude, he unlocks the cupboard and a box in the cupboard and a drawer in that box, and produces three volumes bound in brown leather, and places them solemnly in the middle of the table. The covers are weather-worn and tinged with an algal green – for once they sojourned in a ditch and some of the pages have been washed blank by dirty water. The landlord sits down in an armchair, fills a long clay pipe slowly – gloating over the books the while. Then he pulls one towards him and opens it, and begins to study it – turning over the leaves backwards and forwards.

His brows are knit and his lips move painfully. 'Hex, little two up in the air, cross and a fiddle-de-dee.* Lord! what a one he was for intellect!'

Presently he relaxes and leans back, and blinks through his smoke across the room at things invisible to other eyes. 'Full of secrets,' he says. 'Wonderful secrets!

'Once I get the haul of them – *Lord*!

'I wouldn't do what *he* did; I'd just – well!' He pulls at his pipe.

So he lapses into a dream, the undying wonderful dream of his life. And though Kemp has fished unceasingly, and Adye has questioned closely, no human being save the landlord knows those books are there, with the subtle secret of invisibility and a dozen other strange secrets written therein. And none other will know of them until he dies.

APPENDIX

Authorial Preface to The Scientific Romances of
H. G. Wells *(London: Gollancz, 1933), pp. vii–x*

Mr Gollancz has asked me to write a preface to this collection
of my fantastic stories. They are put in chronological order, but
let me say here right at the beginning of the book, that for
anyone who does not as yet know anything of my work it will
probably be more agreeable to begin with *The Invisible Man* or
The War of the Worlds. The Time Machine is a little bit stiff
about the fourth dimension and *The Island of Dr Moreau* rather
painful.

These tales have been compared with the work of Jules Verne
and there was a disposition on the part of literary journalists at
one time to call me the English Jules Verne. As a matter of fact
there is no literary resemblance whatever between the anticipa-
tory inventions of the great Frenchman and these fantasies. His
work dealt almost always with actual possibilities of invention
and discovery, and he made some remarkable forecasts. The
interest he invoked was a practical one; he wrote and believed
and told that this or that thing could be done, which was not at
that time done. He helped his reader to imagine it done and to
realise what fun, excitement or mischief would ensue. Many of
his inventions have 'come true'. But these stories of mine
collected here do not pretend to deal with possible things; they
are exercises of the imagination in a quite different field. They
belong to a class of writing which includes the *Golden Ass of
Apuleius*, the *True Histories of Lucian, Peter Schlemil* and the
story of *Frankenstein*. It includes too some admirable inventions
by Mr David Garnett, *Lady into Fox* for instance. They are all
fantasies; they do not aim to project a serious possibility; they
aim indeed only at the same amount of conviction as one gets in
a good gripping dream. They have to hold the reader to the end
by art and illusion and not by proof and argument, and the

moment he closes the cover and reflects he wakes up to their impossibility.

In all this type of story the living interest lies in their non-fantastic elements and not in the invention itself. They are appeals for human sympathy quite as much as any 'sympathetic' novel, and the fantastic element, the strange property or the strange world, is used only to throw up and intensify our natural reactions of wonder, fear or perplexity. The invention is nothing in itself and when this kind of thing is attempted by clumsy writers who do not understand this elementary principle nothing could be conceived more silly and extravagant. Anyone can invent human beings inside out or worlds like dumb-bells or a gravitation that repels. The thing that makes such imaginations interesting is their translation into commonplace terms and a rigid exclusion of other marvels from the story. Then it becomes human. 'How would you feel and what might not happen to you,' is the typical question, if for instance pigs could fly and one came rocketing over a hedge at you? How would you feel and what might not happen to you if suddenly you were changed into an ass and couldn't tell anyone about it? Or if you became invisible? But no one would think twice about the answer if hedges and houses also began to fly, or if people changed into lions, tigers, cats and dogs left and right, or if everyone could vanish anyhow. Nothing remains interesting where anything may happen.

For the writer of fantastic stories to help the reader to play the game properly, he must help him in every possible unobtrusive way to *domesticate* the impossible hypothesis. He must trick him into an unwary concession to some plausible assumption and get on with his story while the illusion holds. And that is where there was a certain slight novelty in my stories when first they appeared. Hitherto, except in exploration fantasies, the fantastic element was brought in by magic. Frankenstein even, used some jiggery-pokery magic to animate his artificial monster. There was trouble about the thing's soul. But by the end of last century it had become difficult to squeeze even a monetary belief out of magic any longer. It occurred to me that instead of the usual interview with the devil or a magician, an ingenious use of scientific patter might with advantage be subsituted. That was no great discovery. I simply brought the fetish stuff up to date, and made it as near actual theory as possible.

As soon as the magic trick has been done the whole business of the fantasy writer is to keep everything else human and real. Touches of prosaic detail are imperative and a rigorous adherence to the hypothesis. Any *extra* fantasy outside the cardinal assumption immediately gives a touch of irresponsible silliness to the invention. So soon as the hypothesis is launched the whole interest becomes the interest of looking at human feelings and human ways, from the new angle that has been acquired. One can keep the story within the bounds of a few individual experiences as Chamisso does in *Peter Schlemil*, or one can expand it to a broad criticism of human institutions and limitations as in *Gulliver's Travels*. My early, profound and lifelong admiration for Swift, appears again and again in this collection, and it is particularly evident in a predisposition to make the stories reflect upon contemporary political and social discussions. It is an incurable habit with literary critics to lament some lost artistry and innocence in my early work and to accuse me of having become polemical in my later years. That habit is of such old standing that the late Mr Zangwill in a review in 1895 complained that my first book, *The Time Machine*, concerned itself with 'our present discontents'. *The Time Machine* is indeed quite as philosophical and polemical and critical of life and so forth, as *Men like Gods* written twenty-eight years later. No more and no less. I have never been able to get away from life in the mass and life in general as distinguished from life in the individual experience, in any book I have ever written. I differ from contemporary criticism in finding them inseparable.

For some years I produced one or more of these 'scientific fantasies,' as they were called, every year. In my student days we were much exercised by talk about a possible fourth dimension of space; the fairly obvious idea that events could be presented in a rigid four dimensional space time framework had occurred to me, and this is used as the magic trick for a glimpse of the future that ran counter to the placid assumption of that time that Evolution was a pro-human force making things better and better for mankind. *The Island of Dr Moreau* is an exercise in youthful blasphemy. Now and then, though I rarely admit it, the universe projects itself towards me in a hideous grimace. It grimaced that time, and I did my best to express my vision of the aimless torture in creation. *The War of the Worlds* like *The Time Machine* was another assault on human self-satisfaction.

All these three books are consciously grim, under the influence of Swift's tradition. But I am neither a pessimist nor an optimist at bottom. This is an entirely indifferent world in which wilful wisdom seems to have a perfectly fair chance. It is after all rather cheap to get force of presentation by loading the scales on the sinister side. Horror stories are easier to write than gay and exalting stories. In *The First Men in the Moon* I tried an improvement on Jules Verne's shot, in order to look at mankind from a distance and burlesque the effects of specialisation. Verne never landed on the moon because he never knew of radio and of the possibility of sending back a message. So it was his shot that came back. But equipped with radio, which had just come out then, I was able to land and even see something of the planet.

The three later books are distinctly on the optimistic side. *The Food of the Gods* is a fantasia on the change of scale in human affairs. Everybody nowadays realises that change of scale; we see the whole world in disorder through it; but in 1904 it was not a very prevalent idea. I had hit upon it while working out the possibilities of the near future in a book of speculations called *Anticipations* (1901).

The last two stories are Utopian. The world is gassed and cleaned up morally by the benevolent tail of a comet in one, and the reader is taken through a dimensional trap door with a weekend party of politicians, into a world of naked truth and deliberate beauty in the other. *Men like Gods* is almost the last of my scientific fantasies. It did not horrify or frighten, was not much of a success, and by that time I had tired of talking in playful parables to a world engaged in destroying itself. I was becoming too convinced of the strong probability of very strenuous and painful human experiences in the near future to play about with them much more. But I did two other sarcastic fantasies, not included here, *Mr Blettsworthy on Rampole Island* and *The Autocracy of Mr Parham*, in which there is I think a certain gay bitterness, before I desisted altogether.

The Autocracy of Mr Parham is all about dictators, and dictators are all about us, but it has never struggled through to a really cheap edition. Work of this sort gets so stupidly reviewed nowadays that it has little chance of being properly read. People are simply warned that there are ideas in my books and advised not to read them, and so a fatal suspicion has wrapped about the later ones. 'Ware stimulants!' It is no good my saying that they are quite as easy to read as the earlier ones and much more timely.

It becomes a bore doing imaginative books that do not touch imaginations, and at length one stops even planning them. I think I am better employed now nearer reality, trying to make a working analysis of our deepening social perplexities in such labours as *The Work, Wealth and Happiness of Mankind* and *After Democracy*. The world in the presence of cataclysmal realities has no need for fresh cataclysmal fantasies. That game is over. Who wants the invented humours of Mr Parham in Whitehall, when day by day we can watch Mr Hitler in Germany? What human invention can pit itself against the fantastic fun of the Fates? I am wrong in grumbling at reviewers. Reality has taken a leaf from my book and set itself to supersede me.

H.G.W.

NOTES

Title page   A Grotesque Romance: Wells's subtitle has frequently been dropped from editions of the novel, but is clearly a vital pointer to the spirit in which he wished it to be understood. See the Introduction for a discussion of its implications.

Title Page   'Being but dark earth though made diaphanall': From 'The Trinity illustrated by a three-square perspective Glasse', a sonnet by John Davies, in *Wittes Pilgrimage* (1605?), which begins: 'If in a three-square Glasse, as thick, as cleare, / (Being but dark Earth, though made Diaphanall) / Beauties divine, that ravish Sence, appeare, / Making the Soule, with joy, in Trance to fall...'. Like the subtitle, it has usually been omitted from reprints of the novel. Wells added it in the American edition.

p. 3   early in February: a date contradicted by the beginning of Chapter 3 (p. 13), where we are told that the stranger arrives on the twenty-ninth of February. The description of the arrival derives something from that of Dr Nebogipfel in Llyddwdd in Wells's early story, 'The Chronic Argonauts' (1888), reprinted in Bernard Bergonzi, *The Early H. G. Wells: A Study of the Scientific Romances* (Manchester: Manchester University Press, 1961) pp. 187–214.

p. 3   down: rolling upland.

p. 3   Bramblehurst: with a few exceptions (noted below) the place names in the novel are fictitious.

p. 3   the Coach and Horses: a pub.

p. 3   sovereigns: gold coins worth one pound, or twenty shillings, each.

p. 3   Iping: a village on the edge of the Sussex Downs, three miles west of Midhurst (at whose Grammar School Wells was a pupil and then Undermaster between 1881 and 1884), and sixty miles from London.

p. 3   lymphatic: sluggish.

p. 3   *éclat*: ostentation (French).

p. 4   side-lights: pieces of glass at right angles to the main lenses of spectacles, which have the effect of obscuring a view of the eyes.

p. 4   side-whisker: facial hair grown in front of the ear.

p. 6 clothes-horse: a wooden frame on which laundry is hung to dry.

p. 6 taters: potatoes. Sussex dialect is frequently, but not rigorously, reproduced throughout the novel.

p. 6 upsettled: turned over (dialect).

p. 7 jest: just (dialect).

p. 7 regular: really (dialect).

p. 7 them as had the doing for him: those who had to look after him.

p. 8 clock-jobber: a person who mends clocks.

p. 8 My sakes!: a mild expletive, suggesting astonishment.

p. 8 like adverse railway signals: i.e. red. Cf. the discussion about the pigmentation at the back of the eye which Griffin and Kemp have in Chapter 20 (p. 87).

p. 9 he says: here, as elsewhere, the narrator assumes the periodic guise of one relating events told to him directly by those involved in them.

p. 10 humbugging: cheating or deceiving. The suggestion is that Henfrey is deliberately attempting to make the job seem more complex than it is.

p. 11 sure lie: 'surely'; one of Wells's occasional attempts to transcribe Sussex pronunciation.

p. 11 wropped: wrapped (dialect). The first American edition misprints this as 'wrooped', but all other editions agree.

p. 11 'stopping a bit': i.e. to drink.

p. 11 'Ow do: how are you doing (dialect).

p. 11 a rum un: an odd person (slang).

p. 11 stones in boxes: Henfrey is suggesting to Hall that the stranger may be a professional thief. 'Stones in boxes' would give the appearance of possessions, and their removal would allow Hall's property to be concealed in the boxes.

p. 11 Hastings: a residential town and seaside resort, on the English Channel, in East Sussex.

p. 11 Get up, old girl: Hall addresses the mare which draws the conveyance.

p. 11   rated: berated, chided.

p. 12   to show that the stranger wasn't master there: this bizarre intrusion is rather difficult to believe, but other descriptions of the parlour in the novel do not suggest that it has more than one room.

p. 13   twenty-ninth: see the first note to p. 3. The events of the novel thus take place in a leap year and, because they postdate the Golden Jubilee of 1887, mentioned in chapter VII (see the third note to p. 30), the possibilities are narrowed to 1888, 1892 or 1896. The mention of the scientist Röntgen in Chapter 20 (see note to p. 86) suggests that the last of these dates is the most likely. It is not necessarily legitimate, however, to assume chronological consistency on Wells's part.

p. 13   *dilettante:* in this context the meaning seems to be 'half-hearted' (the Italian word means 'amateur').

p. 14   en: him (dialect).

p. 15   chiffonier: chest of drawers.

p. 16   hobnails: short nails inserted into the soles of heavy boots to protect them.

p. 16   crepitation: creaking.

p. 17   Iping Hanger: a place name which had already featured in Wells's *The Wonderful Visit* (1895).

p. 19   the Scarlet Coat: a pub.

p. 19   bogies: evil spirits.

p. 19   National School: a school run by the National Society, founded in 1811 to promote the education of the poor.

p. 19   Anarchist: According to David Miller (ed.), *The Blackwell Encyclopaedia of Political Thought* (Oxford: Blackwell, 1987), p. 13, anarchism 'in the 1880s and 1890s ... came to mean individual acts of terror, for example the assassination of political leaders or prominent industrialists. This was the period in which the popular image of anarchists as ruthless men with bombs under their coats became fixed in the public mind.' Wells himself exploited as well as satirised the stereotype. He had already published an amusing story, 'The Stolen Bacillus' (1894), about an anarchist who swallows a sample of what he thinks is the cholera bacteria, in an attempt to poison the water of London with it. The sample turns out not to be cholera at all, and its only effect is to turn him blue. A story more closely related to *The Invisible Man* is that of the lonely experimentalist in 'The Diamond Maker', who in numerous respects (such as suspicion that he is an anarchist) is a prototype for the Invisible Man. Wells's friend Joseph Conrad (1857–1924), who was much impressed by *The Invisible Man* (see the Introduction), was undoubtedly influenced by it in his famous portrait of the anarchist, explosives-manufacturing professor in *The Secret Agent* (1907).

p. 20   **the man with one talent:** who dug a hole in the ground and buried his talent instead of putting it to use (see Matthew's gospel, 25:14–30).

p. 20   **Whitsuntide:** the week that begins with Whit Sunday, the seventh Sunday after Easter, which commemorates the descent of the Holy Ghost to the apostles on the day of Pentecost.

p. 21   **ammonite:** a fossil, used commonly as a paperweight.

p. 22   **scratch:** without an advantage.

p. 25   **coal-scuttle:** a metal container for coal, usually kept beside the fire.

p. 26   **something to do with the specific gravity of their beer:** the density of beer relative to water is legally fixed: the passage suggests that the Halls may surreptitiously be diluting their beer.

p. 26   **sarsaparilla:** a non-alcoholic drink. 'Sarsaparilla hides watered beer's loss of tang and colour,' points out Leon Stover in *The Shaving of Karl Marx* (Lake Forest, Illinois: The Chinon Press, 1982), p. 67.

p. 28   **horseshoes:** commonly believed to ward off misfortune. There is some humour here: Wadgers does not miss the opportunity to peddle his wares.

p. 30   *piqué:* stitched (French).

p. 30   **the Purple Fawn:** a pub.

p. 30   **the Jubilee:** the Golden Jubilee of 1887, commemorating the fiftieth anniversary of Queen Victoria's ascendancy to the throne. Victoria celebrated her Diamond Jubilee in the month that *The Invisible Man* began to be serialised (June 1897).

p. 32   **hobbledehoy:** clumsy youth (archaic).

p. 33   **babel:** a noisy confusion. Compare the reverse effects of the Holy Ghost's arrival on the Pentecost: 'And they were all filled with the Holy

Ghost, and began to speak with other tongues, as the Spirit gave them utterance. And there were dwelling at Jerusalem Jews, devout men, out of every nation under heaven. Now when this was noised abroad, the multitude came together, and were confounded, because that every man heard them speak in his own language. And they were all amazed and marvelled' (Acts 2:4-7).

p. 34   goal-keeper for the offensive: in other words, he hangs back while his colleagues surge forward.

p. 36   *mêlée*: riot, brawl (French).

p. 37   as a gust scatters dead leaves: an echo of Shelley's 'Ode to the West Wind' (1819): 'O, wild West Wind, though breath of Autumn's being,/ Thou, from whose unseen presence the leaves dead/Are driven, like ghosts from an enchanter fleeing . . .' Shelley was a hero of Wells's.

p. 39   Mr Thomas Marvel: a figure who lives up to his name in his initial reaction to the Invisible Man, and who bears some relation to the 'Respectable Tramp slumbering peacefully among the wild-flower' encountered by the Angel in Chapter 30 of Wells's *The Wonderful Visit* (London: Dent, 1895), p. 141.

p. 39   embonpoint: stoutness (French).

p. 42   *Vox et – :* Marvel is improbably half-remembering the Latin phrase *Vox et praeterea nihil* ('A voice and nothing more').

p. 42   bearded face: a feature which raises some problems for Wells. We learn a few lines later that material 'not quite assimilated into the system' remains visible, and, in Chapter 17 (p. 73), that blood becomes visible when it leaves the Invisible Man's body. The sustained invisibility of 'dead' material like hair is thus puzzlingly unaccounted for.

p. 42   If this don't beat cock-fighting!: i.e. for excitement. Cock-fighting was illegal.

p. 42   not quite assimilated into the system: Marvel apparently sees the pale remnants of the Invisible Man's meal floating in mid-air.

p. 43   I was wandering, mad with rage ... And I saw you: there is probably an intentionally bathetic glance at the mad Lear's meeting on the heath with Edgar in this speech. Cf. Shakespeare, *King Lear*, III.iv.

p. 43   dizzy: 'all in a dizzy spin' is a common phrase, expressing a state of confusion.

p. 45 **assumed**: feigned. Marvel seems to be attempting to give the 'innocent' impression that he has simply had a drink in the inn.

p. 47 **cypher**: secret writing, code.

p. 48 **'Tap?'**: 'Is this the taproom?' (i.e. bar).

p. 48 **'Stand clear!'**: it transpires that this is an instruction to the Invisible Man, who has gained entry to the parlour by means of Marvel's charade.

p. 50 **dooce**: deuce.

p. 50 *sotto voce:* in an undertone (Italian).

p. 51 **pell-mell**: in a disorderly manner, headlong.

p. 58 **saving his regard**: apart from what he was looking at.

p. 59 **Alteration**: the mariner's solecism for 'altercation'.

p. 60 **if he took a drop over and above**: if he had too much to drink.

p. 62 **rouleaux**: cylinders formed by stacking coins on top of one another.

p. 63 **belvedere**: a turret on the top of a house, usually built to afford a fine view.

p. 64 **glairy**: slimy, like the white of an egg.

p. 65 **The Jolly Cricketers**: a pub.

p. 65 **talked of horses with an anaemic cabman**: hansom cabs were horsedrawn.

p. 65 **Burton**: a brand of ale.

p. 65 **American**: i.e. an American accent.

p. 67 **'out of frocks'**: a colloquialism meaning 'grown up' (i.e. 'I no longer wear childish clothes').

p. 69 **the time dimension**: a 'scientific' explanation of the fourth dimension is offered by the Time Traveller in Chapter 1 of Wells's *The Time Machine* (1895).

p. 70 **runaway ring**: practical joke played by children, who ring a doorbell and run off before the ring is answered.

p. 70 **quill**: pen (made of goose quill).

p. 72 Griffin: the first mention of the Invisible Man's name. In the context of the novel, multiple associations seem to attach to it. The primary connection may be with the 'fabulous animal usually represented as having the head and wings of an eagle and the body and hind quarters of a lion' (*OED*) – Griffin is similarly hard to categorise, and equally fearsome. But the word was also used in Anglo-Indian parlance to describe 'a European newly arrived in India, and unaccustomed to Indian ways and peculiarities' (*OED*) – a situation somewhat analogous to Griffin's own in West Sussex. It is difficult to know how far to extend such associations, however: more obscurely (but perhaps pertinently, given the novel's dealings with bodily colour) the word was also used in the United States (particularly Louisiana), to denote 'a mulatto' (*OED*).

p. 72 University College: one of the colleges of the University of London.

p. 72 albino: a person born without pigmentation in the skin and hair (which are white) and eyes (which are pink). The term was first applied by the Portuguese to white African Negroes.

p. 73 Drawers: underpants.

p. 73 I always like to get something about me before I eat: The reasons for this preference have already been explained in Chapter 9 (p. 42): the food Griffin eats remains visible until it is fully digested. He presents the preference to Kemp as a mere personal idiosyncrasy, presumably because he is embarrassed at not having anticipated this unfortunate effect.

p. 73 Gets visible as it coagulates, I see: blood coagulates, or clots, at the opening of a wound, thus preventing its own flow.

p. 74 pharynx and nares: the cavity at the back of the mouth, and the nostrils, respectively.

p. 74 after the first collapse: after the initial shock.

p. 77 Has the world gone mad – or have I? Here and elsewhere Kemp veers between attempting rationally to understand the phenomenon of invisibility and believing it a product of insanity. These are precisely the reactions, when confronted with an invisible being, of the narrator of 'Le Horla' (1887) by Guy de Maupassant (1850–93), a short story which was an undoubted influence on Wells's novel (see the Introduction).

p. 77 nauplii and tornarias: two types of larvae.

p. 78 *cum grano:* with reservations; *cum grano salis* means 'with a grain of salt' (Latin).

p. 81 Chesilstowe: we learn later in this chapter (p. 84) that Griffin worked here, 'teaching fools in a provincial college', and that he left London seven years prior to this conversation.

p. 81 refractive index: the refractive index of a medium is the ratio of the velocity of electromagnetic waves in free space to that in the medium.

p. 81 a valuable stone: such as a diamond, prized partly for its beautiful refractive qualities.

p. 86 Röntgen: Wells is being deliberately up-to-date. Wilhelm Konrad von Röntgen (1845–1923) had in 1895 achieved fame as the discoverer of X-rays, for which work he was jointly awarded the Rumford medal in 1896. There was much discussion of X-rays in Britain at the time: in 1896 John Macintyre achieved the first X-ray cinematograph at Glasgow's Royal Infirmary. In the same year, William J. Morton and Edwin W. Hammer published *The X Ray, or Photography of the Invisible and Its Value in Surgery* (London: Simpkin, Marshall, Hamilton, Kent and Co., 1896), which reprinted Röntgen's 'Preliminary communication to the Würzburg Physico-Medical Society' of December 1895, and a large number of ghostly radiographic plates, mostly of the human frame. (See also the first note to p. 13).

p. 87 truckle-bed: a low bed on wheels, usually stowed under a larger bed, and commonly used by servants.

p. 87 to get her to wash: a necessity, as the pigmentation of dirt would not become invisible. The cat evidently washes thoroughly.

p. 87 *Tapetum:* reflective layer at the back of the retina in some vertebrates. The phenomenon is often remarked of cats; in humans, it is most obviously noticeable in the 'red eye' sometimes produced by flash photography.

p. 87 chloroform: a colourless liquid, produced from ethanol and calcium chlorate, whose vapours cause unconsciousness. Discovered by Justus von Liebeg (1803–73) in 1831, its place as an anaesthetic in Britain was ensured when Queen Victoria allowed it to be administered to her during the birth of Prince Leopold in 1853.

p. 88 bustle: commotion.

p. 89 strychnine: a strong poison. It was used in small doses as a stimulus to the appetite and the central nervous system.

p. 89 palaeolithic: i.e. the palaeolithic period. Kemp's point is that the drug is crude and its use primitive.

p. 89 The laws of this country against vivisection were very severe: Britain was the first country to legislate against experimentation on living animals. Few today would consider that the Cruelty to Animals Act of 1876 was severe, however: by the time it was repealed (in 1986) not a single prosecution had been brought under it. For accounts of the practice in Britain at the time, see Stewart Richards, 'Vicarious Suffering, Necessary Pain: Physiological Method in Late Nineteenth-century Britain' and Nicolaas Rupke, 'Pro-vivisection in England in the early 1880s: Arguments and Motives', both in Nicolaas A. Rupke (ed.), *Vivisection in Historical Perspective* (London: Croom Helm, 1987), pp. 125–48, 188–208 respectively. Wells was a supporter of vivisection. He engaged in a public controversy on the issue with George Bernard Shaw, a vocal anti-vivisectionist, in 1927. For a brief account of their debate, see Michael Coren, *The Invisible Man: The Life and Liberties of H. G. Wells* (London: Bloomsbury, 1993), pp 178–81.

p. 91 my transparent eyelids: In his essay 'El Primer Wells' ('The First Wells') (1946), the famous Argentinian writer Jorge Luis Borges remarks, 'The harassed invisible man who has to sleep as though his eyes were wide open because his eyelids do not exclude light is our solitude and our terror', (trans. Ruth L. C. Simms; reprinted in Patrick Parrinder (ed.), *H. G. Wells: The Critical Heritage* (London: Routledge and Kegan Paul, 1972), p. 331. But, in fact, Wells makes nothing of the potential horror of not being able to close one's eyes and enjoy a private darkness. On the other hand, Garcin, in Jean Paul Sartre's play, *Huis Clos (In Camera)* (1944), believes that this is one of the torments of the hell he is in (my translation): 'A little flash of darkness, a blind that falls then opens again: a break. The eyes moisten themselves, the world is blotted out for an instant. Can you imagine what a relief that was? Four thousand breaks every hour. Four thousand temporary escapes. And when I say four thousand . . . So I must live with no eyelids? You needn't pretend that you don't follow me. No eyelids, no sleep, isn't that right? I'll never sleep again . . . But how will I manage to bear it?'

p. 92 *patois:* regional dialect (French).

p. 92 against: in anticipation of.

p. 92 register: an adjustable plate that controls the flow of air into a chimney.

p. 92 costermonger: a seller of fruit and vegetables from a barrow.

p. 95 hansom: a two-wheeled, one-horse carriage designed by J. A. Hansom (1803–82).

p. 95 ... the weather and all its consequences: as Bernard Bergonzi has pointed out, in *The Early H. G. Wells: A Study of the Scientific Romances* (Manchester: Manchester University Press, 1961), p. 120, 'it seems a serious flaw in Wells's narrative – though necessary for the "plot" – that Griffin so inexplicably neglected to make his clothes invisible, and thus had to go out naked.' After all, we have recently seen him, in Chapter 20, make a piece of white wool invisible (p. 86).

p. 95 Mudie's: one of the main commercial lending libraries of the period.

p. 95 the Museum: the British Museum.

p. 96 Salvation Army: the evangelistic Christian organisation, first known as the Christian Revival Association, was founded by William Booth (1829–1912) in 1865. It changed its name in 1878.

p. 96 'When shall we see his Face?': Wells may be remembering the last verse of the Methodist hymn, 'We have not known Thee as we ought', by Thomas Benson Pollock (1836–96): 'When shall we know Thee as we ought,/And fear, and love, and serve aright?/When shall we, out of trial brought,/Be perfect in the land of light?/Lord, may we day by day prepare/To see Thy face and serve Thee there.'

p. 96 his foot was a-bleeding: it is not clear why, in the next paragraph, the boys do not therefore see the blood as well as the mud on Griffin's foot.

p. 97 Crusoe's solitary discovery: For Crusoe's discovery of 'the print of a man's naked foot on the shore' of the island he believes deserted, see Daniel Defoe, *The Life and Times of Robinson Crusoe* (1719; Harmondsworth, Penguin, 1965), p. 162. The fact that the Defoe print belongs to a black man has been seen as important by at least one critic, Robert F. Fleissner: see the quotation from his work in Wells and His Critics p. 157.

p. 101 comforter: a woollen scarf.

p. 101 slouch hat: soft hat with a brim that can be pulled down over the ears.

p. 102 Dust to dust, earth to earth: A misquotation of 'The Order for the Burial of the Dead' in *The Book of Common Prayer*: 'earth to earth, ashes to ashes, dust to dust'. Had Griffin been more familiar with the text of the Order he may have been aware that it includes Psalm 39, one verse of which reads: 'O spare me a little, that I may recover my strength: before I go hence, and be no more seen.'

p. 106   Drury Lane: the famous street of theatres in London's West End.

p. 106   cheval glass: a full length mirror, mounted in a frame on hinges that permit it to be swivelled.

p. 106   'Damn the boys!': the proprietor thinks himself the victim of a 'runaway ring' (cf. the second note to p. 69).

p. 109   a Louis Quatorze vest: a garment in fashion during the reign (1643–1715) of Louis XIV of France (1638–1715).

p. 110   benzoline: a commercial name for impure benzene, used, among other things, as a solvent.

p. 110   turpentine: a white spirit, used to thin and remove paint.

p. 110   calico dominoes: hooded cloaks made of plain white fabric; they were designed to disguise the wearer, as they were usually worn with an eye mask at masquerades.

p. 110   cashmere scarfs: so-called because imported from Cashmere or Kashmir, part of the British Empire until 1947.

p. 112   when her name must needs be Delilah: i.e. when she would make it a test of love that she be told the secret of one's strength; Delilah's betrayal of Samson is recounted in Judges 16:4–21.

p. 118   Halstead: town in Kent, south-east of Wells's birthplace, Bromley.

p. 118   powdered glass: ironically, Kemp suggests trapping Griffin by using a substance with an incidentally high refractive index. Cf. Griffin's use of powdered glass as an example in Chapter 19 (p. 82).

p. 119   ken: knowledge.

p. 120   we can know nothing of the details of the encounter: once more, the usually omniscient narrator pretends to a limited knowledge of events.

p. 123   pillar box: i.e. the post box in which Griffin has posted his letter.

p. 123   2d. to pay: i.e. the recipient is requested to pay two pennies for the postage, because the sender did not put a stamp on the card. The note would have been added by a post office official.

p. 123   the letter had come by the one o'clock post: this is not an unduly speedy delivery. There were several postal deliveries a day in this period. Mail was much quicker in the nineteenth century than it is in our own.

p. 124   *contra mundum:* against the world (Latin).

p. 125   **hard by:** nearby.

p. 129   **He's killed Adye. Shot him anyhow:** readers of the serial version and first English edition were thus left undecided as to whether or not Adye is dead. The Epilogue, which Wells added to the first American edition, makes it clear that he survives (see p. 138).

p. 129   **Sidney Cooper:** Wells perhaps refers to Thomas Sydney Cooper (1803–1902), an animal painter.

p. 130   **poker clubbed:** holding the poker like a club.

p. 130   **Doctor Kemp's a hero:** the first American edition unaccountably prints 'Doctor Kemp's in here', which is either a misreading or a correction prompted by failure to register the irony of what is being said. The error was replicated in many subsequent editions. As the American text makes no sense, I have adopted the reading of the English first edition.

p. 132   **French windows:** a pair of casement windows which extend to floor level.

p. 133   **fag end:** the last and worst and consequently little-frequented part.

p. 133   **tram horses:** like cabs, trams were horsedrawn.

p. 134   **Rugby football:** Wells's capitalisation emphasises the connection of the sport with the Warwickshire public school where it was first played in 1823.

p. 135   **shamming:** pretending (i.e. to be unconscious).

p. 136   **garnets:** hard, glassy minerals.

p. 136   **they carried him into that house:** thus ended the serial version and first English edition (see the Note on the Text).

p. 137   **treasure trove:** valuable items of unknown ownership, so designated, become the property of the Crown.

p. 138   **Cobbett:** William Cobbett (1763–1835), author of *Rural Rides* (1830), was born in Farnham, Surrey, and was a long-time resident of Hampshire.

p. 138   **Hex, little two up in the air, cross and a fiddle-de-dee:** Marvel's attempt to verbalise Griffin's algebraic notation gets no further than '$X^2 +$'.

WELLS AND HIS CRITICS

Wells's reputation today is rather more ambiguous than some of his contemporaries, impressed by his prodigious output and enormous commercial success, might have imagined it would be. The history of Wells's commentary displays considerable difficulties in categorising a writer whose output was multi-faceted and heterogeneous, as much journalistic and polemical as artistic; whose literary texts cannot without major qualification be labelled 'realistic' or 'modernist'; and who worked in a variety of genres which span the 'popular culture'/'high art' divide. Canonical status has not, as a consequence, been something Wells has enjoyed, and there has therefore been a relative lack, until fairly recently, of serious scholarly attention to his work. John Huntington, in the introduction to his edited collection, *Critical Essays on H. G. Wells* (Boston: G. K. Hall, 1991), has noted that Wells is 'important in a number of areas but, at least to current tastes, he is supreme in none. Unlike James Joyce, whose every thought and gesture the age finds admirable, Wells's accomplishment is always in question':

> Much of the commentary written on Wells has assumed that the points he makes are clear and has spent its primary energies summarizing and defending him. Moreover, since Wells engaged in a wide variety of literary pursuits, critical attention to his work has been dissipated by being spread thinly. He has been discussed as the originator of the scientific romance, the father of anticipation and futurology, a comic social novelist, an autobiographer, an international activist, a journalist, an educator, and finally, not commonly held up for admiration but nevertheless relevant to any understanding of what he meant to his age, a notorious philanderer. If Wells's literary stature were to be evaluated on the basis of sheer abundance, on the sustained outpouring of energy, he would doubtless be ranked as one of our greatest novelists.

This is not to say that commentators on Wells have remained silent. A 'Bibliography of Writings About Wells, 1895–1986' occupies 412 pages of William J. Scheik and J. Randolph Cox's *H. G. Wells: A Reference Guide* (Boston: G. K. Hall, 1988). However, the vast majority of the 3019 items abstracted therein are journalistic or anecdotal rather than scholarly. Many of the early reviews, in fact, give more sustained attention to the book than several recent volume-length studies of Wells (see Suggestions for Further Reading for examples of such studies). This might be considered a cause for celebration, in a contemporary cultural climate in which few texts have escaped the fate of being 'definitively' colonised and recolonised by successive generations of critics. It certainly means that even today's reader of *The Invisible Man* does not come to it with a huge critical legacy pressing on his or her interpretation: the novel is there to be read and, largely, made of what you will.

It had a rather lukewarm reception on publication. Ingvald Raknem, in a somewhat partisan (that is, pro-Wells) summary of this response in her *H. G. Wells and His Critics* (London: George Allen and Unwin, 1962), quotes Wells's refutation of various charges that the novel contained 'slovenly writing': 'The "slush" effort,' Wells remarked, 'came to more than 100,000 words; the final outcome of it amounts to about 55,000. My first tendency was to make it shorter still' (for the interview in which Wells made this comment, see 'A.H.L.', 'Realism *v.* Romance', *Today*, 11 September 1897). However, it was not conciseness that the critics found wanting. The reviewer in the *Daily Telegraph* (22 September, 1897) pointed to some weaknesses and 'unessential improbabilities' in the realistic parts of the novel, while praising its general energy and wit:

> 'The Invisible Man' is not on a level with the author's best work. There are signs of hurried writing; there are details, such as the thousand and one bottles, which fit very inadequately into the tissue of the tale; there are unessential improbabilities, as when Mr Marvel, tramp by trade and education, describes the hero as 'vox et – jabber'; there are also occasions on which Sussex rustics forget to maintain their dialect. Further, the tale is slighter, less ambitious, less imaginative than the book which made the author's name. 'The Invisible Man' cannot compete with 'The Time Machine'; indeed, is not meant to. It is, as described by the author,

a grotesque romance, which, more often than not, sinks into broad farce. But, as such and no more, it must be judged to fulfil its part excellently. There is displayed throughout a wealth of that faculty which distinguished the writings of Dean Swift. The Lilliputians once invented, all their ways and thoughts appear to result inevitably from their definition, and your admiration is moved less by the preliminary imagination than by the rigour of the logical process. The people behave, in fact, as they should, and the truth of their behaviour gives the story its pleasing smack of probability . . .

The book is naturally, in accordance with the theme, little more than a series of co-ordinate scenes, but each is so fresh, ingenious, and humorous that interest is never allowed to flag until the final hunt and visible calamity in the neighbourhood of the 'Jolly Cricketers'. The tastes of the world at large are well consulted; there is creeping horror for those who love the horrible, there are scientific explanation and plausible use of technical terms for the ingenious and throughout the whole an ebullient flow of humour as rare as it is welcome.

Three days later *The Athenaeum* (25 September, 1897) subjected the novel to the terser opinions of an anonymous critic (the review, probably by A. B. Bence-Jones, is quoted here in full):

Mr H. G. Wells correctly speaks of this volume as a grotesque romance. Halfway through the book we are told that the invisible man is Mr Griffin, a medical student of University College, who by strictly scientific methods has succeeded in rendering himself invisible. His clothes he cannot deal with in the same manner, and the story tells how many and various are the complications which follow. As a literary *tour de force* the book has considerable merit; but it does not become interesting or attractive at any point. The writer's skill in depicting the conduct of the inhabitants of a village in which the invisible man endeavours to reside in peace is hardly equal to the occasion.

C. L. Graves wrote more substantially, and with greater favour, in *The Spectator* of the same day:

The central notion of Mr H. G. Wells's grotesque romance, as he has frankly admitted, has been utilised by Mr Gilbert in one of the *Bab Ballads*, being that of a man endowed with invisibility but susceptible to heat and cold, and therefore obliged to wear clothes.

But while Mr Gilbert treated the theme in a spirit of fantastic farce, Mr Wells has worked it out with that sombre humour and remorseless logic which stamp him as a disciple, conscious or unconscious, of the author of *Gulliver*. Swift, however, excelled in the logical conduct to its extreme consequences of some absurd proposition; Mr Wells's method is in its essentials much more realistic. He does not posit his invisible man; he tells us how he became invisible as the result of a discovery in physiology based upon actual scientific data, for Mr Wells is no dabbler but deeply versed in these studies. It is characteristic, again, of his method that his invisible man should be neither a buffoon nor a humourist [*sic*], but a moody, irritable egotist, with a violent and vindictive temper ... As, however, he is so strong in realistic detail, we may be allowed to ask whether it is not the case that his invisible man, as an albino, would have been handicapped by short sight. To sum up, *The Invisible Man* is an amazingly clever performance, of engrossing interest throughout; we should call it fascinating were it not that the element of geniality, which lent unexpected charm to *The Wheels of Chance*, is here conspicuously absent.

Clement Shorter, writing in *The Bookman* (London, October 1897), was another enthusiast:

Mr Wells's 'Invisible Man' – Griffin is his name – has succeeded in rendering his body invisible, although it retains its corporeal character. Yet what misery this 'triumph of science' entails on its discoverer will be learned by many an eager reader. Griffin had thought to lord it over all his race. To have 'a good time' was the motive of his experiments, but one misfortune follows upon another until the wretched man hates his fellows and becomes findish [*sic*] in his attempts to war with them. Scientific research is indeed vanity if we are to accept Mr Wells as a guide. That is only one interpretation of his book. The important thing to note is that the author has conceived of his creation with a splendid mastery of detail. Point after point helps to fix Griffin in his wanderings vividly upon the imagination, and at every turn we learn most realistically how disastrous his new power must be to him. Only children, for example, to whom life offers no mysteries, would have followed the footprints of the hunted man. But to write all this is perhaps to treat the matter too seriously. The story, which is bound to be popular, has not a suspicion of preaching about it, and in a quite unpretentious way will help to pass an amusing

hour or so. I have not been so fascinated by a new book for many
a day.

But, on the whole, the book's entry into the world was not an
auspicious one and, although its fortunes improved with age,
Wells was always laconic about it. When the novel was reprinted
alongside *The War of the Worlds* in volume three of the Atlantic
edition of his works (T. Fisher Unwin, 1924), Wells prefatorily
remarked, 'There is very little to be said about either work. They
tell their own stories.' He then spent a page on *The War of the
Worlds*, but said no more about *The Invisible Man*. Nine years
later, in the preface to *The Scientific Romances of H. G. Wells*
(London: Gollancz, 1933), he said nothing specific about it
other than to recommend 'that for anyone who does not as
yet know anything of my work it will probably be more
agreeable to begin with *The Invisible Man* or *The War of the
Worlds*' (this preface is reproduced in the Appendix to the
present edition).

David C. Smith summarises the novel's changing fortunes in
H. G. Wells: Desperately Mortal: A Biography (New Haven:
Yale University Press, 1986):

> The book probably provided the novelist Ralph Ellison, an
> important black observer of America, with the title for his work
> *Invisible Man* (1952), and perhaps with its theme, that blacks in
> America remain invisible while going about their daily lives,
> although promising that their emergence will be significant . . .
>
> The book is an interesting phenomenon in another way. It sold
> well for a month, after which sales collapsed entirely, yet it was a
> steady producer of revenue throughout Wells's life, especially in
> the US. Every six months a royalty cheque arrived. As late as
> January 1935 (at the height of the Depression) the cheque was for
> £42. 17s. 5d., for example. In the 1920s the film rights to the
> book became valuable, and gave Wells an opportunity to increase
> his income substantially. Famous Players offered to buy the work
> outright, but Wells, wise in the ways of the world, said he did not
> believe in such sales; he preferred to grant options on a short-term
> basis, with each successive option bringing in more funds. Wells
> asked £4,000 for an option for a reasonable number of years,
> while the Hollywood magnates offered $25,000 with $2,000
> deductible if they took up the option to film within sixty days; this
> last Wells accepted. The film, when made in 1933, starred Claude

Rains, and was a modest hit. The Invisible Man certainly brought in visible funds.

Despite this undoubted commercial success, recent assessments of the novel remain every bit as mixed as the early ones. Alfred Borrello focuses on the relationship between Griffin and Kemp in his brief analysis of the novel in *H. G. Wells: Author in Agony* (Carbondale: Southern Illinois University Press, 1972):

> Kemp represents just one of the many flat, monodimensional antagonists Wells creates out of his insatiable desire to identify those forces which stand in the way of progress. These forces are self-satisfied, as Kemp; they are filled with a sense of their own worth, yet nevertheless, their dignity is slightly absurd. More significantly, they are dangerous because they are completely beyond the protagonists' understanding or sympathy. And, all too often, they are beyond the protagonists' control. Griffin cannot understand Kemp's lack of vision and daring, qualities he possesses in large proportions and qualities he expects to be possessed by any scientist. Nor can any of Wells's protagonists comprehend in any way other than the negative the particular forces which oppose them. They cannot comprehend because Wells creates his protagonists, ironically, as peculiarly self-centred yet intellectually gifted individuals who believe themselves interested in the welfare of the masses they somewhat paranoically proclaim to represent . . .
>
> Griffin's death serves as an object lesson to all god-men. Each, Wells warns us, must confront the consequences of his actions to better himself and the world alone, unprotected, and naked to the world. Those who expect recognition of their contribution and adulation for effort expended are only deluding themselves. No god-man can hope for such recognition nor can he expect help, even when it is logical to expect help from those of like disposition. Kemp's perfidy, like Pendick's [*sic*], even though well intentioned, accents Wells's less than subtle message that mankind is not generally equipped for nor desirous of accepting the unknown. This rejection of the strange and the foreign occurs even when man has been conditioned to receive and accept what his senses and his reason deny.

Thus is *The Invisible Man* read to yield a fairly conventional moral and 'less than subtle' message. Michael Draper, in

H. G. Wells (London: Macmillan, 1987), similarly focuses on the relationship between Kemp and Griffin, and also draws a parallel with the relationship between Prendick and Moreau in Wells's earlier novel, *The Island of Doctor Moreau* (1896):

> Kemp was once a fellow student of Griffin's. His distaste for strychnine is equivalent to the abstinence from alcohol of Prendick, and he resembles Prendick too in being a Good Scientist with a responsible attitude, brought in as a foil to the Bad Scientist. Yet, rather more explicitly than Prendick, he is implicated in the unhealthy world view he opposes. Early in our acquaintance with Kemp we see him gazing up at the stars in reverie, speculating about the social conditions of the future and about the time dimension. This readiness to take on startling new points of view marks his mental kinship with Griffin, who had also turned to stare at the stars when he first realised he might make himself invisible.
>
> Griffin mentions this incident after a bullet wound has forced him to take refuge in Kemp's house. Griffin's retrospective account of his adventures, which explain the mysteries of the first part of the book and prepare us for the conclusion to come, do something to draw us in to his point of view, but his outbursts of callousness and Kemp's interjections qualify our sympathy. However, we must regard Kemp ambivalently too, for his hostility to Griffin seems to be based less on superior morality than on his superior position in the social order. While the brilliant Griffin is a shabby demonstrator at a provincial college, Kemp is respected and secure. He has a large house, servants and a private income. He shows no understanding of the outcast and is equally ruthless. When he offers Griffin a chair it is not out of genuine concern but in order to place him where he cannot see the police coming.
>
> Kemp's betrayal of Griffin, and abuse of his confidences when giving the police advice on how to harass him, arouse our sympathy for the fugitive. This in turn is dispelled by news that Griffin broke a child's ankle as he fled from Kemp's house. The events of the story are carefully balanced so that we are unsure whether to regard Griffin as inhuman or afflicted, hateful or pitiful. Although Griffin's own attacks on society are crude and unsuccessful, Wells's development of their implications calls into question some of the categorisation society employs.

Romolo Runcini too, in 'H. G. Wells and Futurity as the Only Creative Space in a Programmed Society', in Patrick Parrinder and Christopher Rolfe (eds.), *H. G. Wells Under Revision: Proceedings of the International H. G. Wells Symposium, London, July 1986* (Selinsgrove: Susquehanna University Press, 1990), sees the relationship between Kemp and Griffin as the key to the book's meaning, but feels that the characterisation of Griffin is a little too crude:

> ... while Griffin seems to be the last dangerous incarnation of the medieval alchemist, Kemp embodies, in his self-sacrifice and serious-mindedness, the true modern scientist. Unlike the central character of *The Time Machine*, Griffin is sympathetic neither by virtue of his scientific research nor of his style of life; he is, however, the main device of a plot introducing elements of the 'marvellous' into a world besieged by banality.
>
> In this story, not without pathos in itself, the conflict between good and evil seems established as a polarity of fixed extremes and does not achieve tragic intensity (in spite of Griffin's catastrophic end) because of the weak psychological characterisation of the protagonist and the exaggerated stereotyping of his alter ego, Dr Kemp. We are some distance from the tragic dimension of the relationship between Jekyll and Hyde.
>
> Thus, while the Time Traveller has captivated the reader with his profusion of technical information and through the exciting prospect of a future (or a past) at hand, Griffin is presented from the beginning as nothing but a crafty mystifier, a maniac, a dangerous man. With the discovery of invisibility (implicit, if only marginal in the story of *The Time Machine*), the reader is faced with a defined menace, namely the state of anarchy that will follow if scientific methodologies are employed without adequate social control.

Darko Suvin, in a chapter in *The Metamorphosis of Science Fiction* (New Haven: Yale University Press, 1979) also finds *The Invisible Man* 'less felicitous' than Wells's earlier work:

> ... the delineation of Griffin hesitates between a man in advance of his time within an indifferent society and the symbol of a humanity that does not know how to use science. This makes of him almost an old-fashioned 'mad scientist', and yet he is too important and too sinned against to be comic relief. The vigor of the narration, which unfolds in the form of a hunt, and the

strengths of an inverted fairy tale cannot compensate for the
failure of the supposedly omniscient author to explain why Griffin
had got into the position of being his own Frankenstein and
Monster at the same time. In this context, the dubious scientific
premises (an invisible eye cannot see, and so forth) become
distressing and tend to deprive the story of the needed suspension
of disbelief.

John Batchelor, in his *H. G. Wells* (Cambridge: Cambridge
University Press, 1985) is similarly unimpressed:

> Griffin's will to power is the product of early conditioning; he was
> a 'shabby, poverty-struck, hemmed-in demonstrator, teaching
> fools in a provincial college'. He seems, then at first, to be a figure
> like Mr Lewisham, from *Love and Mr Lewisham*, who has the
> gifts of the Time Traveller; a socially disadvantaged figure who
> uses science to free himself from his circumstances. The reader's
> sympathies for much of the novel are *for* Griffin and against, for
> example, the oafish inhabitants of Iping, where his early attempts
> to gain control are entirely comic in their effect. Half-way through
> his novel Wells forces it against the grain of our sympathies – and
> severely damages it, in my view – by turning Griffin into an
> obvious maniac, raving about a 'Reign of Terror' and the necessity
> of killing all who disobey him. The best of the novel's intentions
> are all calculated to enlist the reader's sympathy firmly *with*
> Griffin by exploring the details and hazards of invisibility; the
> retina of his eyes and undigested food in his stomach remain
> visible, he causes hysteria in dogs, and so forth. Further, the reader
> inevitably responds to the anarchic pleasures – the opportunities
> for beating the system – that invisibility confers, and is disap-
> pointed when Wells turns against the implications of his invention
> and bends the knee to a conventional morality in which he clearly
> has no real faith.

Less harshly, Mark R. Hillegas, in *The Future as Nightmare:
H. G. Wells and the Anti-Utopians* (New York: Oxford University Press, 1967), concludes that the novel's moralistic elements
are subsidiary to its comic intentions:

> In Griffin, the invisible man, we have the blood brother of Dr
> Moreau: again, the scientist who has pursued knowledge and lost
> all human sympathy. But *The Invisible Man* is the closest of
> Wells's five great scientific romances to being a work of 'sheer

exuberance'. Its serious meaning is almost completely 'dissolved in the narrative' of the extraordinary adventures of the invisible man.

Wells's point of departure is, as usual, the everyday and familiar, only in this case it continues to be present in the foreground to a much greater extent than in the other scientific romances. The everyday and familiar is at first the sleepy and matter-of-fact village of Iping, to which Griffin comes to take up lodgings. His comic encounters with the villagers and others are handled with great skill, and in this respect the romance is a forerunner of Wells's masterpieces of lower-middle-class life, *Kipps* and *The History of Mr Polly*. Altogether it is a greatly entertaining book, and chiefly a brilliant effervescence of the creative imagination.

Yet there are darker meanings within the narrative. Most obviously, in the ruthlessness of Griffin, who will rob and kill rather than have his wishes frustrated, we see illustrated, as Wells himself tells us, 'the dangers of power without control, the development of the intelligence at the expense of human sympathy'. Like *The Island of Dr Moreau*, *The Invisible Man* thus foreshadows a major anti-utopian theme: the need for ethical control over the use of science and its discoveries. And how perfect a symbol of science without humanity is an invisible man without scruples!

Roslynn D. Haynes further explores the comic dimension of the novel in *H. G. Wells: Discoverer of the Future: The Influence of Science on His Thought* (London: Macmillan, 1980). Briefly tracing the parallels between Griffin and Marlowe's Dr Faustus, she none the less indicates that:

unlike Marlowe, Wells does not trust to a supernatural scheme of punishment; Griffin's nemesis springs inevitably from his own actions and attitudes. The things he reaches for recede before his Tantalus-like grasp; cold, hungry, pursued, and in dire danger of being run over, he remains unrepentant even at death. But Wells wreaks a further and perhaps more severe punishment on Griffin, one which Faustus was not forced to endure. Unlike Moreau, Griffin is, from the first, presented as faintly absurd and the suspicion of this is never fully overcome even in the scenes of his 'reign of terror' and the final brutal chase. It is not easy to be sure how far this was intended by Wells as a further level of meaning in the story and how far it resulted from his exuberant inability to pass by an opportunity for the vivacious situational humour which the particular circumstances of this story offered, but it seems reasonable to see it as an extension of the warning already inherent in 'The Moth' – the insanity to which obsession with an evil motive potentially leads. To condemn Griffin out of his own mouth is damning enough, but to render him, as well, a semi-comic figure is a greater and more humiliating indictment.

Bruce Beiderwell, in 'The Grotesque in Wells's *The Invisible Man*', *Extrapolation* 24, 4 (1983), sees the mixture of comic and serious and strange and familiar elements as producing a generally grotesque experience for the reader:

> For most readers of *Moreau*, disgust effectively stifles laughter. The comic fares far better in *The Invisible Man*. But the difference should not obscure an essential similarity. In some respects *Moreau* mirrors *The Invisible Man*; both books rest upon the structure of the grotesque, but the latter book reverses the tension between the strange and the familiar. In *Moreau* Pendrick [*sic*] – a 'man alone' – is brought to a world which shows him things he cannot accept. Moreau's creatures force the profoundly ominous element upon Pendrick's vision. In *The Invisible Man*, Griffin – a 'stranger' – is the ominous element. He intrudes into our familiar world and upsets our faith in it. This reversal accounts for the unrelentingly grim and disturbing tone of *Moreau*. We are forced to identify exclusively with Pendrick, the sole narrator, and fully share his nightmare. In *Moreau*, a lone man confronts terror; in *The Invisible Man*, a lone terror confronts man. In *Moreau*, only Pendrick (and the reader with him) experiences the power of the grotesque; in *The Invisible Man*, the power of the grotesque is more diffused. Griffin commands a portion of our sympathy by his reckless individuality, but only a portion. He remains a nameless stranger throughout the first half of the book, and achieves a full human identity only in death. Faced with the threat Griffin represents, we can always retreat to the relative security of belonging to the mob.

Recent critics have brought to light some of the wider social themes tapped by the novel. Robert F. Fleissner, in 'H. G. Wells and Ralph Ellison: Need the Effect of One *Invisible Man* On Another Be *Itself* Invisible?', *Extrapolation* 33, 4 (1992), suggests that 'at least three passages in *The Invisible Man* glance prominently ahead of Ellison's own more substantial or "visible" treatment of the notion of blackness in *Invisible Man*:

> The first relevant passage occurs early in the Wells story. In the third chapter, Griffin, the Invisible Man, happens to be abruptly mistaken for a black. When onlookers fail to find flesh beneath his clothing, but rather what appears to be a hole, they readily jump to their impressionistic conclusion that they are experiencing something black. Now such a reaction, if taken as stereotypical, would easily enough have lent itself to Ellison's cardinal theme, one upon which his own follow-up novel is based, namely that blacks are too much thought of as being no more than 'anonymous', that all too often they appear to look alike (to use the old bromide) and are, in that respect, likewise invisible men . . .
>
> The second passage in the Wells's work worth considering shows Griffin relating himself to a black. He observes that the obsequious way he has to go 'to work' and thereby truckle to others has made him feel just like a black slave. Surely Ellison made a mental note of this description . . .
>
> The third passage worth considering is somewhat subtler, but the best so far. When Wells's uncanny invisible outcast leaves footprint traces, they are forthwith compared with those of a non-Caucasian, the native Friday in Defoe's own adventure novel, *Robinson Crusoe*: 'a footprint as isolated and incomprehensible . . . as Crusoe's solitary discovery'. By implanting such clues in the soil, Wells's invisible protagonist lets others know of his being present, so such a Crusoe correlation is not merely a desultory one, incidentally pointing again to what may now be designated 'the black factor' in the Wells novel. In the final comparative analysis, the total imprint, let us say, is rather more than that of a foot (or even footnote), is thus not merely pedestrian, because it indicates a causative effect upon Ellison.

Jeanne Murray Walker's 'Exchange Short-Circuited: The Isolated Scientist in H. G. Wells's *The Invisible Man*', *The Journal of Narrative Technique* 15, 2 (1985), argues that the novel combines the detective novel with the dramatic monologue, to help us to think about the way in which knowledge is constructed, and how it relates to moral judgment:

> The reader is drawn into the problem of how evidence relates to conclusions, not only through the detective novel format, but also

through the style of the narrative. The novel is peppered with attributive phrases which make the story seem like evidence at a trial. 'Mrs Hall asserts', the narrator writes, and 'it is stated by an anonymous bystander'. Chapter 26, 'The Wicksteed Murder', is a model of such judicial language. 'If our supposition ... is correct', and 'Of course we can know nothing of the details of the encounter', and 'But this is pure hypothesis'. These recurring refusals to transgress the limits of narrative omniscience call attention to the task which observers in the novel must perform to discover the truth. And they remind the reader that he functions like a jury which sits in final judgment over conclusions already reached by witnesses.

It might be argued that the detective form which shapes the first half of the novel fails in the second half. By then the people of Iping understand that the curious dress and behaviour of the stranger arise from his invisibility. They also realise that he is a social misfit. But these superficial data do not satisfy the real question about the stranger's identity. Therefore, in the middle of the novel Wells introduces the intellectually credible physician, Kemp, to interrogate the stranger. As a result of this interrogation the invisible man confesses.

... Wells used the form of the dramatic monologue – whether he got it from Mary Shelley or Tennyson or Browning – to extend the novel's statement about the problem of knowledge. As Robert Langbaum observed about dramatic monologues, they work most successfully when the speaker is unquestionably guilty. Through the speaker's special pleading – extenuating circumstances, terrible need, or even simple malice – the reader is fixed in an ambivalent position between sympathy and judgment. In this position, it is impossible for the listener to make an unbiased judgment; the point is precisely that judgment has to be deferred. Or if it is made, it is forced in the teeth, either of compelling need on the one hand, or of guilt on the other. By definition, the dramatic monologue suspends the reader's ability to come to a judgment solely on the basis of facts.

Bernard Bergonzi, in *The Early H. G. Wells: A Study of the Scientific Romances* (Manchester: Manchester University Press, 1960), indicates that *The Invisible Man* was, in an important respect, a new departure for Wells:

The significance of *The Invisible Man* in terms of Wells's fictional development is that, for the first time in his romances, we are shown a recognizable society in being which engages our sympathy and interest for its own sake. Instead of seeing a society, albeit a small one, through the eyes of a strange visitor, as in *The Wonderful Visit*, we see the strange visitor – to begin with – through the eyes of the society. And, as Wells emphasises, it is a smug, settled and apparently prosperous little community. Later, Griffin is to disturb its peace in the farcical events of Whit Monday when he goes berserk and inflicts widespread – if minor – damage to property and injury to its inhabitants. Thematically, *The Invisible Man* relates those romances in which the interest is centred in the heuristic perceptions of a single figure – the Time Traveller, the Angel, Prendick – to *The War of the Worlds*, where attention is focused on society as a whole as it is subject to the unwelcome attentions of not one but a multitude of alien visitants . . .

It is arguable that the transitions in mood in *The Invisible Man* are too abrupt, and that the attempted combination, as it were, of Thurber and Kafka, is ultimately unsatisfactory. Yet, as I have suggested, all the changes in feeling with which Griffin is associated do point in one direction: namely, that of making him seem more and more an outcast from the kind of everyday society whose weight and solidity Wells is at such pains to establish. One contemporary reviewer wrote of the book:

> The tragedy is always on the brink of farce until we reach the last page and a piece of wholly pathetic tragedy. The hunted terror of society is caught at last, and most pitiful is the re-entry he makes into the visible world he left so boldly. [*Saturday Review*, 18 September 1897]

One is reminded here of the concept of 'tragic farce' that T. S. Eliot [*Selected Essays* (London: Faber, 1953), p. 123] applied to Marlowe's *Jew of Malta*, and this certainly seems as good a description as any of *The Invisible Man*: Griffin, like Barabas, is both farcical and murderous.

Finally, Frank McConnell is one of the few critics to relate *The Invisible Man* to Wells's earlier and later short stories. In *The Science Fiction of H. G. Wells* (New York: Oxford University Press, 1981) he points out the relations between the novel and

Wells's 'The Stolen Bacillus' (1895) and 'The Country of the
Blind' (1911). He also valuably ponders the significance in the
narrative of the tramp Marvel, and particularly of his place in
the Epilogue which Wells added (see the Note on the Text) to
the American first edition:

> Marvel is a rogue, a coward, and the character around whom
> most of the comic elements of *The Invisible Man* revolve. He is,
> in fact, one of Wells's most unusual figures, a lower-class clown
> (in both the ancient and modern senses of the word), nearly
> untouched by elements of sensibility or tragedy. And yet it is
> Marvel, in all the unthinking self-confidence of his ordinariness,
> who is the last person we see in the book. After Griffin has been
> killed and Kemp and Kemp's society vindicated in their trust in
> the normal conventions of humanity, Marvel is – absurdly but
> somehow appropriately – rewarded with some money Griffin has
> stolen, since no one can determine from whom he originally stole
> it. More crucially, though, Marvel has secured the three volumes
> of notes Griffin has made about the secret of invisibility – volumes
> of immense importance to the scientific world, but totally incomp-
> rehensible to Marvel, who nevertheless refuses to disclose their
> existence to anyone . . .
>
> It is a strange ending for a strange book. Why should Marvel,
> that most crass and unredeemed member of the working (or non-
> working) class, be the heir, the final actor, of the struggle between
> Griffin's anarchist revolutionism and Kemp's humane conserva-
> tism? Perhaps because Wells wishes to insist that neither Griffin
> *nor* Kemp, ultimately, is right, that neither the pure individual *nor*
> the committed group man is quite the figure needed to carry on
> and advance the course of human civilisation. So that the magic
> books . . . are given in the end to a man too stupid to use them,
> but also too ordinarily decent to try and exploit them. They are
> given to Marvel, that is, just because marvel is the embodiment,
> not of a utopian intelligence, but of an anti-utopian, generous
> ignorance that knows its own limits, and in recognising its own
> limits asserts or incarnates something important about the limits
> of human capability.

The selection of comment offered here may give the
impression that *The Invisible Man* has attracted a great deal of
attention. In conclusion, it is therefore worth repeating that,
with one or two exceptions, the critics here cited seldom develop

their insights beyond those they offer in the passages quoted. *The Invisible Man* remains a territory relatively uncharted by Wells scholars (who typically see it as a minor work), commentators on the modern novel (who universally ignore it), and students of science fiction (who, if they deal with it, do so in passing). To merely human critics, the novel itself has been somewhat invisible, leaving only an odd faint footprint in their annals; more dog-like readers, on the other hand, seldom fail to notice its presence.

SUGGESTIONS FOR FURTHER READING

Bibliographies of Wells's work include J. R. Hammond, *Herbert George Wells: An Annotated Bibliography of His Works* (New York: Garland Publishing, 1977) and *H. G. Wells: A Comprehensive Bibliography* (4th ed., London: The H. G. Wells Society, 1986). William J. Scheik and J. Randolph Cox, *H. G. Wells: A Reference Guide* (Boston: G. K. Hall, 1988), is almost entirely a bibliography (with useful abstracts) of writings about Wells published between 1895 and 1986. Unfortunately, however, the *Guide* does not include Wells's works in its index, thus making it impossible to use it to locate comment on individual Wells texts. Ingvald Raknem has a section entitled 'Reviews of Wells's Writings' in her *H. G. Wells and His Critics* (London: George Allen and Unwin, 1962), which lists early reviews according to the work under review; early reactions to *The Invisible Man* by Clement Shorter, Joseph Conrad and W. T. Stead are reprinted in Patrick Parrinder, *H. G. Wells: The Critical Heritage* (London: Routledge and Kegan Paul, 1972).

On Wells's life, see Norman and Jean MacKenzie, *The Time Traveller: The Life of H. G. Wells* (rev. ed., London: Hogarth Press, 1987) and David C. Smith, *H. G. Wells: Desperately Mortal: A Biography* (New Haven: Yale University Press, 1986). Those interested in Wells's scientific ideas around the time of publication of *The Invisible Man* should consult Robert M. Philmus and David Y. Hughes (eds.), *H. G. Wells: Early Writings in Science and Science Fiction* (Berkeley: University of California Press, 1975).

There are several general books on Wells which attempt to convey the immense range of his output: Brian Murray's *H. G. Wells* (New York: Continuum, 1990) is one of the most recent and most concise, but it has little to say about *The Invisible Man* beyond mere summary. Michael Draper's *H. G. Wells* (London: Macmillan, 1987) devotes a couple of pages to *The Invisible Man* in a very readable general survey, as do John

Batchelor, *H. G. Wells* (Cambridge: Cambridge University Press, 1985), Roslynn D. Haynes, *H. G. Wells: Discoverer of the Future: The Influence of Science on His Thought* (London: Macmillan, 1980), Alfred Borrello, *H. G. Wells: Author in Agony* (Carbondale: Southern Illinois University Press, 1972) and Mark R. Hillegas, *The Future as Nightmare: H. G. Wells and the Anti-Utopians* (New York: Oxford University Press, 1967). J. R. Hammond's *H. G. Wells and the Modern Novel* (London: Macmillan, 1988) is more ambitious than the five books just mentioned, but virtually ignores *The Invisible Man* altogether. This is effectively true of an otherwise excellent collection of essays, *H. G. Wells Under Revision: Proceedings of the International H. G. Wells Symposium, London, July 1986* (Selinsgrove: Susquehanna University Press, 1990), edited by Patrick Parrinder and Christopher Rolfe.

It is in books with a narrower focus that more prolonged attention to *The Invisible Man* is found. This is true of Frank D. McConnell's *The Science Fiction of H. G. Wells* (New York: Oxford University Press, 1981) and Bernard Bergonzi, *The Early H. G. Wells: A Study of the Scientific Romances* (Manchester: Manchester University Press, 1961), both of which devote substantial sections to the novel. Chapter three of Thomas C. Renzi's *H. G. Wells: Six Scientific Romances Adapted for Film* (Metuchen: The Scarecrow Press, 1992) offers an account of the translation of Wells's narrative for the film medium in James Whale's movie, *The Invisible Man* (Universal Pictures, 1933).

Articles on *The Invisible Man* include: David J. Lake, 'The Whiteness of Griffin and H. G. Wells's Images of Death, 1897–1914', *Science-Fiction Studies* 8 (1981), pp. 12–18; Bruce Beiderwell, 'The Grotesque in Wells's *The Invisible Man*', *Extrapolation* 24, 4 (1983), pp. 301–10; Jeanne Murray Walker, 'Exchange Short-Circuited: The Isolated Scientist in H. G. Wells's *The Invisible Man*', *The Journal of Narrative Technique* 15, 2 (1985), pp. 156–68; Philip Holt, 'H. G. Wells and the Ring of Gyges', *Science-Fiction Studies* 19 (July 1992), pp. 236–47; and Robert F. Fleissner, 'H. G. Wells and Ralph Ellison: Need the Effect of One *Invisible Man* On Another Be *Itself* Invisible?', *Extrapolation* 33, 4 (1992), pp. 346–50.

Finally, that large class of readers who combine a sense of humour with an interest in revolutionary politics should not overlook Leon Stover, *The Shaving of Karl Marx: An Instant Novel of Ideas, After the Manner of Thomas Love Peacock, in which Lenin and H. G. Wells Talk about the Political Meaning of the Scientific Romances* (Lake Forest, Illinois: The Chinon Press, 1982), pp. 57–76 of which deal with *The Invisible Man*.

TEXT SUMMARY

Chapter 1: The Strange Man's Arrival
A mysterious stranger arrives at Mrs Hall's inn and rents the parlour room there. His identity is impossible to determine, as his face is covered in bandages, and he maintains a hostile resistance to Mrs Hall's enquiries.

Chapter 2: Mr Teddy Henfrey's First Impressions
Mrs Hall asks Teddy Henfrey to mend the clock in the stranger's room. Teddy tries unsuccessfully to engage the stranger in conversation. On the way home he meets Mrs Hall's husband, and attempts to raise his suspicions about his guest. Hall and his wife have words about the matter.

Chapter 3: The Thousand and One Bottles
The stranger's voluminous luggage, including his experimental equipment, is delivered. The carter's dog bites at the stranger and rips his trousers. The stranger rushes to the parlour. When Mr Hall follows him to find out if he is hurt he is forcibly thrown out. When his crates and trunks are unpacked, the stranger settles with intensity to his work. Mrs Hall complains about the mess he is making and is told simply to add it to the bill. The carter, Fearenside, speculates that the stranger is 'a kind of half-breed, and the colour's come off patchy instead of mixing'.

Chapter 4: Mr Cuss Interviews the Stranger
Two and a half months pass, in which the villagers engage in much unconfirmed speculation about the stranger. The local doctor, Cuss, unable to resist his own curiosity, visits the stranger on a pretext. Assuming that the stranger has lost an arm, he quizzes him as to how, although his sleeve seems empty, it remains open. The stranger menacingly tweaks Cuss's nose with fingers that seem not to be there. In terror, Cuss runs out of the inn to the vicarage, where he relates the story to Bunting, the vicar.

Chapter 5: The Burglary at the Vicarage
Early on Whit Monday, Bunting the vicar and his wife are wakened by
the sounds of a burglar in the vicarage. They attempt to confront the
criminal, but discover no one, although the housekeeping money has
been taken and a burning candle left in the study.

Chapter 6: The Furniture That Went Mad
At around the time of the vicarage burglary, Mr and Mrs Hall notice
that their front door is unbolted, and that the parlour is empty. As they
examine it, the contents of the room seem to move and attack them of
their own accord. Mrs Hall suspects that the stranger has conjured up
unfriendly ghosts. They seek out the aid of their neighbours, but when
the latter come round, the stranger reappears mysteriously from the
parlour, displaying his usual aggressive refusal to account for himself.

Chapter 7: The Unveiling of the Stranger
The next day, Mrs Hall deliberately fails to bring the stranger his meals
and, when he complains, she demands payment for his lodging and
certain explanations as to his behaviour. The stranger becomes exasperated and removes the wrappings on his face to reveal that he is invisible.
Those who witness this run in horror from the inn, and soon the entire
village, busy because of the festival, is in uproar. Mrs Hall returns with
a policeman with a warrant to arrest the stranger for the vicarage
burglary. There is a struggle in the inn, the stranger eventually escaping
by removing his clothes to assume complete invisibility.

Chapter 8: In Transit
Gibbins, a local amateur naturalist, is unnerved by the phantom sounds
of a man coughing, sneezing and swearing on the utterly desolate downs.

Chapter 9: Mr Thomas Marvel
Thomas Marvel, a local tramp, encounters the Invisible Man on the
downs. He thinks he is suffering from an alcoholic hallucination, that
he is going mad, or that he has met a ghost. The Invisible Man bullies
and persuades him into accepting the truth, but does not reply to
Marvel's requests to explain how he has managed to become invisible.
He informs Marvel that he has decided to enlist his assistance, and
promising him rich rewards: 'An invisible man is a man of power'. The
fearful Marvel agrees.

Chapter 10: Mr Marvel's Visit to Iping
Back in Iping, despite the extraordinary events of the morning, the
Club festival is in full swing. Marvel comes into the village, and is

observed by several witnesses as looking very uneasy. He goes into the Coach and Horses briefly. He is then seen entering the yard of the inn by Huxter, the tobacconist. When he emerges with a bundle and three books, Huxter raises the alarm and gives chase, but is tripped and sent flying by the Invisible Man.

Chapter 11: In the Coach and Horses
The events inside the Coach and Horses from the moment Huxter first sees Marvel are described. Cuss and Bunting are in the parlour, looking through the Invisible Man's possessions. Marvel enters the inn and opens the parlour, thus allowing the Invisible Man entry. Cuss and Bunting redirect him to the bar, and he leaves. The Invisible Man behaves very threateningly to Cuss and Bunting, complains about their intrusion into his privacy, and demands clothing, accommodation, and his books.

Chapter 12: The Invisible Man Loses His Temper
The scene changes to the bar. Henfrey and Hall hear violent noises coming from the parlour, and attempt to investigate, only to be diverted by Mrs Hall. Hearing Huxter raise the alarm, most of those in the bar give chase to Marvel, but are impeded by the Invisible Man, who has left the inn by the parlour window, giving Marvel the books and a bundle containing Bunting's clothes, and proceeding to assault everyone who follows him. The festival ends in chaos as the entire village attempts to flee the wrath of the Invisible Man, who commits various acts of vandalism before leaving the village.

Chapter 13: Mr Marvel Discusses His Resignation
On the road to Bramblehurst, the Invisible Man threatens to kill Marvel, whom he suspects of having tried to escape from him. Marvel pleads to be let go, but the Invisible Man ignores him. They go through Bramblehurst silently.

Chapter 14: At Port Stowe
The next morning, Marvel is greeted by a mariner at an inn outside Port Stowe. The mariner recounts newspaper stories of the Invisible Man. Marvel is on the point of telling him what he knows about the stories when the Invisible Man intercedes. The mariner is incensed when Marvel tells him that the story is a hoax, but the Invisible Man drags the former away. Shortly afterwards the mariner hears one of many rumours about money moving 'without visible agency' all over the district.

Chapter 15: The Man Who Was Running
Doctor Kemp, a scientist who is contemptuous of rumours of the Invisible Man, sees Marvel running towards Burdock from his house above the town. The town's inhabitants are not so sceptical: at Marvel's warning of the approach of the Invisible Man they lock themselves indoors.

Chapter 16: In The Jolly Cricketers
Marvel seeks refuge in the Jolly Cricketers in Burdock, and is locked in the bar parlour. An American customer produces a revolver and unbolts the front door, but the Invisible Man gains entry from the yard. There is another bar-room brawl as the Invisible Man tries, but fails, to drag Marvel away. As the Invisible Man retreats into the night the American fires five gunshots after him.

Chapter 17: Doctor Kemp's Visitor
Dr Kemp hears the gunshots in Burdock, but goes on working. When he goes to bed at 2 a.m. he discovers that the Invisible Man is in his bedroom. He has a minor gunshot wound. By coincidence, the Invisible Man (whose name we discover to be Griffin) turns out to have been a fellow medical student of Kemp's at University College. Griffin tells Kemp some of his story while eating, smoking and drinking, but he is near exhaustion. Kemp offers to let him sleep in the room for the night.

Chapter 18: The Invisible Man Sleeps
Kemp gives Griffin his word that his presence will remain a secret, but the latter still suspiciously checks his possible escape routes before retiring. While Griffin sleeps, Kemp wonders about what he has discovered, and re-reads the previous day's newspaper stories about the Invisible Man. He is still awake at dawn, when he tells his servant to set breakfast for two in the study and then not to enter it. He sends out for all the morning papers, which include incomplete stories about the previous evening's events in Burdock. He begins to fear that Griffin has become a violent maniac. After deliberating, he sends a note to Colonel Adye, the chief of the Burdock police, just as he hears Griffin waking upstairs.

Chapter 19: Certain First Principles
Over breakfast, Griffin begins to tell Kemp at length how he discovered the secret of invisibility. We also learn that, after leaving London seven years previously, he earned a living and had access to experimental resources as a demonstrator in a college in Chesilstowe. He none the less ran out of finance for his work, and stole money from his father

which did not, in fact, belong to him. His father committed suicide as a consequence.

Chapter 20: At the House in Great Portland Street
Griffin continues with his story. Back in London, he buried his father with very little remorse, and pushed his experimental work towards its conclusion. He successfully rendered a neighbour's cat invisible, causing it great pain in the process, lying to its owner when asked about it, and eventually setting it loose. He was eventually challenged by his landlord, who served an eviction notice. This event and his near-bankruptcy precipitated Griffin's decision to make himself invisible. Having done so, but not before forwarding his cheque book and notebooks to a *poste restante* address, he covered his trail by destroying his experimental equipment and deliberately setting fire to the building.

Chapter 21: In Oxford Street
Griffin recounts his adventures immediately after escaping from his lodgings. These were not the 'wonderful things' he had fantasised about, but a series of calamities and accidents experienced as, naked and invisible, he attempted to negotiate the busy streets of Central London. Coming full circle, he witnessed his lodgings ablaze, and realised, 'I had burnt my boats – if ever a man did!'

Chapter 22: In the Emporium
Griffin continues, telling how he took overnight shelter in a department store, with the intention of clothing himself so that he might reclaim his notebooks and cheque book. He slept in the bedding department, but was discovered by staff in the morning, and was only able to escape by discarding his clothing and assuming invisibility once more.

Chapter 23: In Drury Lane
Griffin goes on to explain that he began to realise the unanticipated disadvantages of being invisible. He went to a theatrical costumiers to obtain a wig, a mask, spectacles and a costume so that he might assume 'perhaps a grotesque but still credible figure'. Unable to negotiate the inquisitive and persistent shop proprietor, however, he resorted to knocking him unconscious and tying him up. Kemp openly remonstrates with Griffin about the ethics of both this action and Griffin's subsequent robbery of the shop owner. Griffin defends himself by referring to the desperateness of his situation. Griffin relates how, disguised, he went out once more into the city, only to realise that, although invisibility made it possible to obtain desirable things, 'it made it impossible to enjoy them when they are got'. Thus, he

eventually decided to go to the country to experiment with ways of restoring himself to visibility.

Chapter 24: *The Plan That Failed*

Kemp, who has deliberately kept Griffin talking, notices the approach to the house of Colonel Adye and two other men. Unaware of this, Griffin outlines the plan he had to go to southern Europe or north Africa, where the heat would allow him to remain invisible indefinitely. Marvel's escape with his books and the stolen money, he explains, has made this plan impossible. He now proposes that Kemp hide him, maintain him, and assist him in his investigations. Meanwhile, he proposes to establish a 'Reign of Terror' which will command obedience from the local community, including the exemplary murder of individuals who refuse to submit. At this point, the three men enter the house, and Griffin realises that Kemp has betrayed him. He manages, with difficulty, to escape from the house.

Chapter 25: *The Hunting of the Invisible Man*

Kemp issues swift instructions to Adye for the preparation of a civilian and military campaign to capture Griffin.

Chapter 26: *The Wicksteed Murder*

The narrator presents evidence to suggest that, after leaving Kemp's house, Griffin proceeded to Hintondean, where he murdered Lord Burdock's steward, Mr Wicksteed. After this he seems to have gone on to the downland where, the campaign to track him down now in full swing, he lies low.

Chapter 27: *The Siege of Kemp's House*

The following afternoon, Kemp receives a letter from Griffin, written in apocalyptic language, which announces 'day one of year one of the new epoch – the Epoch of the Invisible Man', and promises to inaugurate the epoch with the murder of Kemp. Shortly afterwards, Griffin lays siege to Kemp's house, shooting Adye in the process. Kemp is defended by two policemen, one of whom injures Griffin.

Chapter 28: *The Hunter Hunted*

Kemp flees, pursued by Griffin, towards the house of his neighbour, Mr Heelas. Heelas locks him out, so that he has to go on to the hill-road and run for safety into Burdock. As he approaches the entire town seems to be barring him entry. However, people gradually emerge and collectively catch and beat Griffin to death. In death, his invisible albino body gradually materialises again. His body is carried into the Jolly Cricketers.

The Epilogue
The reader who wishes to know more is instructed to go to the Invisible Man, an inn in Port Stowe, of which the affluent Marvel is now the landlord, and where, every Sunday morning, he secretly pores over Griffin's three notebooks.

ACKNOWLEDGEMENTS

Acknowledgement is due to the copyright holders of the extracts reproduced in the Wells and his Critics section of this book.